**CUT AND DRIED**

# CUT AND DRIED

C. A. Shilton

Published by
COPSE CORNER BOOKS

First Published in Great Britain in 2016
By Copse Corner Books

Copyright © C.A. Shilton, 2016

The right of C.A. Shilton to be identified as author of this work has been asserted by him in accordance with the Copyright, Designs and Patents Act 1988.

All Rights Reserved. No part of this publication may be reproduced, stored in a retrieval system, or transmitted, in any form or by any means, electronic, mechanical, photocopying, recording or otherwise, without the prior permission of the copyright owner. Any person who does any unauthorised act in relation to this publication may be liable to criminal prosecution and civil claims for damages.

ISBN   978-0-9926013-1-7

Cover Design by Rachael Gracie Carver
Type-set by Green Door Design for Publishing

Many thanks to all who have given me help and encouragement during the writing of this novel. Special thanks go to Ann Dixon, Joy Hodge, Maureen Scollan and Elisabeth Skoda.

Thanks also to Peter Whent, for keeping me on track with his expertise on the use of DNA, relatively new at the time of this novel.

# Chapter 1

The house stood over a mile from the road, partway up a narrow, rutted lane. It was an old house - really more like a cottage - with thick stone walls and small deeply recessed windows. With the exception of the farmhouse at the far end of the lane there were no other dwellings in the area. The glow from the house window was the only glimmer of light visible for miles around.

In the lounge, Bill and Sue Bishop sat side by side on the sofa, he reading a newspaper, she a book. Oscar, their cocker spaniel, was curled up on the rug. Presently Bill dropped his paper onto the floor, stood and walked over to the front window. He pulled one curtain across, then paused and stood gazing out. After a moment he crossed the room and pressed the light switch, plunging the lounge into darkness.

'Oi!' said Sue's indignant voice. 'I was reading.'

'Sorry,' said Bill absently.

'What are you doing?' asked Sue.

'Looking out.'

'At what?'

'At nothing.'

'You're standing at the window of a darkened room, looking out at nothing?' said Sue slowly.

'Yes. Because there's nothing to look at. Nothing to see for miles around - not even a glimmer. I can't even see the darn sleet hammering on the window.'

Sue stood up and moved cautiously across the dark room to join him at the window. He put his arm round her waist, pulling her close. After a moment Sue freed herself, moved over to the switch and restored the lights before going back to the sofa. Bill came over, turfed Oscar back onto the floor and sat next to her.

'It really is a bit too remote here, Sue,' he said.

'I know, but it's not for long Bill - just while we look round and find something to buy, or maybe rent short-term. Anyway, don't you think it's nice to be surrounded by lovely countryside and wild-life?'

Bill picked up the newspaper again. 'Maybe in the summer. Right now we're surrounded by pitch darkness and gloomy trees.'

'Ah - is little Billy frightened of the big, bad dark?' She laughed as he hit her with a cushion. 'Anyway you must admit the cost of this place is pretty good.'

Bill chuckled at that. 'Couldn't be better.' The house was a holiday home belonging to friends, who had loaned it rent free until Easter.

Sue cuddled into him. 'Come on Bill - stop being such a misery guts and give your wife a cuddle. I don't start my new job until Monday; we have the whole romantic weekend ahead of us. We can split a bottle of wine and have a cosy relaxing evening.' She stroked his arm. 'Or maybe we could have an early night.'

Bill laughed, put down the newspaper and pulled her into his arms.

Ten miles away, Police Sergeant Tim Hawkins was hurrying across the car park of Fairfield Police Station, head down against the needles of icy sleet driving into his face. He pushed open the heavy swing doors, escaping into the warmth of the front enquiry office with a sigh of relief. Jim Taylor was behind the counter, wearing his ancient, battered Barbour coat over his uniform. Next to him, Mandy Cornwell was shrugging herself into her very smart designer shower proof.

Tim chuckled. 'You'll need more than that to keep this lot off, Mandy. It's evil out there.'

Neither Mandy nor Jim made any response; they seemed pre-occupied, lost in their own little world. But Tim had no time to worry about that at the moment - it was almost 11 pm and he was ten minutes later than he should have been. Pete was going to be thoroughly pissed off, but a collision between a car and a bus had blocked the road and caused a long detour; the roads were treacherous with black ice.

Tim hurried down the main corridor and turned into the secured side corridor that led to the custody office. He pressed the button on the wall and the door clicked open. A few yards brought him to the heavy metal door of the custody suite itself. Again he pressed the button, but without result. He waited a few seconds, then tried again - still no response. He pressed the button on the opposite wall and this time the intercom crackled into life.

'Control room.'

'Tim Hawkins. Can you buzz me through? I think Sergeant Ashbourne's gone on strike.'

The buzzer sounded and Tim walked through into the custody office. There was no one behind the adjacent counter and for a moment he thought the room was empty. Then he realised that there was someone there; a heavily built man, scruffy and unshaven - a civilian, not a police officer - kneeling on the floor in the far corner, staring towards the door. At the sight of Tim he came quickly to his feet.

Shock mingled with disbelief as Tim registered what the man had been kneeling over. Pete Ashbourne was lying motionless, face down on the floor. His blue shirt was soaked in blood and the hilt of a knife protruded from his back.

# Chapter 2

Eight hours previously Pete Ashbourne had been hurrying across the crowded car park of Fairfield Police Station, splashing his way through the slushy puddles. The weather was worsening - it had been raining all day and now the wind had risen and a sharp drop in temperature was turning the rain to sleet. It was, he supposed, a good day to be working inside, but he would have preferred not to be working anywhere at all. There had been a time when he had enjoyed coming to work, but that was a long time ago. The job had changed since then and so had he. Back in the sixties he had been proud to be a copper, strong and fit, carrying the uniform well. Now it was 1987 and he was pushing fifty, balding and running to fat.

He heaved open the swing doors and walked through into the warmth of the public enquiry office, shaking the excess water off his cap and his long black trench coat. The room was spacious and functional, but dull - grey tiles on the floor, grey chairs against the wall, and a lighter grey emulsion on the walls. The building had been completed in the mid-60's and was, in Pete's view, a concrete monstrosity.

Mandy was behind the desk - WPC Mandy Cornwell, aged twenty one, with short blond hair and eyes like a scared spaniel. She was in shirt sleeves and Pete's small blue eyes gleamed appreciatively. Mandy was very well endowed.

'Afternoon Mandy,' he said.

She looked up. 'Oh – good afternoon sergeant.' She didn't seem overjoyed to see him.

'Any female prisoners in today?'

'One. She's due for another visit in half an hour.'

Pete nodded. Maybe this shift wouldn't be a total waste of

time, with young Mandy on hand for a bit of amusement. He crossed behind the counter and entered the main corridor, then turned down the side corridor towards the cell block - custody suite as it was now called. Load of old rubbish! A cell was still a cell, and most of them were still occupied by toe-rags and low-life, who thoroughly deserved to be there. Pete had no truck with the namby pamby way you had to treat the prisoners nowadays. He pressed a button on the wall. The intercom crackled to life.

'Yes?'

'Pete.' he said briefly.

There was a buzz as the heavy door unlocked and Pete walked through. The room he entered was divided by a long counter, higher than the norm, behind which were shelving and a couple of high stools. The uniformed sergeant standing behind the counter looked up at Pete's entrance.

'Pete – good to see you. It's always good to see my relief.' He looked at Pete's coat, still dripping water. 'You never walked here in this weather?'

Pete gave a non-committal grunt as he took off his coat and cap and hung them behind the counter. 'Not much use driving in on this shift, car park's always full of civvies and nine-to-fivers. Who's in?'

'Just two. There's a woman in for public order; young Mandy's looking after her and she's due a visit around half three if she hasn't been bailed before that. Then there's Burford – burglary again. Martin Attwood's got him out for interview. And that's it – nothing else to report. With a bit of luck you'll have a quiet shift.'

'What? On a Friday night!'

'You might be lucky, it's bloody cold and the forecast's for more sleet and snow. Anyway I'm off - the kettle's just boiled.' He was shrugging himself into his civilian coat as he spoke. Thirty seconds later he was out of the door.

Pete looked glumly around the place where he spent his entire working life, eight hours a day - or night – five or six days a week. The room was spartan. The wall opposite the counter comprised wall to ceiling bars, accessed by a door of similar design. In one corner was a tiny sink, next to a small, battered fridge supporting a kettle, coffee and a few mis-matched mugs. There was a narrow bench along the side wall. Above the bench was a clock, showing 3 pm.

The whole place stank, as it always did, of stale air and unwashed bodies. No windows, so no natural light, just the never-ending glare of the strip lights. God, what a dump! Pete couldn't wait for the next year to pass; then he could get out of the job and start drawing his well-earned pension.

The wall buzzer sounded, indicating that someone in the corridor wanted in. He pressed the intercom button.

'Yes?'

'Superintendent,' crackled from the intercom.

Pete pressed the button that opened the doors. Superintendent Michael Horner strolled into the room.

'Afternoon sergeant,' he said affably.

'Good afternoon sir.' Pete's expression was wooden.

Superintendent Horner was tall and enviably slim, with thick, dark brown hair and even but unremarkable features. A product of the graduate entry scheme, he had been rushed through the lower ranks, gaining his promotion to superintendent whilst still in his early thirties. Ridiculous, in Pete's view. To be fair, Horner was always polite to his underlings, not arrogant like some of these high flyers; but how in the world could he have the experience necessary to run a sub-division properly? And why should his privileged background give him the right to lord it over proper, honest to goodness coppers who had got their experience the hard way, out on the streets?

The superintendent had wandered round the counter. To Pete's mind he always seemed to stroll and wander, his manner pleasant, but irritatingly vague. He began to thumb his way through the custody records.

'I see you've got a woman in. Who's looking after her?'

'Mandy sir – WPC Cornwell.'

'Ah yes. How long do you expect her to be here?'

'Not too long now. George Haines is just writing up his statement, then she'll be charged and bailed.'

'Good, good. Ah – there's one other thing sergeant. Your annual appraisal is due.'

Pete frowned. 'Hardly seems worth it; I've only got a year to go.'

'Yes, well, the rules still say you need an annual appraisal. I thought we might have a chat about it this evening, perhaps your meal relief can cover for you a little longer. Shall we say seven o'clock?'

'Yes sir.' Pete just stopped himself from shrugging. What a waste of time, and what did this wet-behind-the-ears boy know about him?

The superintendent signed the custody sheets, then drifted out of the door. Pete pulled the daily paper from his briefcase. The buzzer sounded again.

'Yes?'

'It's Mandy, sarge.'

Pete glanced at the clock – almost 3.30 pm. He smiled as Mandy came in, looking apprehensive.

'I've just come to visit the prisoner, sarge.'

'You know the way!'

Mandy picked up the keys and disappeared into the cell block. A few minutes later she was back.

'She's fine – doesn't want anything.'

'Good. She's not getting anything.'

Mandy hung up the keys and started to fill in the record. Pete walked up behind her, then moved up close and pushed himself against her buttocks.

'Sarge, please – '

'Please what? This?'

He reached round with one hand to fondle her breast, over her shirt. Then he pushed himself onto her even harder, forcing her forward against the desk.

'Sarge, stop it! If you don't stop it I'll report you – I swear I will!' Her face was fiery red, and she sounded close to tears.

Stupid little bitch! It wasn't as if he was hurting her or doing her any harm.

'I don't think you will, you know. You'll never prove anything, and you're still on your probation, aren't you? I could make things very difficult for you.'

The buzzer sounded and he swore softly. He let go of Mandy and moved over to the intercom.

'Yes!'

'Martin, Pete - with Burford.'

"Martin" was Detective Sergeant Martin Attwood. Pete scowled as he pressed the admission button. Martin was all right – he was another old-style copper – but he had a damnable sense of timing. And Pete preferred to be addressed as 'sergeant' in front of prisoners. These CID types were too bloody casual.

Mandy was already round the counter, waiting near the door. She made her escape as the detective sergeant came in with his prisoner.

# Chapter 3

The panda car was parked up at the back of Roy's transport cafe. Inside the vehicle PC Jim Taylor and his colleague PC Tony Woodford were thoroughly enjoying Roy's best bacon sandwiches when the police radio suddenly crackled into life.

'November Foxtrot 6, position please.'

Jim swore as he jumped and dropped a large and fatty chunk of bacon onto the log he was completing. Tony scooped up the receiver.

'Main Street, just by the transport cafe.'

'November Foxtrot 6, make your way to number 12 Kings Crescent, report of woman screaming, believed violent domestic dispute. We'll get back-up on the way to you.'

'Any complainant?' asked Tony.

'Negative to that. Anonymous call.'

Jim groaned as Tony acknowledged the message. 'Bloody Robbie Nichols again. He'll do for that woman one of these days. Blues and twos eh?'

'Blues anyway,' said Tony. Panda cars were fitted with a blue flashing light, but no siren. They pushed the remainder of their sandwiches into the paper bag. Jim swung the car off the café forecourt and headed for Kings Crescent, blue light flashing. As they shot across the traffic lights at the edge of town they could hear control seeking other vehicles in the vicinity.

It was a little after four o'clock, the beginning of the weekend rush hour. Luckily Kings Crescent lay towards the centre of the little market town, just a five minute drive away. Jim skidded the car into the crescent and brought it to an untidy halt outside number 12. Everything was quiet now. The street was deserted.

Tony glanced at the houses, rooms lit, curtains drawn.

'No one about,' he said superfluously.

'Yeah,' agreed Jim, 'but you can see the curtains twitching. Whoever called'll stay out of the way - they're all scared of Nichols.'

In fact all the curtains were not drawn, those of number 12 were open and the lights were on, giving a good view into the lounge. They could see no-one in the room. They exchanged glances and both men pulled out their truncheons. Tony knocked firmly on the front door.

'Robbie' he shouted.

'Fuck off!'

Jim nodded and Tony turned the handle of the front door, which opened easily. 'Careful,' cautioned Jim. The empty hall yawned at them as they headed towards the kitchen at the end of the hall. Both of them knew the geography of the house well, it was by no means their first visit.

Robbie Nichols was in the kitchen, leaning against the sink, holding a knife which appeared to be a stiletto. As they entered the room he lifted it threateningly and pointed it towards them. Even from the doorway they could see the blade was covered in blood. Blood also spattered the floor and the table. A woman was huddled in the corner behind the door, sobbing and moaning, the sleeve of her blouse heavily stained with red.

Tony swung a kitchen chair across in front of him and positioned himself between Nichols and the woman. Nichols glared at him but made no move. Jim kept a wary eye on them whilst he grabbed a nearby tea towel. He bent over the woman on the floor.

'My arm,' she whimpered. 'He slashed me up - said he'd do my face next time.'

Jim gently pulled her hands away and looked at the wound, which was still bleeding sluggishly. He folded the towel and pushed it over the wound. 'Here love, you keep that pushed up against your arm - nice and tight.' He pressed the call button on his radio.

'November Foxtrot 6 to control. Ambulance to 12 Kings Crescent.'

'Acknowledged November Foxtrot 6. What injuries?'

'Stab wound to upper arm.'

'Roger,' acknowledged control. 'Back-up en route.'

In the middle of the kitchen, Tony and Nichols were still facing each other. Nichols made a slight movement with the knife. 'Come on then copper, I can take you two out anytime.'

'Don't be daft Robbie - back-up's already on the way.' As if on cue they heard the slamming of car doors from outside. Two more constables raced into the room. Nichols snarled, then tossed the knife onto the kitchen table. Tony and one of the newcomers quickly handcuffed him. Nichols continued to swear and struggle as they moved him away from the table and the weapon, but it was only a token resistance.

'Robbie,' said Tony, 'I'm arresting you on suspicion of wounding.' He added the caution. Nichols shrugged his shoulders but made no further response.

Tony recovered the knife, holding it cautiously by the blade, then went across to check on Mrs Nichols. Jim had thrown off his tunic and his hands and shirt were thoroughly blood-stained, but the bleeding had slowed to a trickle. Mrs Nichols was still conscious but in shock. The skin around one eye was red and puffy, in contrast to the rest of her face, which was dead white. Blood was still welling from a split lip.

Jim stood up and turned to one of the newcomers. 'Jock, can you stay with her while we get him back to the nick? Ambulance is on the way so it shouldn't be long.'

'No problem,' said Jock easily. 'Come on love, let's see if we can't do something to help you a bit.' He and his colleague set about making the injured woman more comfortable while Tony and Jim took Nichols out to the waiting panda. There was still no-one about, but several pairs of curtains were now conspicuously twitching.

Tony placed Nichols in the back of the car behind the empty passenger seat then sat next to him, watching him carefully. Nichols was securely cuffed, but both men knew from experience how unpredictable he could be. As the ambulance came screaming into the road, Jim thumbed the switch on his radio. 'Control? November Foxtrot 6. Can you inform custody office we're bringing Nichols in. ETA about thirty minutes.'

# Chapter 4

Back in the custody office at Fairfield Station, Martin Attwood was returning his prisoner to his cell whilst Pete completed the custody record. Martin was in his late thirties, quick moving, slimly built and of average height. He had dark brown curly hair and smoky-blue eyes that looked black in the harsh fluorescent light. He came back into the office and hung the heavy keys on their hook behind the counter.

'Kettle hot?' he asked.

'Help yourself.'

'Want one?'

'Might as well. What's happening with your prisoner?'

Martin moved over to the fridge and started spooning coffee into two cups. 'He's ready, inspector says we can charge him and he can be on his way.' He paused. 'What was wrong with Mandy?'

'What?'

'Mandy. She looked as if she was about to burst into tears.'

Pete shrugged. 'How should I know? Maybe it's her love life.'

Martin walked back to the counter, carrying two mugs. 'Are you touching her up?'

'Of course not. Well, I might have a bit of fun sometimes, but nothing serious. She needs to grow up a bit. For God's sake Martin! In the old days she'd have been held over a desk and had her knickers round her ankles while we put the station stamp on her bum. And don't tell me you've never done that!'

Martin grinned. 'Well, maybe, a long time ago. But seriously Pete, things are different now. And you need to be careful who you have fun with, Mandy's not the type. You'll get into really hot water if you're not careful.'

'Phewie! And are you saying you hold with the way things are now? Bloody women getting above themselves! Do you want a woman in charge of the sub-division?'

Martin frowned. 'Perish the thought! I don't mind women in the service so long as they keep to doing what they do well, but all this pseudo equality – they've got a female inspector on the shifts now, over at Central.'

'Who?'

'Sandy Rawlings.'

Pete snorted. 'Oh, her! I thought you said a female inspector – she's a dyke; she's more butch than most of the men.'

'Yeah, but it's still the thin end of the wedge. There'll be a woman chief constable one day, you mark my words.'

'At least I'll be retired before that happens - if it ever does.' Pete leered at Martin. 'Probably be a detective inspector before too long though – I'd like to hear you calling a woman "guvnor."'

Martin grunted. 'Not bloody likely!'

Pete swigged back the last of his coffee. 'Well, I suppose I'd better get ready for the influx. It's Friday night. All the local pond life'll be out on the piss.'

'Yeah, well, right now I wish I was out on the piss!'

'So what's ruffled your feathers?'

'Bloody detective inspector's board, for the vacancy on the west,' said Martin bitterly.

'They've never turned you down again? You've been doing the job for three months, for God's sake.'

Martin slammed his mug down on the counter. 'Tell me about it!'

Pete swung the custody records round and started checking the previous entries. 'Tell you what Martin, I dunno why anybody'd want to be a DI, now this PACE shit's come in.'

Martin picked up his mug again and stared gloomily at its contents. 'Bloody PACE, makes you wonder if they want us to get the scroats put away.' PACE was the Police and Criminal

Evidence Act; recently passed legislation that imposed strict rules and regulations regarding – amongst other things - the treatment of prisoners. It was almost universally detested by the detectives in CID.

Pete gave a resigned sigh. 'It's made the charge sergeant's job bloody difficult as well.'

'Custody sergeant, you mean. And don't forget this is the custody suite, not the cell block.'

Pete scowled. 'Suite be damned. Don't know why they don't call it a bloody hotel and be done with it. Make sure the prisoner has three meals a day; make sure the prisoner has eight hours uninterrupted sleep; make an entry on the custody sheet if the prisoner goes for a pee. Load of bollocks! Anyway, what about this board of yours? Why'd they fail you this time?'

Martin shrugged. 'Well, they never really tell you the truth, do they? They asked me a lot about PACE, and what I thought about it. So I told them.'

'What'd you say?' asked Pete.

'What I thought. I couldn't sit there and say I agreed with rules that tie us up hand and foot. The criminals don't follow any rules, do they? Look Pete, I'm a damned good detective, but PACE is making it impossible. The only way to get results is to use the same tactics the crooks do.'

'And you said that to the promotion board? Mad bugger!' said Pete unsympathetically.

Martin shrugged. 'Yeah – well – I always was, wasn't I? I guess I just have to accept I'll never make detective inspector now. I wouldn't mind so much, but as you said I've been acting DI for three months, and doing a good job of it too.'

'Yeah, well,' said Pete, 'you can bet it'd be different if you were a woman, or black. So who got the job? Do you know?'

'Only that he's from outside the force. Manchester or West Mids – somewhere like that. One of the big metropolitan forces, anyway. Can't say I really care.

They were interrupted by the burr of the telephone. Pete picked it up.

'Ashbourne, custody office. Right - got it.' He dropped the receiver back onto its rest. 'Well, here we go. Weren't thinking of going home, were you?'

'One coming in?'

Pete nodded. 'Robbie Nichols. Wounding, on his missus.'

Martin groaned. 'Not again! How bad is it this time?'

'Gone to hospital with stab wounds to her arm. God almighty, why does the stupid bitch stay with him?'

'Who's bringing him in?' asked Martin.

'That little faggot Woodford - and you needn't pull a face like that. What's the matter with you? You know I've no time for bloody queers.'

'Oh for God's sake!' said Martin.

'What?' asked Pete. 'Don't tell me you're in favour of the likes of him? You of all people.'

Martin shrugged. 'Quite frankly I don't give a damn, so long as he doesn't bother me and he does his job. I'm telling you Pete, you'll open that mouth of yours too wide one of these days. Besides, Tony's okay - got the makings of a good copper.'

'Not if I have owt to do with it,' said Pete sourly. 'Anyway, they'll be here in twenty minutes - let's get Burford bailed and on his way.'

The outside buzzer sounded at quarter past five. Pete pressed the intercom button.

'Yes!'

'PC Woodford sergeant, with prisoner.'

Pete grunted and opened the door. Tony Woodford walked in, preceded by Nichols. Slightly built and quietly spoken, Tony was almost thirty, but having joined the service late he was only just out of his probation. Pete openly detested him. His mild manner masked what Pete regarded as a stupid obstinacy; he wouldn't bend the rules, he wouldn't swear. Worst of all in Pete's eyes, he was widely believed to be gay, an accusation Tony didn't even trouble himself to deny.

'Evening sergeant,' said Tony politely.

Pete didn't respond to the greeting. He pulled the custody record towards him.

'Well?' he said.

Tony indicated Nichols. 'I've just arrested this man for wounding on his wife, Mary Nichols.'

'Evidence?'

'We were called to the house because neighbours had reported Mrs Nichols screaming for help. When we got there it was quiet, but the front door was unlocked so we went in. Nichols was in the kitchen and his wife was lying on the floor, bleeding from stab wounds to her arm. Nichols was still holding the knife. This knife.'

He laid the stiletto-style knife on the counter, out of Nichols' reach, handling it carefully by the blade and avoiding the handle. Pete lifted it in the same way and put it on the rear shelf.

'All right,' he said. 'I'm authorising detention so this matter can be further investigated.' He turned to the prisoner. 'Nichols, you listen to me. You have the right to have a friend informed of your detention. You have the right to consult a solicitor . .'

'I know all that shit,' interrupted Nichols. He was about forty, heavily built, with scrubby grey hair and a chin decorated with bristly stubble. His arms and his light grey pullover were liberally flecked with blood.

Pete continued as if there had been no interruption. 'You have the right to consult the codes of practice. I also need to remind you that you're under caution and that you do not have to say anything unless you wish to do so, but what you say may be given in evidence.'

'Bullshit.' responded Nichols.

Pete recorded the word onto the custody record. 'Anything else to say?'

'I hope I've killed the bitch!'

Pete ignored that and pushed a piece of paper across the desk. 'This is a copy of your rights; sign here to say you've got it. Right, now empty your pockets onto the desk here.'

Nichols grunted. He pulled a dirty handkerchief, a crumpled packet of cigarettes and a lighter out of one pocket; a number of coins out of the other. Pete listed them all and put them carefully into a transparent bag.

'Right, now get your jumper off. Woodford, search him.'

'Why the hell should I? said Nichols.

'Because I told you to.'

'Well, you can piss off. It's freezing in here.'

Pete reached across the counter and gave Nichols a back-handed slap across the face. Tony stepped forward.

'Now hang on, sarge.'

'You can shut up.' grunted Pete. 'I don't ask toe-rags like him twice. Search him.'

Looking mutinous, Tony complied. 'Nothing else sarge.'

'Right. Now get that knife and jumper bagged up while I finish with him.'

He picked up the heavy keys and pushed Nichols towards the iron bars. He unlocked the door and disappeared into the cell block with his prisoner. There was the rattle of keys and the sound of a heavy door opening. Then Pete's voice.

'Get your shoes off.'

'Bollocks.'

There was the smack of a blow, and a gasp of pain from Nichols.

'Ow! You fucking bastard. I'll bloody do for you some day copper.'

'In your dreams, sunshine,' said Pete. He emerged from the cell block and started to write on the custody record. 'Watch how you handle that knife Woodford, I don't want your dabs all over it!'

Tony sealed the bag. 'I'm sorry sergeant, but this just isn't on.'

'What isn't on?'

'Thumping prisoners.' Tony had picked up the custody record and was reading through it. He stiffened. 'Oh now, just a minute. I'm not going along with that.'

'What?' grunted Pete.

'What you've put down here – on arrival, prisoner had visible injuries, bruising to right eye, split lip, all injuries sustained on arrest.'

Pete shrugged. 'So? What's your problem?'

'My problem is that he didn't come in with any visible injuries. You did that, just now.'

Pete snorted in contempt. 'And he just might have a bit more bruising on his wrists too – those cuffs were tight.'

'They were not!'

'They were just before I took them off. God, you are such a boy scout; he's just put his missus in hospital for the umpteenth time, for God's sake! The man's just scum.'

Tony's mouth set obstinately. 'Maybe. But I'm still not standing by and seeing prisoners thumped.'

'Oh, really. And just what do you think you can do about it?'

'I can report it.' responded Tony grimly.

'You sanctimonious little nark. Mind your own business and go and get on with that statement of arrest. I want it back here in half an hour so DS Attwood can interview.'

'I can do that.' protested Tony. 'For goodness sake, sarge, it's a bang to rights case.'

'It's a wounding. CID will handle it.' He paused and stared at Tony maliciously. 'I want it done properly.' He glanced at the clock. 'It's half past five now – I want you back here by six o'clock, with your statement of arrest.'

'That's cutting it a bit fine sarge; I've got an appraisal appointment at six o'clock.'

'Then you'd better get on with the statement now, hadn't you?' He pointed his pen at Tony. 'And hear this, you bloody little arse-grabber - you try putting the finger on me and I'll make sure I fix you, one way or another.'

Tony shrugged and stalked out of the room, just as the telephone rang. Pete snatched it up.

'Yes!' he snapped.

'Sarge? Control room. Sergeant Harris has just rung to say

he'll be late relieving you; he's got tied up with a sudden death.'

'Oh bugger! What time will he be in?'

'He said a bit after half six.'

Pete hung up. That was a bummer; it gave him about twenty minutes of his meal break before his appraisal interview at seven o'clock. So much for forty five minutes uninterrupted. He sighed and shook his head. Oh well, maybe Harris would relieve him for a bit longer and that juvenile excuse for a superintendent would agree to bring the appraisal forward by half an hour. Meanwhile, he had to arrange meals for his reluctant guest, not to mention room service. A bloody hotel flunkey, that's all he was nowadays.

# Chapter 5

'You're very quiet!'

Mandy Cornwell was on her meal break, with her new fiancé Jim Taylor. Jim was on the same shift as Mandy; they had first met at training school and since then romance had quickly blossomed.

Mandy shrugged her shoulders and stared at the half-eaten sandwich on the table in front of her.

'What's up love?' asked Jim. 'Come on Mand – you're never like this. What's upset you?'

Mandy turned away from him. 'I can't tell you Jim. You can't help.'

'Come on Mand, spill the beans. Something's really put you out. I'm your fiancé, for goodness sake. We're supposed to share things, remember?'

She shook her head. 'I'm scared to tell you Jim; you'd just go ape.'

'Well, now you've got to tell me!'

Mandy looked around furtively, but they were alone in the little canteen.

'All right. But listen Jim, you've got to promise not to lose your rag. I'm scared you'll do something silly, like go and sort – someone – out.'

'Who? Come on Mand, spill it!'

Mandy turned away from him and surreptitiously wiped away a tear. 'Sergeant Ashbourne, Pete Ashbourne.'

'Ashbourne?' His voice sharpened as he pulled her round to face him. 'Has that bastard been pestering you Mand?'

'She nodded, looking at the floor.

'How? What's he done? Has he been touching you up?'

Mandy nodded, tears now streaming. 'He won't leave me alone, Jim; every chance he gets. I've told him I'll report him and he just threatens to fix things so they won't confirm my probation.'

'That bloody bastard! I'll fix him.' Jim was already up out of his chair. Mandy grabbed his arm.

'Jim – please! Please wait a minute. Oh God! I knew you'd react like this.'

'How the bloody hell am I supposed to react when some sick bastard's touching up my fiancée?'

'I know. But please Jim, wait. I need your help. Rushing off and punching Pete Ashbourne isn't the answer.'

'It's what he bloody deserves.'

'I know. Look Jim, I'm trying to get up the courage to make a complaint about him; an official complaint. But I'm scared to do it. He's bound to deny it, they might not believe me. And if they do, they'll think it's just a lot of fuss over nothing. And anyway I can't prove anything. I don't know what to do.'

'I bloody do!'

Mandy was in tears. 'Please, Jim, please wait. Please calm down; you'll make things worse.'

Jim sat down, still smouldering. 'Look Mand, you've got to do something about this. You can bet it's not just you; how many others do you think he's touched up, who're scared to do anything about it? The man's nothing but a sick bully.'

Mandy sniffed, then nodded. 'All right, I will do something about it, but let's at least talk it over first. And Jim, please promise me, you won't rush off and do anything stupid, like confronting Pete Ashbourne.'

'Confront him! I'd like to wipe him round the floor of the cell block.'

'I know, but please don't. It won't help.'

Jim frowned darkly, then they both fell silent as the door swung open and Martin Attwood entered the canteen.

# Chapter 6

It was 9.30 pm. Back in the custody office, Martin and his colleague DC Paul Redman had just brought Nichols back from interview. Pete handed the keys to Redman.

'Put him back!' he said. He glanced towards the clock. 'I don't suppose you'll want him again tonight?'

Martin shook his head. 'No, I've got pretty much all I need from Mr Nichols here. I'd have to have a good reason to interview him much later than this.'

'Too right!' asserted Nichols sneeringly. 'I know my rights – uninterrupted sleep I'm entitled to.'

Pete snorted. 'Huh! I suppose you wouldn't like tea in bed as well?'

'Not if it's like that pig-swill you called dinner.'

Redman took him down to the cells, then hung the heavy keys back on their hook. Pete sighed and looked at the dirty plates and cups stacked by the tiny sink.

'And now I've got to wash up after him,' he muttered.

'Make him do it,' suggested Martin.

'Oh yeah, that's very likely. Some prisoners I get to do the washing up, but not him. He'd chuck the plates across the room, as like as not, just for the hell of it. Put your moniker on this. Coffee before you go?'

Martin glanced in the fridge. 'Milk's out Pete. Anyway, I'd rather have a pint.' He scrawled his signature on the custody record. 'Okay Pete, that's it for me, we're off home. Well, off to the pub anyway.'

'Lucky blighters,' grunted Pete.

'Sometimes. See you Pete.'

He picked up his file and he and Redman left the room. Pete

sighed and went over to tackle the pile of dirty crockery. The clock on the wall showed 9.35 pm.

# Chapter 7

Midnight. Fairfield Police Station was usually hushed at this hour, especially on a hostile winter's night. Tonight was different. The main entrance had been re-opened, the police officer on duty directing visitors appropriately. A uniformed police officer guarded the entrance to the custody office corridor, recording the names of all who entered and forbidding entry to anyone not concerned with the examination of the scene.

In the custody office, Pete Ashbourne's body still lay where it had fallen. The police surgeon had arrived and was examining the body, whilst members of the force's forensic department were carrying out a detailed examination of the room. The cells were empty, Nichols having been arrested on suspicion of murder and whisked off to the nearest police station to await interview.

In his first floor office Superintendent Michael Horner was gazing abstractedly out of the window. Heavy footsteps sounded on the stairs and Detective Chief Superintendent David Wallace walked into the room. Wallace was in his mid-forties, not tall but stockily built, greying hair thinning but ruthlessly cropped. He was in overall charge of the force's CID. Horner turned back from the window.

'David, come in and grab a chair. Coffee?'

'Thanks, strong and black please. Hell of a business Michael.'

'As you say.' He handed the mug to the detective. 'Have you seen the body?'

'From a distance - they wouldn't let me into the custody office. Quite right too! We both know how many crime scenes have been ruined by well meaning coppers tramping all over the place with their size tens.'

Horner nodded slowly. 'True enough, though this one seems pretty cut and dried.'

'Certainly does on the face of it, but how the hell did that prisoner get his hands on that knife? There's a few questions to be answered here Michael.'

Horner nodded. 'And Pete the only man who could have answered them.'

'Nichols can answer them too,' said Wallace grimly. 'Now then, let's look at the investigating officer for this one. I'll take overall charge of course, but we need a DI or DCI to take direct charge of the investigation. What's the position with your men? Is DI Smith still on sick leave?'

'Yes - and it's looking unlikely he'll be coming back.'

'Shit! And the DCI's on extended leave in bloody Australia. Well, we'll have to appoint from another division.' He thought for a moment. 'Just a minute - I've got the very person. Bishop.'

'Bishop?' queried Horner.

Wallace nodded. 'New to you. From out of force - just been appointed to the vacancy on the west, due to start Monday. Well, the DS on the west can keep acting up and Bishop can start here. Tonight.'

Horner looked doubtful. 'An outsider? Who won't know anyone or anything about the area?'

'Better I think, in a situation like this. No danger of any bias, don't you see? It's an open and shut case anyhow, if ever anything was. Martin Attwood can be the right hand man, he's got all the local knowledge necessary. Get on the phone and get him in here.'

Horner frowned. 'That'll really go down well, given he's been acting DI for three months and this Bishop has just pipped him to the job.'

Wallace snorted. 'He'll just have to get on with it, won't he? Attwood wouldn't have got the job in any case, he takes too many risky short cuts. That might have been okay for a DC or DS in the past, but not any more and definitely not for a DI. Whether we like it or not we're stuck with PACE and we'll just have to work with it.'

He banged his mug down on the table and stood up.

'Right. I'll get back to FHQ. I'll get Bishop out of bed, to report directly to you, here, as soon as possible. I'll get an incident room set up at FHQ and get a couple of men to do the donkey work. I'll call you with an update as soon as I can.'

'FHQ? You're running the incident room from headquarters?'

'Right! I don't want it to be here - too many nosy buggers trying to find out what's going on. HQ's only a couple of miles up the road.'

He nodded, picked up his briefcase and left the office. Horner heaved a deep sigh and picked up the telephone to call DS Martin Attwood.

# Chapter 8

The strident ringing of the telephone pulled Sue from a deep sleep. The room was pitch black and she groped blindly around on the bedside table, trying to find the phone before Bill woke up. Disorientated by the sudden awakening, she almost overset the bedside lamp. Damn! Where was the dratted phone? She switched on the lamp and finally located the instrument.

'Hello?' She glanced at the clock on the bedside table – it showed quarter to one in the morning.

'May I speak to Detective Inspector Bishop?' The voice was male, gruff and vaguely familiar.

'Speaking,' said Sue. Next to her, Bill stirred restlessly.

'Ah, good morning inspector, this is Detective Chief Superintendent Wallace. We met at your selection board, if you remember.'

'Oh, yes sir.' Sue remembered Superintendent Wallace well; direct and incisive, he had been the most challenging of the three interviewers.

'Sorry to call you at such an unearthly hour, but I'm afraid we need your services.'

'What – now?'

Next to her, Bill was stirring. 'Who the devil is it?' He mumbled. Sue shushed him and held the receiver closer to her ear.

'Right away, I'm afraid,' continued Wallace. 'Soon as you can. I know you're not due to start until Monday, but you're on strength now and we need you. There's been a murder, on Fairfield Sub-division.'

Sue frowned, trying to remember the various subdivisions of her new force. 'Fairfield? Isn't that on the northern division, sir?'

'You're quite right, it is. I know you should be starting on the west, but Fairfield's DCI is abroad on leave and the DI is sick, so we need you. There are other reasons too, which you'll understand later. Can you find it, do you think?'

'Directions would help!'

'Right, grab a pen! You're near the divisional boundary so Fairfield is only about ten miles from you, twenty minutes at the most, this time of night. Ready?'

Sue was fully awake now, the adrenalin pumping as she scribbled directions with her free hand. Even as she wrote, her mind was buzzing. A murder! She was being put in charge of a murder, on a sub-division she had never heard of, on her first day in her new force.

'Got it sir.' She willed her voice to sound calm and efficient.

'Good. The sub-divisional superintendent will be expecting you; that's Superintendent Michael Horner. How long will you be?'

'About forty minutes, if I don't get lost.'

He chuckled. 'You won't – it's very straightforward. They'll probably have locked the main entrance again but just ring the bell and someone will let you in. Sorry to throw you in the deep end like this, but we really do need someone from the outside for this one.' He paused. 'It looks like a cut and dried case - good one to cut your teeth on. Coffee and explanations will be waiting. Best of luck!'

There was a click as he hung up. 'Best of luck!' he had said. Well, she'd be needing all of that. She swung her legs out of bed. Next to her, Bill was sitting up, blinking the sleep out of his eyes.

'You're going to the station? At this hour?'

'Fraid so!'

'But – you don't even start working on the force until Monday.'

'I know. But I'm already officially on strength, so they can call me if they need me.' Sue was already heading for the bathroom.

'How long will you be?' said Bill plaintively.

'No idea,' came Sue's muffled voice. The splashing of the shower rendered further speech impossible.

Ten minutes later, Sue emerged from the bathroom and rummaged quickly in the wardrobe. Smart dark green trouser-suit, she thought. Power dressing, and at the moment she felt she needed all the power she could get. Bill had donned his dressing gown and was sitting on the edge of the bed, looking distinctly unhappy. He stood up and moved over to her, standing behind her as she checked her appearance in the mirror. There was considerable disparity in their appearance. Bill was thirty, six feet two inches and built in proportion, his light brown hair already beginning to thin a little. Sue was twenty eight and barely reached his shoulder; by standing very upright she just managed five feet four inches. She had thick copper coloured hair, cropped short, and eyes of an indeterminate blue/green.

'Terry and Sarah are coming over tomorrow, for lunch,' Bill said.

'I know. You'll probably have to give them my apologies.'

'They'll expect you to be here.'

'I can't help that.' She finished buttoning her blouse and shrugged herself into the jacket.

'When will you be home?'

Sue groaned. 'Bill, for God's sake, I've no idea. I'm a newly appointed detective inspector here, I've been called out on a murder investigation. I can hardly delegate everything and bugger off for the weekend, can I? I have to go!'

She opened the bedroom door and clattered off down the stairs. Bill shook his head, then climbed out of bed and followed her down, catching up with her as she opened the front door. He pulled her back and gave her a hug. 'Good luck, Detective Inspector Bishop; go and give 'em hell!'

Sue laughed nervously. 'Bill, I'm shitting myself. But they'll never know it, I swear!' She broke away from his embrace and ran out to the car. Bill stood in the doorway, watching until the red tail-lights had disappeared from view. He heaved a sigh and headed for the kitchen, and tea.

# Chapter 9

Back at Fairfield Station Superintendent Horner was looking distinctly frayed around the edges as he poured his third cup of strong black coffee. Footsteps sounded on the stairs, followed by a tap on the already open door.

Horner turned. 'Ah, Martin. Come in and pour yourself a coffee. You've been downstairs? How's it going?'

Martin helped himself to coffee. 'Thanks sir, I could do with this. Forensic operations are well under way and the police surgeon's nearly done. I've asked him to call us when he's through.'

'Good. I want to speak to him of course, but right now I'm waiting for a call from your big boss.'

'Mr Wallace?'

'The same. He's just sorting out the DI to take on the Investigating Officer's job.'

Martin seated himself in the proffered chair. 'Christ, yes - I'd forgotten that. We'll have to poach someone from another division.'

'Already sorted,' said Horner. The telephone buzzed and he pressed the intercom button. 'Horner.'

The amplified voice of David Wallace boomed out. 'Mike, I've sorted out your investigating officer, Bishop should be with you around half one. Have you got hold of Attwood?'

'Yes,' responded Horner. 'He's sitting right opposite me.'

'Good. I've sorted out the incident room and a couple of lads to help out in the preliminary stages; we can sort out a full team when we know where we're at. I'll expect Bishop and Attwood in my office, ten o'clock in the morning.'

Martin pulled a face and glanced at the clock, which showed

1.15 am. Horner nodded.

'Er - Mr Wallace - it's after one now and Bishop hasn't arrived yet. It's going to be at least three in the morning before we've spoken to the police surgeon and forensic team.'

'The team will be working through the night in any case. Sorry Mike but we have to crack on with interviewing Nichols as soon as we decently can. Bishop and Attwood will just have to catch up on their sleep later - and if Attwood can hear me, tell him to stop pulling that hard-done-by face. Goodnight Mike.'

The line went dead and Martin gave a rueful smile. 'Who's Bishop? I don't think I know him.'

'Er - no. He's from outside the force - the new appointment.'

'Bloody hell, that's all we need.'

Horner sighed. 'Yes, well, Mr Wallace feels there may be advantages to having an outsider on this one. More objectivity.'

'But he'll know jack shit about the people involved, or the area.'

Horner frowned at him. 'With a cut and dried case like this, does that matter? In any case the decision's been made and you can provide him with all the local knowledge he needs. Look Martin, you're this bloke's right hand man and he's going to need your support. I do understand how you must feel but I'm relying on you to be professional about this.'

'Yes sir,' responded a poker faced Martin.

'All right. Get yourself down to the custody suite and see how the surgeon's getting along. I'll wait here for Bishop and bring him down to you.' Martin nodded and left the office.

Shortly after 1.30 am Sue was parking her red VW polo outside Fairfield Station. The car park was quiet, with just a handful of vehicles parked nearest to the building. She sat for a moment looking towards the station and wondering what awaited her on the other side of those doors, then left the car and walked round to the main entrance. The sleet had abated for the time being, but there was still a biting wind. A grizzle-haired sergeant responded to her ring.

*Cut and Dried*

'Can I help you?'

'I'm Mrs Bishop - I think the superintendent is expecting me.'

The sergeant looked at her blankly.

'Bishop,' she repeated. 'Detective Inspector Bishop. Superintendent Horner should be expecting me.'

'Oh. Oh - yes - er - ma'am. Yes, he is. Come this way please.'

He led the way down the corridor and up the stairs, their footsteps echoing in the strange, eerie hush that almost deserted buildings take on at night. At the top of the stairs he turned into a corridor and tapped smartly on the first door on the right.

'Come in!'

The sergeant opened the door. 'Detective Inspector Bishop, sir.' He stood aside for Sue to enter, then closed the door behind her. His footsteps faded away down the stairs.

The uniformed superintendent behind the desk stood up as she entered; he looked a little confused.

'Good morning sir,' said Sue. 'I believe you're expecting me?'

He came forward, holding out his hand as he did so. He was a nice-looking man, she thought, with a pleasant manner. Much younger than she had expected, given his rank.

'Yes – yes, of course we are. Come in, inspector, and welcome to Fairfield Police Station. I'm Superintendent Horner – Michael Horner - the sub-divisional commander. Please, sit down.'

Sue sat in the proffered chair. The superintendent returned to his chair behind the desk, still looking a little awkward. Sue remembered the confusion of the sergeant who had escorted her up the stairs.

'Didn't Mr Wallace tell you I was a woman?' she asked.

He hesitated, then laughed.

'No, in fact he didn't; and of course there's no reason why he should have to, no reason at all. Please forgive my surprise, inspector. Coffee?'

'Please.'

He busied himself with the coffee cups, talking as he did so. 'Let me just fill you in quickly on the basics of what's happened, then we need to get downstairs and talk to the police surgeon. Sorry you've been plunged in at the deep end like this, but we have a nasty murder on our hands. Of course, all murders are nasty, but this one is rather close to home. In fact, very close to home. In the family, you might say.'

Sue stiffened. 'Not a police officer?'

'Indeed. And right here, in the station.' He came across and put the mug of coffee into her hand. 'It's the custody sergeant. He was found dead on the floor of his own custody office.'

'Good grief! And it's definitely a murder?'

He nodded gloomily. 'Not a doubt of it. His relief found him, lying there on the floor, stabbed in the back.'

'In the custody office? But – isn't that kept secure?'

'Oh yes! And of course that narrows the number of suspects considerably.'

'To how many?' asked Sue.

'Well, realistically, to just one. A prisoner was found standing over him and the knife in his back belonged to the prisoner. It's really pretty much an open-and-shut case, but it's still a murder, so we need a DI to run it with the DS.' He gave a tired smile, unwittingly echoing Wallace. 'At least it'll be an easy one to cut your teeth on, so to speak.'

'Sounds like it,' said Sue cautiously, 'but I'd rather not jump to any conclusions.'

'Proper order too.' he approved.

Sue frowned. 'Am I the best person for this? I don't know any of the people involved.'

'Exactly. That's one reason Mr Wallace wanted you on the case. He could have called in the DI from the neighbouring division for this one, but he preferred you. You have no prior knowledge and no pre-conceptions, so you can be completely objective. With a local DI who knows everyone involved, Mr Wallace feels the investigation could be a little – well - incestuous. Kind of like family investigating family.'

*Cut and Dried*

Sue frowned, some instinct telling her that there was more to this than met the eye. 'Can I see the murder scene?' she asked. 'And the body, of course.'

'Sure. The police surgeon's down there waiting for us. I'll take you down now to have a word with him and take a look around. DS Martin Attwood is already down there, so he'll be able to fill in the details for you.'

'Good man?' asked Sue.'

'Sorry?'

'The DS,' she clarified.

'Oh – yes. Yes, Martin's an excellent detective. But he's very much an old-style copper who hasn't adapted too well to the demands of PACE. He's always got results, but by his own sometimes questionable methods.' He chuckled. 'He went up for the DI's assessment board last month and some of his views were decidedly out of line with the demands of today's service. A little – shall we say – unorthodox.'

Sue frowned. 'He went for the DI's post? The one I've got?'

'That's right.'

'So he's not going to be a very happy bunny.'

The superintendent shrugged. 'He'll just have to live with that, won't he? There were six people up for one job, which means that five of them had to be disappointed. In any case, Martin wouldn't have got the job, even if he'd been the only runner.' He frowned. 'Even though he's been doing the job for three months.'

Sue frowned. 'That sounds a bit hard on him.'

'I know, and I agree. And fair play to him, he's worked hard as acting DI and the men like him. But we've had to sort out a few problems along the way. As I said, he takes too many short cuts, and I'm afraid the days of short cuts are numbered.'

'So far as I'm concerned, the days of short cuts are gone,' said Sue bluntly. 'Short cuts just lead to lost cases, in the long run. Not to mention damaging publicity for the service.'

'Yes, well, I'm afraid you might have your work cut out convincing some of your detectives of that one.' He swallowed the last of his coffee. 'Right, the police surgeon will be wanting his bed; we'd better get down to the custody suite and see what he has to say.'

It was quiet down in the custody office. There was still quite a bit of activity, but it was subdued activity. Pete's body hadn't yet been moved and forensic teams were still combing the rest of the room. Other than essential personnel the room was still a no-go area, and a uniformed officer still presided over the entrance. Next to him two men were talking quietly. One of them, wearing a dark suit, had his back towards them and Sue could only see that he was slim, medium height, with curly dark hair. The other man, facing them, was chubby and middle-aged, casually dressed in jeans and polo-neck sweater. Superintendent Horner approached them.

'Martin?' he said.

The man in the suit looked round and Sue regarded him with interest - this was to be her right-hand man, the man whose support was crucial to her. She guessed that he was in his mid-thirties, with a thin face and watchful eyes.

'Oh, there you are, sir,' he said. 'I believe you've met Dr. Clarke?'

'Indeed yes.' The superintendent shook hands with the doctor, then turned to Sue. 'May I introduce you to our police surgeon, Dr. Henry Clarke; and Detective Sergeant Martin Attwood. Gentlemen, this is Detective Inspector Sue Bishop.'

'Bloody hell!' exclaimed Martin.

'I beg your pardon, sergeant?' Horner's tone was unusually frosty.

Martin shook his head in confusion. 'Sorry, sir – er – ma'am. No offence, but you took me by surprise.'

'Obviously.' said Sue dryly. She turned her attention to the police surgeon. 'I'm pleased to meet you, Dr. Clarke.'

They shook hands and Horner gestured towards the door at the far end of the corridor. 'Perhaps somewhere a little more private?'

He led the way to the main admin office, deserted at this

time of night. 'Well, doctor? What can you tell us?'

The doctor perched on one of the desks. 'Cause of death is fairly self-evident. Just one stab wound to the back, but the knife had gone right through the heart, clean as a whistle. I couldn't have done better myself. The wound is consistent with having been made with the stiletto the prisoner was holding, but of course I can't comment on the blood match before analysis.' He smiled. 'I wouldn't like to bet anything on its NOT matching though.'

'Time of death?' asked Sue.

'Ah! Now that's a bit of a tricky one. I understand the body was found just before 11 pm, with this man Nichols standing over him? Well, I'd have put the death at somewhat earlier than that. More like 10 pm, give or take a quarter of an hour.'

Martin frowned. 'Nichols would hardly have been standing over him for that length of time.'

'I agree,' said Horner. 'Doctor, could you be mistaken about the time of death?'

The doctor shrugged. 'Of course - it isn't a very exact science. But frankly I wouldn't expect to be too far out with this one. I was here by quarter to midnight, within 45 minutes of the body being found.'

'The cold?' suggested Horner. 'Could that make it seem longer?'

'It could.' said the doctor dryly. 'Except that it isn't cold; not in there anyway. The temperature is a nice, steady 70 degrees Fahrenheit.' He shrugged. 'It's a bit of an anomaly, certainly, we may know a little more after the post mortem.' He looked at his watch. 'I don't think there's much more I can do here, I'll let you have my preliminary report in the morning of course. In the meantime, I'm happy for the body to be moved to the mortuary, once the forensic team are through.'

When the doctor had gone Sue went back to the custody office, where the forensic team grudgingly allowed her to look at the body. A pointless exercise really, she thought. The experts would have gathered all possible evidence, both seen and unseen.

Pete Ashbourne still lay where he had fallen, the blood on the back of his shirt now dried almost to black. There was a pool of blood on the floor and specks of blood spattered around; on the side of the sink, the nearest wall. Smashed crockery was scattered around the area.

After a few minutes she left the custody office, having first established that the scene would remain sealed for the time being. That, too, was probably a pointless exercise, she thought. Damage – if any – had probably already been done, in those crucial first few minutes after the crime was discovered. That was the time when most evidence was inadvertently destroyed, when the prosecution case was most often weakened, sometimes fatally. And it wasn't always civilians who caused the damage; as often as not it was police officers, including highly trained police officers. Those first few minutes when excitement and adrenalin kicked into action, and objectivity went into neutral.

The doctor having left, Horner turned to Sue. 'Where are we going from here, inspector?'

'Nichols!' interrupted Martin. 'We need to talk to Nichols. As soon as we can, I'd say.'

Sue looked into his watchful and slightly hostile eyes, then glanced at her watch. 'You're suggesting we haul him out of his cell and start interviewing him? At three o'clock in the morning?'

'Sure – why not? He's tired? Good! Tired men make mistakes.'

'Tired detectives make mistakes too,' Sue pointed out. 'In any case, you can't justify waking him up and interviewing him now; not without a cast iron reason.'

'Such as murder?' suggested Martin.

'Such as someone being at immediate risk, such as evidence being destroyed. It won't wash, detective sergeant.'

'I quite agree.' said Horner crisply. 'So what now?'

'Well, I suggest we leave the experts to their job of gathering evidence and reconvene in the morning. We need to set up an incident room . . .'

'Already done,' said Horner. 'Mr Wallace is sorting all that;

he wants to see both of you in his office at FHQ, ten o'clock in the morning.'

Sue looked doubtful. 'There's an awful lot I need to know - and we should certainly be interviewing Nichols as soon as we can, once he's had his eight hours. DS Attwood's right about that.'

'Mr Wallace appreciates that, but he wants to see you first. I suppose he wants to establish a game plan. In the meantime, I've got Sergeant Tim Hawkins waiting in the sergeants' office downstairs - he's the one who found the body and he'll go to the post-mortem in the morning. Once you've spoken to him, why don't you both get yourselves home to bed? There's really nothing more you can do tonight, that you can't do just as well in the morning. Oh - do you know the way to FHQ?'

Sue nodded. 'I had my interview there.'

'Of course you did. Right, let's go back up to my office, I'd like a brief chat before you see Tim.' He turned to Martin. 'And if you'd like to wait in your office, I need a quick word with you too. I shan't be long.'

Martin nodded and Horner and Sue left him and headed back to the superintendent's office. Once there, Horner gave a tired smile.

'What's your first name inspector?'

'Susan. Sue.'

'Is it all right to call you Sue, when we're alone and being informal? Nothing to do with your being a woman, I assure you, I tend to use first names for most people. Unless they object, of course.'

'No problem with that sir,' said Sue.

'Good. I'm sorry about Martin's reaction downstairs, I'll certainly be having a few words with him about it. He'll come round, given time. He's a good DS, on the whole. He'll give this investigation his best shot, I'm sure.'

'I hope you're right.'

He frowned. 'If not, I want to know about it. I mean that Sue. You have my full support in this - if there's any insubordination,

I need to know.'

'I can handle Sergeant Attwood,' said Sue shortly.

'I don't doubt it. Well, goodnight Sue - or should I say good morning. I'll take you down to the sergeants' office where Tim is, then I'll go and have those words with Martin Attwood.'

Tim Hawkins was alone in the sergeants' office, already working on his statement. Sue introduced herself and they shook hands. The sergeant didn't react at all to her being a woman and Sue suspected he'd already been warned - probably by Martin Attwood.

Sue sat down opposite Tim. 'Sergeant, I appreciate that you're doing a full statement in any case, but could you just talk me through what happened.'

'No problem. As you doubtless know I was due to be custody sergeant on the night shift, eleven through to seven. Normally I'd relieve Pete around quarter to eleven, but I got held up by a traffic accident so I was late. I steamed into the front office about five to eleven, just before they locked the main door.

Normally I'd have popped into control room to see what was going on, but I knew Pete would be pretty pissed off, so I headed straight for the custody office. The corridor entrance was locked, so I guessed there was at least one prisoner in. Control buzzed me through as usual, then I rang the custody office bell. There was no answer, which was a bit unusual, so I buzzed again, and shouted. When there was still no answer I buzzed the control room to let me through.'

Sue interrupted him. Tell me about the security system and the buzzers.'

'Sure. Well, when there's a prisoner in, the side corridor and the custody office are both supposed to be secured. There's a button each side of the corridor entrance door, so you can buzz to be let in or out of the corridor. Both go direct to the control room.'

'Speech only, or speech and video?'

'Just speech, on the corridor ones.'

'Okay. What about the actual custody office entrance?'

'That has two buttons. One is just heard inside the custody office, the other one goes to control. Again, they're just speech - no video.'

'Any other security buttons?'

'Yes. There's one by the door that leads to the prisoners' yard, and another in the yard outside. Both go direct to control. The inside one is just speech, but the one outside in the yard has a camera on it. I suppose the logic is that we're more concerned with who comes in, than with who goes out.'

'Thank you - sorry to interrupt. Now then, you said you shouted through to Sergeant Ashbourne. What did you shout? Can you remember?'

'Just "Pete!"'

'All right. Then you buzzed the control room and they let you through.'

'Yes. When I walked in - well, I think I struggled to take in what I was seeing. The first thing I registered was a bloke kneeling in the corner of the office, near the sink'. He shuddered. 'It took a second or two before I really took in what he was kneeling over and when I did it just made my blood run cold. It was Pete, lying on his front. I could see straight away that the back of his shirt was covered in blood. Then I recognised the bloke as Nichols - everybody here knows him. He was staring up at me and I was staring back - you know what it's like at times like that, we seemed to be staring at each other for ages, but it was probably just a couple of seconds. Then as he stood up I noticed the knife sticking out of Pete's back.

'At that point I came to and hit the alarm button. Luckily the night shift were briefing in the parade room just opposite the custody office corridor and there were five blokes there within about ten seconds.'

'What did Nichols do?'

'He just stood there, looking like a rabbit caught in the headlights. Then when the troops arrived he backed against the wall. He was just shaking his head and saying "no - no!" Andy Rye and Sergeant Wright shoved him against the wall and searched him while I went to Pete.' He shook his head. 'I'm no doctor so I can't certify death, but I know a dead body when I see one. And I'll tell you this - Pete was well and truly gone. He was dead white, except where the blood had gathered and made the skin go blue. And he was cold.'

'Cold? Even then?'

Tim nodded. 'Yes. I didn't think about it at the time, but he must have been gone for a while. It hadn't just happened.'

Sue nodded. 'Thanks very much sergeant. I'd be grateful if you could make sure all of that is included in the statement.'

'Will do ma'am.'

Sue left the office to find Martin waiting for her in the parade room. She looked at her watch, which showed 3.30 am. 'Well, the scene is safely preserved, the prime suspect is under lock and key. There's not much more to be done tonight and we need to be at FHQ for ten o'clock. I think we both need to head for home.'

They left the building together, not speaking, and separated on the car park. For a few moments Sue sat quietly in her car, trying to collect her whirling thoughts; but she was too tired really. Time for sleep and a fresh start in the morning.

# Chapter 10

Sue arrived home a little after four o'clock in the morning. The rutted lane leading to the house was treacherous with ice and the blackness of both the lane and the surrounding countryside was total, the thickness of the clouds blocking out moon and stars. There was, however, a rosy glow from the ground floor of the house - the only glimmer of light visible for miles around.

She let herself in quietly. Light flooded into the hallway from the open door of the kitchen, but all the other rooms were in darkness. There was no one in the kitchen - presumably Bill had left the light on so Sue wouldn't have to grope her way through the house in the pitch darkness. Oscar greeted her enthusiastically, tail wagging madly and whining with pleasure. She shushed him, then made her way upstairs. Bill was asleep, snoring softly, and she set her alarm for 9.00 am before climbing quietly into bed, without disturbing him. She slept deeply and dreamlessly, waking only when the alarm shrilled.

She clambered out of bed, still feeling tired despite the five hours sleep. A quick shower, she thought, then downstairs for an equally rushed breakfast.

Bill was in the kitchen, munching toast and dropping crumbs and jam across the daily paper. Oscar sat in his usual breakfast position, waiting patiently for any crumb that might make it past the newspaper. Sue popped more toast into the toaster and sat down opposite Bill.

'Did I wake you when I came in?'

'No, what time was it?'

'Four.' She took the coffee he handed her and drank gratefully. 'Sorry Bill, but it's a quick breakfast, then I have to go back.'

He groaned. 'I was afraid of that. Terry and Sarah will be here at eleven o'clock.'

'Well, I won't be here at eleven o'clock. Look Bill, I'm sorry; but we've been through that. I'm on a murder case; that has to take top priority. And it's not as if we never see Terry and Sarah – they only live three miles away, for God's sake!'

Bill frowned as he turned his coffee cup, abstractedly examining the pattern. 'And is this the way it's going to be here?'

'What do you mean?'

'Well, we've only just arrived and already they've pitched you in right at the deep end. I know you were sometimes called out when you worked in the city, but not like this.'

'Bill, how do I know what it's going to be like - I'm holding a cup of coffee, not a crystal ball. Look, in the City I was a detective sergeant – one of several at the station. Then I was a uniform inspector – one of several. Here I'm a detective inspector – the only one on the subdivision - and in operational charge of a murder. Of course it's going to be different. We knew that.'

He shook his head. 'I don't like it, Sue; I've just got a bad feeling about it. About us.'

'Now you're being ridiculous!'

'Am I? Look Sue, I knew I was marrying a copper. I knew you were ambitious; but I think I'm only just beginning to understand what it's going to mean – to us! It's going to get worse, isn't it? The higher you go, the worse it'll get.' He reached across the table and took her hand. 'Listen Sue, I know you love the job. But I love you and I want some home life too. You're married to me, not the job.'

Sue groaned. 'Oh Bill, not now. I love you; you know I do. And I need your support, Bill, now more than ever. I don't think I can do this without you.'

'Oh God, Sue, I'm sorry. Rough time?'

Sue took a bite of her toast, then pushed it away; she didn't feel like eating. 'I think it might be rough. The DS I'm working with obviously has a problem with a female boss, for a starter;

and I'm sure he won't be the only one.'

'Well, you would insist on going into CID.'

'I know, I know. It'll be okay, Bill, I'm just a bit tired.' She gave a wan smile. 'At least the uniform super seems a good sort, and judging by how young he is I suspect he's come up through the special course too. It's good to know there's someone there I can turn to, but I'd rather handle it myself.' She pushed away her still half-full cup of coffee. 'And look at the time! I have to go.'

She kissed him quickly and hurried out to the car, trying to get their recent conversation out of her mind. This had been coming on for some time, ever since Bill had been made redundant the previous year. He had managed to get another job fairly quickly, but then the detective inspector's vacancy had come up. Sue had applied for it somewhat tongue in cheek, not really expecting to be successful. But she had been, and suddenly they found themselves leaving the City and moving half way across the country to this much smaller, rural force. It meant Bill had to give in his notice and now he was job-hunting again. It was the right move, Sue was sure – or it would be, eventually. Her parents lived an hour's drive away and they already had friends in the area. Quality of life was better here too; better for children, if they ever had any.

Sue groaned, that was yet another bone of contention. Bill wanted children now, Sue wanted to wait. But this wasn't the time to be dwelling on her marital worries; she had other things to think about. 'Come on Sue,' she told herself. 'Focus, woman – focus.'

At ten minutes to ten Sue was turning into the lane leading to the county's headquarters. The main building stood at the end of a long, curving drive, flanked by rhododendron bushes which now hung limply but would be wonderful in the springtime. The building itself, framed by currently leafless trees, still retained the pleasing appearance of the country house it had once been.

She pulled onto the car park and slotted the car into one of the spaces marked 'visitor.' Inside the building the illusion of a country house was immediately dispelled, but the aura of elegance persisted. The floor of the reception area was polished parquet, the walls warmly panelled in wood. Sue approached the uniformed civilian behind the reception desk and produced her warrant card.

'Good morning. I'm Inspector Sue Bishop, to see Chief Superintendent Wallace. He'll be expecting me.'

'Very good ma'am. Just go up the stairs, down the first floor corridor, third door on the left.'

Sue thanked him and ran lightly up the splendid curving staircase. Mr Wallace's door stood open and he saw her before she even had time to knock.

'Mrs Bishop, come in - just waiting for the rest of the team. Martin Attwood will be a bit late because he's picking up some useful bits and pieces from Fairfield en route.'

Sue entered the office. It was a corner room, with windows overlooking the trees at the side and rear of the building; she felt as if they were miles out in the country, rather than within two miles of the town.

'It's a lovely building,' she said, 'with beautiful grounds.'

Wallace nodded. 'You'll only find HQ buildings like this in the small county forces like this one, and even here it's an anachronism. We're due to move at the end of next year - they're starting work on the new HQ in the spring.'

'Seems a shame.'

'In a way, but it really isn't practical any more. Not enough space and means that headquarters departments are dotted all over the county - training in one place, control in another. I'm afraid it's had its day. Ah - here's the rest of the team - come on in. Inspector Bishop, meet your team. DCs Dave Horton and Paul Redman.'

The two men came into the office and shook hands with Sue. Horton was around 35, tall and sandy haired. He had what Sue thought of as a typical CID look - his suit somewhere between smart and scruffy, his casual manner failing to mask an underlying sense of alertness. Redman was older, around mid-40s, plump and balding. His suit was clean but it had a comfortable, lived-in look to it and could certainly not be described as smart. Wallace waved them all to seats.

'I've set up the incident room next door,' he said. 'It's my secretary's office but she can double up with the assistant chief's secretary for the time being. In a minute you can go and get things set up, but there's one thing I need to make clear. There's a reason I decided to run the enquiry from here - and that's security.'

'Boss?' queried Horton.

'Security of the investigation. With any murder people who know the victim are going to be curious; they're going to want to know what's going on. Normally that's not a problem, but here it could be, especially if we tried to run the enquiry from Fairfield. We'd for ever have bobbies pestering for information and poking around the incident room.'

'We could keep it locked,' suggested Sue.

Redman chuckled. 'Cleaners' keys aren't difficult to get hold of on night shift. I remember breaking into the super's office and ferreting through his bin.'

'Whyever?' asked Sue.

'To find my annual appraisal. Oh, that's a long time ago, when I was just a young sprogg. Of course' he said, straight-faced, 'I wouldn't dream of doing such a thing now.'

'Remind me to use my shredder more,' said Wallace dryly. 'But you see what I mean? Boredom on the night shift can lead to all kinds of mischief. On the face of it this case seems to be pretty straight forward, but I'm not jumping to conclusions and I don't expect you to. So - no discussion of this case with anyone other than the team, and me. Clear? And nothing to the press, just refer them to the press officer, who will be thoroughly briefed, by me. Right, go next door, get set up and sort out your game plan. Martin Attwood will be here soon. I'm not going to breathe down your necks - just keep me updated with important developments and make sure I have a full report of progress for Monday morning's briefing.' He nodded to the two men.

'Go and start getting set up - I'll just have a quick word with the inspector.'

The two men exited, closing the door behind them. Wallace turned to Sue. 'Inspector, your first priority is?'

'Nichols,' said Sue promptly. 'The clock's ticking and we need to get at least a preliminary interview under our belts.'

He nodded approval. 'You've got a good team inspector, don't be taken in by Paul Redman's appearance - he's the best interviewer on the force, bar none and he's got a sharp eye for detail. Not much gets past Redman. Anything else you need to know?'

'Not that I can think of at the moment.'

'Good. As I said, I'll keep out of your hair, but I'm here if you want me.'

Sue thanked him and went into the adjacent office, which already bore a laminated sign stating 'Murder Incident Room.' Martin Attwood was just coming down the corridor and she held the door open for him. 'Good morning.'

'Morning ma'am. Sorry to be a bit late, I've picked up a few bits and pieces from Fairfield that I thought might be useful. I've got the custody records from Pete's shift yesterday and the statement from Sergeant Hawkins, who found the body.'

'Did Mr Wallace ask you to do that?' queried Sue.

Martin frowned. 'No. I thought it would save a bit of time so I rang him this morning and said I'd be a bit late. Why? Is it a problem?'

'No - on the contrary - it's a good idea. I was just curious. Let's take a look at them both, then we'd better get over to Butt Lane and have a word with Mr Nichols. Start with the custody record.'

Martin opened his briefcase and extracted a number of documents. 'This is the actual record, but I've done a summary for everyone as well.' He handed round copies and silence fell whilst everyone read through the summary. Sue studied the document with interest - these were the last people to see Pete Ashbourne alive.

*Cut and Dried*

*1450     Sergeant Ashbourne takes over from Sergeant Hopwood. Two prisoners in custody Burford (robbery) and Roberts (female - public order).*

*Burford out for interview with DS Attwood.*

*1520     Superintendent Horner visits and signs custody record*

*1530     WPC Cornwell visits prisoner Roberts.*

*1610     DS Attwood returns Burford to his cell.*

*1630     PC Haines to custody office. Roberts charged and bailed.*

*1700     DS Attwood charges and bails Burford. (now no prisoners in custody)*

*1715     PC Woodward arrives with Nichols, arrested for wounding. Nichols searched and placed in cell. Record of slight injuries to Nichols, sustained during arrest.*

*1800     Nichols provided with meal.*

*1835     Sergeant Harris relieves Sergeant Ashbourne for meal break*

*1845     Nichols given cup of tea*

*1900     Inspector Lee visits Nichols for PACE review.*

*1920     Sergeant Ashbourne returns to custody office.*

*2000     Nichols out for interview with DS Attwood*

*2125     Nichols returned to cell.*

Sue looked up. 'And that's it?'

'That's it for official visitors - the ones we know about, who had a reason for being in the custody suite. I left around twenty to ten and it's likely I was the last one to see Pete alive - except for the murderer of course.'

Redman whistled. 'Oooh - Martin Attwood, prime suspect!'

Martin grinned. 'Could be. Luckily for me I had you with me when I left the nick.' He turned back to Sue. 'We left together and joined the lads in the pub until twenty past eleven.'

'Well,' said Sue, 'that's good to hear. Having my right hand man as a suspect might just cramp the investigation a bit.' She glanced at her watch. 'Martin, you can talk me through this list later. I think it's time we had a few words with Mr Nichols.'

## Chapter 11

The solicitor was already waiting when they arrived at Butt Lane. Martin greeted him as 'Jim' before introducing him to Sue as James Cole; the solicitor and Martin were obviously on familiar terms.

'You've had the opportunity to talk to your client?' asked Sue.

Cole nodded. 'Yes, indeed. But I'd like another brief chat with him, if you don't mind. Five minutes or so.'

'Of course,' Sue agreed. When he had gone, she raised her eyebrows at Martin.

'He's okay,' said Martin. 'On the ball, you might say, but not disruptive. We could have done worse.'

'Does he know Nichols?'

'They all know Nichols,' said Martin dryly.

Ten minutes later, they were in the interview room. An uncharacteristically subdued Nichols sat in the proffered chair, while Martin took his seat next to Sue. The solicitor seated himself next to Nichols.

Martin opened the proceedings. 'Right then Robbie, I'm Detective Sergeant Martin Attwood, this is Detective Inspector Sue Bishop. I have to remind you that you are still under caution, and that you do not ...'

'Yeah – yeah,' interrupted Nichols. 'I know who you are and I don't care who she is. I know all that crap, I've been through it often enough. Just get on with it.'

Martin calmly finished the caution then continued.

'Now then Robbie, will you talk us through what happened yesterday evening, when you were in custody at Fairfield Police Station.'

Nichols shrugged. 'Well, I found that bastard dead, didn't I?'

'We need a bit more detail than that, Robbie. Let me take you back a bit. PC Woodward had arrested you for wounding on your wife … '

'Bitch asked for it. I'd bin out to the pub and had a few, then got home and crashed out for a couple of hours. What do I find when I wake up? F – all, that's what. The bloody missus 'adn't even got no beer in the fridge, like I told 'er to. Then she started whining about 'aving no money, so I thumped 'er; and when she started going on about it, I slashed her arm open for 'er. So what? But of course the nosey buggers next door 'ad to call the fuzz, didn't they? I'll do them over when I get out.'

'You've already been interviewed in connection with that,' said Martin patiently. 'Now, you and PC Woodford arrived at Fairfield Station at 5.15 pm that evening, take me on from there.'

Nichols shrugged. 'We got to the station, and that little shit of a sergeant booked me in. Smacked me across the face when I got gobby.' He pointed to his face. 'See that? That's where he hit me in the mouth when he took me down to the cells. Nasty bastard, he was!'

'Did you make a complaint?' asked Martin.

'Don't be bloody stupid, who do I complain to? Another cop? You buggers all stick together, don't you?' He shrugged. 'Anyway, no point complaining about it now. The bastard's dead, isn't he?'

'All right. So you're in your cell. Then what?'

'Then he brought me my dinner, if you can call that pigswill dinner. And a cup of tea that was bloody nearly cold. Then about half an hour later that other sergeant brought me a cup of decent tea. Then I sat there and did sweet f. a. till you fetched me for interview.'

'And after that?'

'Well, you bloody know that. You were there.'

'But I need to know from you.'

'As you like. You took me back from interview.'

Sue leaned forward. 'Robbie, do you remember what time it was then?'

He shrugged. 'Just before half nine, there was a clock outside the cell block.' He nodded towards Martin. 'He stuck me back in my cell and left me. He'd give me a newspaper, so I looked at it for a few minutes, but the light in those cells is bloody crap to read by so I just lay there doing nothing, most of the time.'

'Did anyone come down to see you?' asked Martin.

'No-one.'

'Did you hear anything?'

Nichols shrugged. 'Bit of noise. There often is down in them cells, specially weekend nights. Other prisoners kicking off, you know.'

'And you heard some noise that evening? What kind of noise?'

Nichols thought about it. 'There was some row, yes. A bit of shouting and yelling.'

'When?'

'Just after I'd got back. I dunno - maybe ten minutes, fifteen minutes? Weren't important to me mate. Like I say, you often get a bit of row down there.'

'Robbie, this is important. Can you remember what was said? Any words?'

He shrugged. 'Dunno, just yelling, couldn't make out no words. Wasn't taking that much notice and anyway the sounds're muffled. Them cell doors're thick.'

'Recognise any voices?'

'No. Like I said, it was muffled anyway, and I weren't really interested.'

'All right. What next?'

'Well, it went quiet and I lay down on the bed and tried to doze. I thought I heard someone outside in the cell block corridor and I heard the keys rattling so I guessed they were bringing another prisoner down, likely enough the guy who'd kicked off in the big room. Then about – oh, I dunno – maybe half an hour, maybe an hour after that, I needed to crap. I rang the bell and the bastard didn't answer, so I played hell with it. Then I went to the door to shout – and the bloody door was open.'

'Open?'

'Well, not wide open, but not quite shut. You could see it weren't locked. Anyway, first thing I did was go for a crap. Then I thought – you know – summat weren't just right. What the hell was my door doing open? I went down the corridor to the cell block doors, and bugger me if they weren't open n'all. Bloody queer! But I thought, bloody hell, if there's no-one there, that's me out of here! So I went out into the big room.'

He stopped. 'And then?' Martin prompted.

'And then? And then I saw the body. Bloody shock mate, I can tell you. Just lying there, still and dead.'

'You knew he was dead? Straight away?'

Nichols shrugged again. 'I knew he weren't moving. I knew he was covered in blood. I knew he had a knife sticking out his back.' He paused. 'And from where I was, it looked like it was my knife.'

'So? What did you do then?'

'I went and bent over him to check and sure enough it was my bloody knife. I touched his face and it was cold - you know, like dead meat. I bin in the army mate, I know a corpse when I see one. I could see he was gone.' He leaned forward. 'Look mate, I hated that bastard. When I saw he was dead, I thought well done somebody, good bloody riddance. I'd love to 'ave stuck a knife in 'im, but I wouldn't 'ave knifed 'im in the back - I'd have give it 'im in the front so the bastard could see it coming. But I didn't do for 'im. I don't know who did, or why, but it weren't me.'

'All right,' said Martin. 'Carry on from there. What did you do?'

'Bloody panicked, that's what I did. I'll tell you straight, I was shitting myself. There I was, stuck in there with a dead body, with my knife sticking out of 'im. What did it look like? Bloody obvious you'd think it were me. I decided I'd better get out of there, double quick.'

'How?'

'Absolutely no bloody idea! I didn't get the chance to even think what to do, let alone do it.

'Did you touch the knife?'

'No, but what difference does that make? My dabs'll be all over it anyway.'

'You don't deny it was your knife?'

'How the devil can I deny it?'

'You say all you could think of was getting out. Did you try to get out?'

Nichols shook his head. 'Didn't have time, did I? I'd hardly started to think about it when the bloody buzzer sounded and that sergeant come in.'

'Did you think about trying to get past him?'

'Course I did, but there wasn't time. I'd hardly stood up before the room was full of bloody coppers.'

There was a pause, during which Martin glanced at Sue. She leaned forward, taking over the conversation.

'Robbie, think back. You're standing there in that room. Look around you. Is there anything else you can remember? Anything at all.'

Nichols shrugged and stared down at the floor.

'Think!' Sue persisted. 'You're saying you didn't do this – help yourself by helping us. Help us to find who did. What else did you see in that room? Anything you can remember.'

'Blood, of course. A lot of blood. The back of his shirt was soaked in it and there was a fair bit on the floor. I trod in some of it so it was on the bottom of my sock. And it was on the wall, by the sink. And there were pots or summat, smashed all over the floor. I remember having to be careful because I was in my socks, the shoes were still outside my cell.'

'And did you move at all? Once you'd come through the door in the bars, you got to the body. Did you go anywhere else?'

Nichols shook his head. 'No. I told you, I hadn't time to do nothing. I'd just thought about going back for my shoes and getting myself out of there, when the buzzer went. I heard somebody say 'Pete' and I just sort of froze. Bloody hell, wouldn't you have done? I was standing over a dead body, for God's sake, and there was nobody else in the room.' He leaned forward. 'Look, I hate all cops and I hated that one worse than any of 'em. But I never did 'im in. I 'ated 'is guts and I ain't sorry somebody did for 'im, but it weren't me.'

Sue nodded and looked back at Martin, who stood up decisively.

'All right Robbie, that's all for now. We need to check out a few things, then we'll need to talk to you again.'

'So what happens now?'

'You go back to your cell, for the present.'

Martin and Nichols left the room, leaving Sue with the solicitor. The latter gathered up his papers, then addressed Sue. 'Detective inspector, when might my client expect to get out of here?'

'I don't know. You do appreciate, Mr Cole, that we're investigating a murder.'

'Indeed. And I hope, inspector, that you appreciate the rules of PACE. Mr Nichols was arrested at 11 pm on the 15th on suspicion of murder. It's now noon on the 16th. The clock is ticking.'

'I'm aware of that Mr Cole, but I'm afraid we won't be releasing Mr Nichols just yet. We'll certainly be seeking detention until tomorrow morning, and probably after that.'

'So you'll be seeking a magistrate's hearing?'

'Almost certainly.'

The solicitor nodded. 'We will of course be objecting to that. You'll keep me updated as to any developments?'

'Of course.'

In that case, good afternoon inspector, for the present.'

He nodded, picked up his briefcase and left the room.

\*

The interview concluded, Sue and Martin were on their way back to FHQ.

'Well,' said Sue, 'what do you think?'

'Of Nichols? Guilty as hell.'

'Mmm. I'm not so sure.'

Martin groaned. 'For God's sake! The man was standing over the body, a knife – his own knife, incidentally – sticking out the back of the corpse, covered in blood. He's as guilty as a puppy standing over a pile of steaming poo.'

'Maybe,' said Sue. But don't forget puppies also like to sniff around other dogs' poo. There are still things that don't fit.'

'Such as?'

'Time of death, for one thing. Not just the doctor's estimate, but Tim Hawkins as well. If Nichols had just killed Pete Ashbourne that body would certainly have been warm.'

Martin gave a non-committal grunt. 'What's to say he had just killed Pete? Why couldn't he have killed him half an hour before - or even longer? It's not impossible.'

'I agree,' said Sue, 'and I'm certainly not suggesting we rule Mr Nichols out. I do think there are question marks though. Come on Martin - put your other hat on and give me counsel for the defence.'

Martin frowned. 'Surgeon's opinion on time of death? Supported by Tim Hawkins.'

'Big point in Nichols' favour. Not cast iron, I admit, but it starts to cast that doubt. And?

'Martin smacked his own forehead, causing the car to swerve dangerously across the road. 'Shit! oh – sorry ma'am. But I must be losing it, mustn't I? Blood!'

'Right!' said Sue. 'Blood, indeed. Or in this case, lack of it. There was a lot of blood on Pete Ashbourne's shirt. There was blood on the knife, on the floor, on the fridge, even on the wall. Whoever stuck that knife into Pete Ashbourne had to be blood-stained. Had to be!' She paused. 'And the blood suggests an earlier time of death too. Even the knife, Martin.'

'There was wet blood on the blade.'

'Of course there was – where it had been stuck in the corpse and not exposed to air. But the blood on the hilt was dry.'

Martin nodded. 'I guess he could have wiped the hilt, but then, what did he wipe it on? And Nichols certainly wasn't blood-stained – not fresh blood anyway. He had a few stains on his shirt, but they were long dried and he had them when I interviewed him. They'd be from his missus.' He wrinkled his brow. 'Unless there was some way he'd got hold of something to keep the blood off him, then got rid of it.'

'Where?' asked Sue.

No idea! But let's follow this one through. Let's just say Nichols did kill Pete, and he did it at the time the police surgeon gave as the most likely time of death. Say around ten o'clock, give or take. He had a fair bit of time before he was found just before eleven o'clock.'

'He'd have tried to run for it, surely.'

'Well, you'd think so, I agree.' He ran his hand through his dark curly hair. 'This whole thing's bizarre! What was he doing out of his cell? When I left he was banged up tight as a – well, tight.'

Sue frowned. 'Pete Ashbourne seems to have been washing up just before he died. Could he have got Nichols out to help him?'

Martin shook his head. 'No way! Not Pete – and certainly not Nichols. I even suggested that to Pete, as a bit of a joke. Pete was moaning about having to wash up after the prisoners, he always hated that, on principle. But he made it pretty clear he'd never have trusted Nichols out of his cell. But he was out of his cell, we know that. Look, let's stay with him as a suspect for the moment. Once he was out of his cell and into the custody office, how would he get past Pete, take his own knife from where it was bagged up . . .'

'Which was where?' interrupted Sue.

'On the back shelf, behind the counter.'

'Shouldn't it have been in the safe?'

Martin shrugged. 'Technically, yes. I'm afraid a lot of the

custody sergeants just bag things up on the back shelf like that, then the night sergeant locks them safely away until the next morning. Anyway, on the back shelf is where it was. I saw it there.'

Sue nodded. 'Which means Nichols would have had to actually go round the counter, open the bag, go back and stab Pete. In the back. Unlikely!'

'Impossible, do you think?' queried Martin.

'No, not impossible - at this stage, nothing's impossible. But Pete Ashbourne wouldn't have just been standing around watching him, would he?'

'Suppose Nichols banged him on the head, stunned him? That would give him time.'

Sue scribbled some more notes as the car turned into the driveway of FHQ. 'It would. We need full reports from forensic and the police surgeon, Martin. For the custody office, and for Pete Ashbourne.'

# Chapter 12

Sue arrived home just before eight o'clock that evening. Oscar greeted her with his usual enthusiasm, charging up and down the hall in order to gather momentum before throwing himself at her. She fought her way to the kitchen, where Bill was sitting at the table reading the evening newspaper. On the table was a dirty dinner plate bearing what looked like the remains of baked beans.

'Had dinner I see,' she commented. Bill made no reply.

'Have you fed Oscar?'

'Of course I have, it wasn't much use waiting for you to come home, was it?' He didn't look up from the newspaper.

She picked up the dirty plate and walked across to the sink. The breakfast dishes were piled up on the draining board, still unwashed, with cereal dried onto the inside of the bowls.

'You might at least have put them in soak, if you couldn't be bothered to wash them up.'

Bill responded with a grunt and returned to his newspaper as Sue began to wash the dishes 'For goodness sake,' said Sue. 'Can't you put that paper down for two minutes? There must be some really fascinating news in there.'

'Oh, there is.' He stood up, folded the newspaper carefully and threw it down on the table. 'Why don't you take a look? I'm going to watch the football.'

He stalked out of the room. Sue sighed and scratched Oscar's ears. He wagged his tail appreciatively - if only husbands were as uncomplicated as dogs.

She sat down at the table and picked up the paper. Her own face peered back at her, severe and unsmiling, short hair neatly cut and brushed, tailored suit and blouse. The very epitome of efficiency. Of all the photographs they could have chosen, it had to be that one. She groaned as she saw the headline next to the picture.

## FORCE APPOINTS FIRST FEMALE DETECTIVE INSPECTOR

*Woman Detective Inspector Susan Bishop has become the force's first female detective inspector and has immediately been placed in charge of a somewhat bizarre murder investigation …*

She threw the newspaper back on the table. She would read it later, right now she wasn't in the mood. She didn't feel like eating either, but she had had nothing since lunchtime. She needed food. She popped bread into the toaster, then recovered the rest of the beans from the tin on the counter top and popped them into the microwave. The meal finished, she popped her head round the door of the lounge. Bill was lounging on the sofa, watching football.

'Coffee?' she asked.

'Might as well.'

She made coffee for them both and took it into the lounge. He received it with a grunt that could have meant anything. Suddenly Sue's quick temper boiled over. She grabbed the remote and pointed it at the TV. Sound and image vanished abruptly.

'Hey!' said Bill.

'Hey yourself. I'm your wife Bill, not a bloody servant. I've been working all day and you've been here all day, and you could at least have washed up. It wouldn't hurt you to put the vacuum cleaner round occasionally either.'

'You always do that.'

'I always did that when we were both at work. Now you're at home, you should at least do something.'

'Why? So you can work even longer hours?'

'Bill, we've been through this, again and again. It's my job.'

'Well, I don't much care for your job, Sue. It comes before everything. It certainly comes before me.'

'That's rubbish!' she exclaimed.

'Is it? Is it rubbish? How long have you spent here at home the past few days?' He set his jaw. 'Sue, I want you to pack the job in.'

She gasped. 'What? Pack the job in, just like that? Bill, we've just moved here. You don't have a job yet, and I'm earning good money. There's no way I can stop working now.'

'Or ever,' muttered Bill.

'What do you mean?'

'What I say. Look at that newspaper headline Sue. You're a trail-blazer, a suffragette, a leader of women. Do you see what it says, towards the end?'

'I haven't even read the bloody thing yet.'

'You should. It talks about you being one of the new breed of women with the drive and initiative to carve out a successful career for themselves. Where will it stop Sue? First woman chief constable in the country, perhaps?'

'Don't be stupid.'

'And where do I fit in? I want a family Sue. I want children.'

'One day Bill. It's too soon.'

'And one day it'll be too late. We're neither of us getting any younger, Sue.'

'For goodness sake, Bill, I'm not even thirty yet.'

'And will it be any different when you're just coming up to forty? I don't think so. I think you've got the bit well and truly between your teeth. I think your career has got hold of you; hook, line and sinker. You're never going to give it up for a baby.'

'It's all very well for you Bill, you don't have to make that choice. You don't have to give up anything to have a family. I do.'

'So you're finally admitting it. You don't want to have a family.'

'I'm just saying I don't want a baby right now.'

'That's not what I'm hearing.'

Sue groaned. 'It's no use talking to you. I'm going to bed. I'm whacked out and I have an early start tomorrow.'

'Well, I shan't disturb you. I'll sleep in the spare room.'

He picked up the remote and flicked the TV on again. Sue walked out of the lounge, closing the door behind her and wishing she could have slammed it with all her force. The thick carpet made that impossible.

# Chapter 13

When Sue arrived in the office on the following day the first thing she saw was the newspaper, folded to the appropriate page and placed prominently on the desk. She dropped it into the wastepaper bin.

There was a tap on the door, followed by Martin. 'Morning ma'am.'

'Good morning Martin – and must you keep calling me ma'am? I feel as if I ought to have a pack of Corgis nipping at my heels.'

'Sorry?'

'The Queen!' Sue clarified.

'Oh, right.' Martin chuckled. 'I see what you mean, but I can hardly call you "sir", can I?'

'I'd rather you didn't, but what do you call your regular DI?'

'Bob, or guvnor – depends on the circumstances.'

'So, can't you do that with me?'

'What - call you Bob?'

'Funny man! It'd probably be preferable to "ma'am", but Sue would be fine, when we're on our own.'

Martin shrugged. 'Fine. Sue works for me – but ma'am in company.'

'Why not guvnor?'

Martin shrugged.

'Come on Martin - spit it out. You obviously have a problem.' Martin hesitated. 'Look ma'am - Sue - I don't want to be rude, but wouldn't it be better to have someone running the case who already knows these people?'

'Do you usually do that?' she asked.

He looked confused. 'What?'

'Have someone running the case who knows the people. Bear in mind Martin, most murder victims don't tend to be police officers who are murdered in their own police stations. Most murders happen outside, don't they? And how often does the investigating officer know the people he or she is investigating? Hardly ever. That's just one facet of the investigation, finding out what makes the suspects and witnesses tick. The fact I don't know the people involved is one of the reasons I'm on this case.'

She put the custody record down and faced him squarely. 'Look, let's put our cards on the table and clear the air. I know you're not keen on having me as a boss. Okay, I understand that. I've got the job you wanted, and I'm a woman. Right?'

He looked surprised at her candour, then nodded. 'Well, not totally, no. Believe it or not, I'm not that pumped up about your getting the job I wanted, I can live with that. Someone has to have the job, and I'm enough of a realist to know it was never going to be mine anyhow. I'm too old school for them.'

'And?' Sue prompted.

'Look, I'm sorry I was rude when we first met, but I admit your being a woman was a bit of a broadside. Okay, I can live with that too – I don't much like it, but I can live with it.' He hesitated.

'Something you CAN'T live with?' Sue queried.

He shrugged. 'Well, can I ask how much service you've got?'

Sue gave an inward sigh. Ah well, it had to come out sooner or later, and maybe it was better to get everything in the open right away. She had to work with this man, and if not him, then someone who would probably have similar views and attitudes.

'All right!' she said. 'Potted history coming up. Joined in 1980, three years as a constable. Two years as a uniform sergeant, one year as a detective sergeant. Promoted to Inspector, one year as an operational inspector. And that's it!'

He stared at her. 'Seven years! You've got just seven years service?'

'Good arithmetic, sergeant!'

'Oh glory! You've like the super, aren't you? You're

accelerated promotion – special course.'

'Yes.' she said crisply.

'Then how the devil can you possibly have the experience to do this job?'

Sue took a deep breath. If she was honest with herself, she'd been wondering the same thing, ever since that early morning phone call had pulled her from sleep and pitched her into the pool at the deep end. She had hoped for time to feel her way, play herself in; but that wasn't the way it had happened.

'Frankly Martin, I don't have the experience. What I do have is the legal knowledge, the intelligence and the determination. The experience, Martin, is where you come in. I need an experienced DS – old school or not, and we'll talk about that later.' She leaned forward. 'Martin, listen to me, we both need to be professional about this. The job has to come first. We have to work together. If you can't do that, I'll ask for you to be taken off the case, with no repercussions and no hard feelings. It's up to you.'

He frowned and ran his hands through his hair, then nodded. 'Fair enough.' he said.

'So are you staying, or going?'

'I'm staying. As you said, we need to be professional. All I ask is that you do me the courtesy of listening to what I say. Do what you like in the end – you're the boss – but at least hear me out.'

'Agreed. Now, can we get on with the job?'

Martin looked at her from under his brows. 'I just want to pop over to Fairfield,' he said. 'Couple of loose ends from the jobs I've had to hand over.'

Sue nodded. She gave an inward sigh as he exited. She had no complaints about Martin's behaviour towards her, or the behaviour of the detectives now under her command. No one had been rude or disrespectful. But in a way, that was one of the problems, everyone was too respectful. They simply weren't comfortable with her as their DI, so they were keeping her very much at arms length. Oh well, it was a new experience for them all. It would take time, she supposed. Unfortunately patience had never been one of her strengths.

There was a tap on the door, followed by the appearance of Colin, one of the civilian staff from Admin.

'Morning ma'am,' he said cheerfully. 'This just came for you, marked urgent and personal.' He handed her an A5 size brown envelope.

Sue took it from him with thanks and slit it open. At last! The preliminary forensic report.

'Colin,' she said. 'Would you do me a favour and see if you can catch Martin Attwood – he's about to drive off to Fairfield Station. Tell him I've got the preliminary forensic report.'

'Pleasure.' said Colin amiably as he hurried off.

Sue settled back to read the report. Some ten minutes later the door swung open to admit Martin, carrying two steaming cups of coffee.

'Thought we might need these,' he said. 'Anything interesting?'

'Very interesting. First of all, on Pete Ashbourne. Signs of recent bruising to his left jaw, scratches to his neck. Slight tearing to shirt collar and button missing, suggesting shirt torn open. Missing button found nearby.'

Martin whistled. 'Well, well! Sounds like some kind of a struggle went on. Anything else?'

Sue nodded. 'Yes. What appears to be traces of hair under his fingernails on his right hand. Dark brown hair.'

'Dark brown? That certainly wouldn't fit with Nichols, he's grey. Can they send it for DNA analysis?'

Sue nodded. 'They can and have, but they don't hold out a lot of hope. Apparently you need the root to get an effective DNA analysis from hair and they don't think they have that. But there's a chance. We'll have to hang fire until we get a result on the DNA, if they do come up with something we can start testing potential suspects.'

'How long?' asked Martin. 'Before we hear back, I mean.'

'Minimum two weeks, maximum three.'

He groaned. 'So long? Can't they treat it as urgent? Don't they know it's a murder enquiry?'

'Yes to both. They do know that, and apparently they are treating it as urgent. Routine enquiries can run into months. So we have to do the best we can without DNA evidence, for the time being anyway.'

Martin shrugged. 'Well, at least we can count out baldies and blonds?' He looked at Sue's expression and sighed. 'We can't, can we?'

She shook her head. 'We can't count anyone out, not at this stage. What we can do is prioritise. In the meantime, keep this report between us. Now then, let's think about hair. Which of the people who were in the station on Friday have dark brown hair?'

Martin thought about it. 'Jim Taylor, George Haines, Roger Mason and the super. And Tim Hawkins, but he wasn't actually here when the murder took place.'

'Okay, that's a start. From your own knowledge, Martin, would any of those people have reason to have a row with Pete Ashbourne? A row that could have come to blows?'

'Well, who really knows? But if you're asking me who had reason to dislike Pete, that's a different question. As you'll soon discover, he wasn't too popular. He gave Tony Woodford a hard time, but Tony's fair haired. I'm pretty sure Pete was touching up young Mandy, but she's blonde too and I can't really see her having a physical fight with him and thumping him on the jaw; definitely not Mandy's style. Jim however, now that's a different kettle of fish. If he knew about Pete groping Mandy, he'd have every reason to go down and sort Pete out.'

'Is he the type who would? Sort Pete out I mean.'

'Oh yes. He's got a bit of a paddy on him, has Jim.'

'And did he know, do you think? That Pete Ashbourne was hitting on his girlfriend?'

Martin nodded. 'A bit more than girlfriend, Sue, they're engaged. And yes, I think he did know. At least, he and Mandy were both very upset about something earlier that evening. I walked in on them in the canteen. But obviously it may have been nothing to do with that, they could have just been rowing about something totally different.'

'Still very interesting,' said Sue. She picked up the report. 'Now then, there's some more interesting stuff here. There were traces of blood elsewhere in the room that matches Pete Ashbourne's blood. It looks as if it was carried on the bottom of someone's shoe.'

'Enough to identify the footwear?'

'Sadly not. But enough to say it was a boot or a shoe - not socks.'

'Ah,' said Martin. 'Nichols was wearing his socks when he was disturbed.'

'Yes. His shoes were still outside his cell, and they're clean. There's a bit of blood on the socks of course, but nothing to indicate that he moved from the vicinity of the body until he was bundled back into his cell, after the murder. But someone carried those stains. And they went back around the counter, and stopped. All right, we can't say definitely it was the murderer, but the odds look pretty good.'

'Right team; let's see what we've got.'

It was after lunch and Sue and Martin were up-dating Chief Superintendent Wallace. Each was armed with a copy of the preliminary forensic report and the report of the police surgeon. Wallace was standing by the pen board, where he had scribbled the words WHAT, WHERE, WHEN, WHY, WHO and HOW. By WHAT and WHERE he had placed a tick. By WHEN was a small question mark.

'I think we can narrow down the 'WHEN' quite a bit,' he said. 'From when Martin left the custody office at 2140, to around 2230. Realistically, probably more like 2215 given the surgeon's report and Sergeant Hawkins' evidence.'

Martin and Sue nodded agreement as he scribbled the times next to WHEN.

'Right, WHY and WHO. They go together to some extent

- if we can get the motive, we'll be a long way towards getting the perpetrator.'

'Nichols is still in the frame, surely?' said Martin.

'In the frame, yes - but maybe not centre frame. Let's leave WHY and WHO for the moment and concentrate on HOW. A knife in the back obviously, but we need a lot more than that if we're going to get anywhere.'

'Reconstruction?' suggested Sue.

'Good idea.' He dropped the pen into its rest and moved across to the coffee machine in the corner. 'Okay, I'm Pete Ashbourne. It's somewhere around 10 pm and I'm standing at the sink in the custody office, washing up. Nichols should be securely locked in his cell, unless Pete had got him out to help wash up.'

'No way,' said Martin. 'Pete was an old campaigner and he knew Nichols only too well - there's no way he'd have let Nichols loose like that.'

'But it's not impossible?'

Martin shook his head. 'I suppose nothing's impossible at this stage, but it's highly unlikely.'

Wallace nodded. 'All right. Nichols is obviously still a prime suspect but just for the moment let's assume it isn't him. Where does that take us?'

'Well, it means the odds are on it being a bobby,' said Martin. 'Someone who Pete knew.'

'Agreed. Whoever it was somehow had to get hold of that knife and get close enough to Pete to stab him in the back. Whether or not there was a scuffle, it suggests Pete wasn't watching too carefully and was taken by surprise.'

'Unless he was knocked out in the scuffle,' suggested Martin.

Wallace scanned the report. 'The surgeon talks about minor bruising, not bad enough to put him out. A scuffle rather than a wallop on the head. I'm not saying the scuffle wasn't part of the killing because it may have been, but for the moment let's assume Pete was off guard before whoever it was got hold of that knife.' He nodded to Sue. 'Inspector, jot down anything that occurs to you as we run through this. Martin, you're the murderer. That desk is the custody office counter, with the knife behind it. I'm at the sink washing up. The window is the cell block. Whoever you are, you've just made the decision to kill me - or maybe got yourself so steamed up you're not thinking rationally. The knife is lying there behind you, bagged up. Take it from there.'

He turned his back and started fiddling with the coffee machine. Martin picked up a paper knife from the desk, which he held out of sight by his side. He walked across the room and came up behind Wallace.

'Consider yourself stabbed, sir - possibly following a bit of a scuffle.'

'Okay. I'm lying dead on the floor. There's a knife in my back and a lot of blood - on my shirt, on the floor and the door of the fridge. On you. What are you going to do?'

Martin looked at the knife in his hand. 'Probably shit myself.'

'Doesn't feel like a carefully pre-planned job,' interjected Sue. 'Stuck here with a dead body, no easy way out and someone could come in any time.'

'Martin?' said Wallace.

'I want to get out of here, quick - and I don't want to leave any traces. I need to wipe the knife.' He paused. 'And I need to point the finger somewhere else, if I can.'

'So what are you going to do?'

'Wipe the knife hilt.' He looked round. 'Tea towel. There should be a tea towel.'

Sue looked on the list. 'There wasn't one when forensic got there.'

'Well there was earlier - I used it to dry up my cup.'

Sue scribbled a note. 'So murderer probably used the tea towel to wipe down the knife. Looking good. Now what?'

Martin thought. 'If I want to put Nichols in the frame, I need to unlock the cell block and his cell door.' Sue took her keys from her bag and dropped them onto the desk. Martin walked across and picked them up.

'Hold it there,' said Wallace. 'You've just walked behind the counter, almost certainly with blood on your shoes. That fits with the forensic report and explains why you had to go behind the counter. It also puts another question mark against Nichols - he was in his socks, his shoes were still by his cell door, with no sign of any blood. The indications are that Nichols hadn't moved from the vicinity of the body. Martin, carry on.'

Martin nodded. 'I should have taken the shoes off before I started moving around but I'm probably still in shock at what I've done. Right, I'm trying to pull myself together now. I'm leaving my shoes here and going across to the cell block in my socks. Avoiding the blood.' He walked across to the window. 'I'm unlocking the cell block, then Nichols' cell. Then I'm going back behind the counter, wiping down the keys and hanging them up.'

Sue scanned the report. 'Still fits. Keys were well and truly wiped. Now then, how are you going to get out?'

'I want to avoid leaving any more blood trail,' said Martin. 'So I'll either rinse off my shoes in the sink or carry them until I can get out of the building.' He paused.
'Shoes? Whoever it was could still have small traces of blood on them. Should we seize shoes?'

Sue frowned. Had it still been the night of the murder she would have seized the shoes of everyone in the building, but it was now three days after the event.

'I'd say not,' she said decisively. 'If the murderer realised he had trodden blood through the custody office, the shoes will be long gone in any case. We'll play a waiting game until we actually have a suspect, then we'll be scooping up every pair of shoes he or she owns.'

'I agree,' said Wallace. 'Carry on Martin - you still need to get out of the building.'

'Okay. It's a filthy night, wet underfoot and sleeting, so I can probably put my shoes back on safely once I get outside.'

'And you get outside, how?'

'Well, I can let myself out of the custody office easily

enough, but then - the only way is to buzz control.'

'Where are you going?' asked Wallace. 'Once you're in the cell block corridor.'

Martin frowned. 'I can't go into the cell yard because I'd be stuck there and there's a video camera. I've got to go into the station, then get down to the back door as quickly as I can.'

Sue leaned forward. 'So you have to buzz control?'

'Yes. Only way.'

'So someone in control might remember who buzzed from the cell block corridor in that crucial half hour. They just might.'

'If they knew', said Martin.

'Surely they should ask for identification before they buzz anyone through,' said Sue.

'They should. Sometimes they don't. It depends who was on.'

Sue groaned as she scribbled down notes. 'Let's hope for the best. Right, so you're buzzing to get out of the cell block corridor.'

Martin moved across to the door. 'And I'm covered in blood, which means I don't want to see anyone. I don't want anyone to even catch a glimpse of me . . .' he stopped abruptly.

'What?' asked Wallace.

'Covered in blood. The last thing I want to do is leave that custody office heavily blood stained. I want to cover up.' He stared at the door in front of him, then fingered the fawn coloured windcheater hanging on the peg. 'I want to cover up!' he repeated. He swung round and picked up his copy of the forensic report.

'What are you looking for?'

'I'm looking at the list of stuff that was in the custody office when forensic went over it.' He looked up. 'And I've found it - or rather, I haven't found it. Pete's cap is listed as being there, but not his coat. His coat is missing.'

'You're sure he had his coat with him on that day?' asked Wallace sharply.

'Positive. I saw it hanging there myself - his long black trench coat that he always wore for filthy weather like that. Whoever killed Pete must have taken that coat, almost certainly to cover up just in case he was spotted on his way out of the building.' He raised his eyebrows and looked across at Sue. 'Well, well - it's beginning to smell like other puppies' poo after all.'

# Chapter 14

The following morning Sue and Martin drove across to Fairfield Station to begin their interviews with the officers and civilians who had been on duty on the day Pete Ashbourne had died. The key witnesses were of course those who had been on duty between 9.30 pm and 11 pm.

'That's a fair few people,' said Martin. 'And of course it's possible the murderer wasn't even on duty. All the bobbies have a key to that back door, which means anybody - absolutely anybody - could have come into the station, buzzed for admittance to the custody office and done the deed.'

'Possible,' agreed Sue, 'but how likely?'

Martin shrugged. 'Highly unlikely I'd say. As you said yesterday, it doesn't have the feel of a carefully pre-planned job. Anybody coming in specially would have taken a chance on being seen in the corridor, being identified by control.'

'We're seeing the control room staff today?'

'Tomorrow - the late shift from the day of Pete's murder are day off today. First on the list is Mandy Cornwell.'

'Tell me about her.'

'Mandy? Young, attractive, naïve. Being CID I've never had a lot to do with her, but Superintendent Horner can fill you in - we're seeing him at nine o'clock. I suppose he wants an update.'

'He can't have one.'

Martin looked surprised. 'The super?'

'Nobody has an update Martin, not even the superintendent. Remember what Mr Wallace said. Everyone here is a potential suspect until they've proven otherwise - and even then their mate might be a potential suspect. I'm serious about that Martin - nothing to be leaked beyond the team.'

Martin nodded. 'Sense in that.'

Superintendent Horner was in his office. He greeted them in his usual amiable manner and waved them to chairs. 'Coffee? How's it going?'

'Thank you, yes,' said Sue. 'We're still very much at the early stages.'

'I understand Nichols has been bailed?'

'Yes. We don't have enough to charge and we couldn't hold him any longer.' She paused, then continued. 'I'm afraid we can't discuss the actual investigation sir - not even with you.'

He laughed. 'Oh, Mr Wallace has already intimated we're to keep our noses out. Proper order too.'

Sue sipped her coffee. 'I hoped you'd understand. But perhaps you can help us with a bit of background information. For example we're talking to Mandy Cornwell at ten; can you tell us a bit more about her?'

'Mandy? Funnily enough I've just been going through her file. Her probation ends in a couple of months, so final reports are due.' He frowned. 'She's very bright, she came top of her course at the training centre so everyone had great expectations of her.'

'But they haven't been realised?'

'Unfortunately not, in fact I think winning the top course prize has worked against her. Some people probably expected too much of her. Others immediately assumed she'd be long on theory and short on practicalities and unfortunately she's proving them right. She's not very mature, even for her young age, and she's very short on confidence. We hoped she'd improve as she settled in, but the opposite is true.' He sighed. 'Quite frankly, the girl's struggling and there are a few question marks over her confirmation of appointment, we're holding a case conference at training HQ next week. I don't think we'll be terminating her service but we're thinking about extending her probation and maybe putting her into the city centre for six months. Throw her in at the deep end, so to speak. It'll either make or break her.'

Martin chipped in. 'Did you ever hear any whispers about

her having problems with any male officers?'

'What kind of problems?'

'Harassment problems. Sexual harassment.'

Horner raised his eyebrows. 'No - and I'd be surprised if any of her shift tried anything like that. Apart from anything else she's engaged to Jim Taylor - he's one of the bobbies who arrested Nichols. Jim'd wipe the floor with anyone who tried it on with Mandy. He's very protective.'

'I'm not thinking of the lads on the shift,' said Martin. 'I'm thinking about Pete Ashbourne. The night Pete was killed Mandy and I passed each other in the custody office and she was obviously upset - almost in tears. I tackled Pete about it and he pretty much admitted he'd been touching her up.'

Horner frowned and shook his head. 'I knew nothing about that. I'd have been down on him like a ton of bricks, believe me.' He paused. 'We really need to know if something like that has been going on because it could well have affected her performance. Maybe she confided in one of the other women - you could ask them.'

Sue nodded. 'But we don't want it to be bandied all over the station. Did she have a special friend among the other women?'

'I wouldn't know. The best person to ask would be Judith Saunders; she's a WPC on E shift and she's got her finger pretty much on the pulse. Twenty years service, very efficient and very forthright. She'd have made a wonderful sergeant if she'd ever seen fit to pass her exam, but the young WPC's tend to treat her like a sergeant anyway. She'd also be discreet.'

Sue nodded and stood up. 'Thanks very much sir. Obviously we'll keep you updated as far as possible, even if we can't tell you very much.' She and Martin left the office and made their way down to the interview room to await the arrival of Mandy Cornwell.

# Chapter 15

Prior to Mandy's arrival Sue and Martin read through her statement. It was short and to the point, telling them nothing they didn't already know. She merely stated that she had checked the prisoner at 15:30 hours and that everything had been in order. She had not visited the custody office after that and had not seen Pete Ashbourne again.

Martin put down the statement. 'Well, I daresay it's accurate enough as far as it goes. But I'm pretty sure there's a lot more she could say.'

'About the murder?'

He shook his head. 'Probably not; but about Pete and her encounters with him. It's all important, if we're going to build up a full picture.'

Sue nodded. 'I agree with you. Martin, from what you say there seems to be evidence that Pete Ashbourne was pestering Mandy, at the very least. You front the interview, I'll just chip in.'

'Right.' he agreed.

There was a gentle tap on the door and Mandy came hesitantly into the room. 'You wanted to see me ma'am?'

'Yes we do. Nothing to worry about Mandy, we just want to put a bit of flesh on the bones of this statement.' She nodded to a chair on the other side of the desk. Mandy perched on the end of it, looking nervous and poised for flight.

Martin opened the interview. 'Mandy, I'm sure you've given us an accurate summary of the last time you saw Sergeant Ashbourne, but it really is a summary. What we'd like now is for you to fill in the blanks – the bit between the lines.'

Mandy shifted uncomfortably. 'I'm sorry sergeant, but I don't know what you mean. I've put everything in the statement.

Everything relevant. I went down and checked the prisoner at half past three and I filled in the custody record. She was bailed soon after that, so I didn't need to go down to the custody office again.'

'That's fine as far as it goes Mandy, but I think there's rather more to be said about your encounters with Sergeant Ashbourne. Listen, I appreciate that this is difficult for you. We're not trying to pry into your private affairs. But we need a full picture here; a full picture of Pete Ashbourne and his dealings with his colleagues.'

Mandy looked at the floor, making no reply. Sue and Martin sat quietly, allowing the silence to build. Eventually Mandy looked up again.

'I don't see its relevance. Sergeant Ashbourne's gone now. Anything that happened between us – well, I'd just rather not discuss it. It's nothing to do with his murder – it can't be. Everyone knows Robbie Nichols was found standing over the body.'

Sue leaned forward. 'Mandy, we're investigating a murder here. At this stage nothing is certain; nothing is known or cast in tablets of stone. Anything and everything may be important. We need you to tell us all you can. Martin?'

Martin took over the conversation. 'Mandy, on the day Pete died, I came into the custody office just as you were leaving. Do you remember?'

'Yes,' she mumbled.

'You seemed upset. In fact, you looked ready to burst into tears. We need you to tell us why.'

Mandy looked down again. 'Well – I'm sure you can guess why.'

'But we need you to tell us.'

The silence stretched out, then Mandy sighed and looked up. 'All right. I was hoping I wouldn't have to say anything about it but – well, yes, I was upset. Sergeant Ashbourne had just assaulted me.'

'You mean an indecent assault?' Mandy nodded. 'Tell us about it, please.'

'Well, he – he pushed me against the desk, from the back. Hard, so I could feel him. Then he started squeezing my breasts over my shirt. Hard enough to hurt. I kept telling him to stop, but he just laughed.'

'And was that the first time?'

'No,' she muttered. 'He's been touching me up for weeks and it's been getting worse and worse.'

Sue chipped in. 'Why didn't you tell someone what was going on?'

Mandy flushed. 'It isn't as easy as that. I didn't have any proof, if I'd said anything he'd have just denied it. And then he'd have made things really unpleasant for me. He'd already threatened that.'

'And is that the only reason you didn't say anything?'

'No.' She sighed. 'It's hard to explain because I don't understand it myself, but - I suppose I wanted to fit in, I wanted to be one of the lads – you know, to be accepted. I didn't want to be put down as a whinger who made a fuss about a little incident.'

'Sounds like rather more than an isolated little incident,' said Sue dryly.

'Yes - well - it was to me. But I wasn't sure how it would look to other people, the bobbies on the shift. I know some of them already think I'm a waste of space. Even so, I had decided to complain, this time. He'd just gone too far. But I wasn't sure who I could go to.'

'One of the other women officers?' suggested Sue.

'Well, maybe, but there's only one other woman on my shift and that's Judith Saunders. She hasn't got much time for me, I can tell she hasn't. I'd pretty well decided to go to the superintendent - Superintendent Horner - he's always nice and easy to talk to. But then Sergeant Ashbourne was killed so there didn't seem to be any point in stirring things up.'

Martin nodded. 'Mandy, did you tell anyone at all about this? I rather think you did.'

She hesitated, then nodded. 'I hadn't told anyone before

that day, but as I said, he just went too far. I had to stop it, somehow. Jim – my fiancé Jim – he noticed I was upset and he got the truth out of me.' She looked at Martin. 'You walked in on us when I was telling him. In the canteen.'

'And how did Jim react?'

'Well, you can imagine. He was furious. I practically had to hold him back, but I made him promise to leave it alone and not go rampaging down to the custody office. I promised him I'd report it and take it through the proper channels. Jim was happy with that. Well, he wasn't exactly happy, but he promised to keep out of it, so long as I made an official complaint.'

'And did Jim keep out of it? So far as you know?'

She nodded. 'Yes. He definitely didn't go down to see Sergeant Ashbourne. We were both on late shift that day and after meal he just did a bit of paperwork, then we went home. And then next day we heard what had happened – that Sergeant Ashbourne had been murdered.' She faced Sue and Martin with a hint of defiance. 'I can't pretend I'm sorry he's dead either.' She flushed. 'Oh God, that's an awful thing to say – you should never be glad someone's dead, especially another police officer. But it was such a load off my mind, it really was.'

Sue nodded. 'I can understand that Mandy. Really, I can. Now then, we really do need a full statement from you about this. Everything you've told us, let us decide what's relevant and what isn't. We'll just wait until Jim arrives, then I'd like you to go and do that statement while we talk to Jim.'

Mandy looked startled. 'You don't think Jim had anything to do with it? You can't think that! I told you – '

'Mandy,' Sue interrupted. 'We're in the preliminary stages of a murder investigation and we'll be talking to everyone who was on duty that day and probably several people who weren't. All we're doing is gathering evidence – as much evidence as we can. You're a police officer, you should understand that. You should also understand that we can't discuss the investigation with anyone, outside the murder incident team.' She nodded to Martin. 'Can you get Jim down here now please?'

# Chapter 16

Shortly afterwards there was a firm knock on the door, which immediately opened to admit Jim Taylor. Sue had already learned he was a former soldier and his appearance bore that out. He was aged around thirty, tall and upright. His dark brown hair was neatly cut and combed and his well pressed uniform suggested a man who took pride in his appearance. He paused inside the doorway, looking surprised to see Mandy there. Sue stood up.

'PC Taylor, please come in. Mandy, thank you – that'll be all for the time being.'

Mandy left the office, exchanging a look with Jim as she did so. Sue walked round the desk and held out her hand.

'I don't believe we've met. I'm Detective Inspector Sue Bishop. Of course you already know Martin.' Martin and Jim nodded to one another. Sue re-seated herself and Jim took the proffered seat opposite.

'I really don't know how I can help you,' he said. 'I was on duty the day Pete Ashbourne died, but I didn't actually see him all day.'

'Not at all?' asked Martin.

'No, not at all.'

'Weren't you involved in the arrest of Robbie Nichols?'

'Yes, I was crewed up with Tony Woodford on the panda when we were sent to the incident. I drove Tony and Nichols back to the station and into the prison yard. Tony took Nichols in, then I left the yard, checked over the panda then parked it up.'

'Did you go out again?' asked Sue.

'No. I went into the station and wrote a statement about the incident. I thought at that time Tony would be dealing with the case because he made the arrest, but I should have known better.'

'Why?' asked Sue.

'Because Pete Ashbourne was custody sergeant, that's why. That would have been a good case for Tony to deal with and he was perfectly capable of dealing with it, but there's no way Pete would let him. Pete hates Tony.'

'Again, why?'

Jim shrugged. 'You'd have to ask Pete that.'

'A little difficult under the circumstances,' said Martin dryly.

Jim nodded. 'Yeah – sorry. Well, Pete has never spelt it out to me, but it's pretty well known around the station. Tony's gay – or at least everyone is pretty sure he is – and Pete couldn't cope with that. I think he'd have disliked Tony in any case though. Tony's straight down the line – you know, does things by the book. He and Pete have had words before about the way Pete treats prisoners. And Tony won't swear or share a dirty joke. Pete didn't like that either.'

'Would you describe Tony as strait-laced?' asked Sue.

'In fact I wouldn't. He's got some pretty rigid standards for himself, but he never tries to impose them on other people. Mind you, he makes it clear he does things the official way and expects other people to do the same; you don't take shortcuts when you work with him. But I mean, he never objects when the lads swear and banter, he just somehow manages not to join in, without being prim and proper about it.'

'All right,' said Sue. 'How long did it take you to write your statement?'

'Only about half an hour. Then I had my meal and stayed in to catch up on paperwork. Tony was off at six – though he had an appointment for his annual appraisal then, so he'd be a bit late leaving.'

'Did you see Tony after he'd booked Nichols in?'

'Yes. We sat in the parade room together and wrote out our statements.'

'And how did Tony feel about being taken off the case?'

Jim shrugged again. 'Pissed off I should think, but he didn't say anything to me. He wouldn't. He was just a bit quiet, that's all. Just before six o'clock he dropped both our statements off to Pete Ashbourne. Then I went for meal and he went up for his annual appraisal.'

'Did you see him after his appraisal?'

'No, I should think he went straight home. As I said, he should have been off at six o'clock.'

Sue nodded. 'Now then, I understand you're engaged to Mandy Cornwell. Can you tell me a bit about her?'

Jim frowned. 'Why? She's got nothing to do with all this.'

'Bear with us,' said Sue.

He shrugged. 'Well, like you say, we're engaged. What else do you want to know?'

'How do you feel about her being in the job?'

'Well, it's up to her. No really, it is. Look, I'm not sexist if that's what you're getting at. I've no problem with women in the job.' He glanced quickly at Sue. 'Or women bosses.'

'But talking specifically about Mandy? As her fiancé, how do you feel about her being in the job?'

Jim shrugged. 'All right. Look, I love Mandy. I want to spend the rest of my life with her for God's sake. But as a copper - I don't really think she's cut out for the job, not as it is now. She'd probably have been a good policewoman as they used to be, but - well, she's still pretty naïve and innocent to be dealing with some of the shit we get. She's had a sheltered background and she's only twenty one. She doesn't have much confidence either.'

'And you're older and - shall we say - less naïve?'

Jim laughed. 'Less naïve? You can say that again. I'm nearly thirty and I did six years in the army before this job.'

'You worry about her?'

'Course I bloody do. Every time she's sent to a job I worry about her. I would anyway seeing she's my fiancée but like I say it's more than that, I don't think she can look after herself, I admit I worry about her getting hurt. I wouldn't try to persuade her to leave but if she decided to quit I'd be relieved, quite honestly.' He shrugged. 'I really don't see what any of that has to do with Pete Ashbourne's murder.'

Sue glanced at Martin, who stopped writing and leaned forward.

'Jim, do you remember my coming into the canteen that day? You were on meal break with Mandy.'

'Yes, I remember.'

'You and Mandy seemed to be arguing.'

'Not arguing, no. We were having a bit of a – well, let's say a bit of a heated discussion.'

'What about?'

Jim flushed. 'I'm sorry, but that's personal.'

'I'm afraid it can't be. I have reason to believe you and Mandy were discussing Pete Ashbourne. It may be relevant.'

'It isn't!'

'We'll judge that when you've answered my question. I'm sorry Jim, but we're investigating a murder here.'

Jim pressed his lips together. 'It's Mandy's business. I've no right to talk to you about her private affairs.'

Sue interrupted. 'PC Taylor, if it makes things any easier for you, we're already aware that Sergeant Ashbourne's behaviour towards Mandy may have been – inappropriate.'

'Inappropriate!' Jim exploded. 'It was a bloody sight more than inappropriate, that bastard was touching her up - had been for weeks. Mandy was really cut up that day - for two pins she'd have put her ticket in. She told me what had been going on with Pete Ashbourne – what he'd been doing.' He leaned forward. 'I'll tell you this, if Mandy hadn't stopped me Pete Ashbourne would probably have been murdered a little bit sooner.' He stood up abruptly and walked round the office. 'Oh, I don't mean that – obviously I don't mean that. But I was all for sorting him out and I'd have done it too, come what may. Mandy stopped me, but I made her promise she'd report him this time. And I'd have made damned sure she did it!'

Sue waited until he had sat down again. 'PC Taylor, are you sure you didn't go down to the custody office that evening? I see you have a pretty good black eye there.'

Jim touched his eye. 'What, this? I'd assisted in the arrest of Robbie Nichols, hadn't I? When you arrest Nichols you're lucky to get away with a black eye.'

Sue nodded. 'Just one more thing PC Taylor - did you see anyone else around the station, say between quarter to ten and the time you knocked off?'

Jim shrugged. 'Well, the rest of the shift of course, when they came in to finish.'

'Which would be when?'

'Around quarter to eleven.'

'No-one came in before then?'

'Not so far as I know - they certainly didn't come in to the parade room. Oh - hang on a minute - Clive Stirling popped his head round the door about ten-ish. Didn't stay though?'

'Who's he?' asked Sue. 'Another PC?'

'Yes. He's working in control room at the moment because he's on light duties, but he wasn't on duty that evening.'

Martin rifled through the file on the desk in front of him. 'He was long weekend,' he said.

'I see,' said Sue. 'Did he say or do anything while he was in the parade room?'

'He just said something like "oh, hello Jim." He didn't do anything - like I said he only popped his head round the door, then went out again.'

'Was he carrying anything?'

Jim shrugged. 'Sorry, I have no idea. I just glanced up when I heard the door open because I thought it was probably Mandy coming in, but I really didn't take any special notice. No reason to.'

Sue and Martin exchanged looks, then Sue spoke again. 'All right PC Taylor, that will be all for the moment. Thank you.'

Jim gave her a searching look, then nodded and stood up. He left the office without saying anything more.

Martin put the finishing touches to his notes then turned to Sue.

'Well? What do you think?'

Sue frowned. 'Can't quite put my finger on it, but I'm not entirely happy with him. Did he have that black eye on Friday, after bringing Nichols in?'

Martin shook his head. 'Don't know, I didn't notice it when I saw him in the canteen. But if Nichols had given him a black eye, Nichols should have been charged with assault police as well as wounding on his wife. Which he wasn't.' He paused. 'Tony will know.'

Sue frowned. 'Will Tony tell us?'

'Oh, I think so. I told you, he's very straight down the line and by-the-book.' He gave her a slightly malicious look. 'Follows PACE to the letter – you'll like him.'

Sue ignored that and checked the to-do list at the front of the active file. Tony Woodford was scheduled for interview the following morning. She closed the file, then checked her watch. It was just coming up to 7 pm.

'Let's call it a day Martin; give ourselves some thinking time. We'll interview Tony tomorrow morning, then thrash out just where we are and plan our way ahead. Oh - and we'd better put PC Stirling on the list of priority interviews, no doubt he's got a perfectly good reason, but nonetheless he was in the station at the relevant time. Get DC Redman to check him out.'

'Right,' agreed Martin. 'Oh – and by the way, I should have mentioned it earlier. Forensic have finished with the custody office. If it's okay by you they can start bringing prisoners in from tomorrow.'

Sue smiled. 'That's fine. In fact I did know because I bumped into Sergeant Hawkins earlier on. He'd been cleaning out the fridge and I think he was planning on making yogurt with the remains of the milk.'

Martin laughed, then stopped abruptly. 'Just a minute – that's not right.'

'What?'

'Milk. What milk? Sue, there shouldn't have been any milk in that fridge.' He shook his head at her puzzled look. 'On that

Friday night, Pete offered me a coffee before I went home. I checked the fridge and there was no milk, so I said no and left. If there's milk there now then either the forensic team stuck some in there – '

'Possible,' said Sue, 'but I'd be very surprised. Did they list the fridge contents?'

Martin burrowed through the files for the relevant paperwork. 'No they didn't. Damn!'

'Well, we'd better check with them, ASAP. You realise what this could mean?'

'Only too well,' said Martin. 'Some time between my leaving the custody office and Pete's death, someone took some milk into that office. Obviously I'm not saying that person murdered Pete, but it's a near certainty whoever it was, was the last person to see him alive. I'll check forensic first and if I draw a blank with them I'll check the control room staff.'

'Why them?'

'Because that's where the custody sergeants tend to get milk from, if they run out after the canteen's shut.'

'Right,' said Sue. 'I'll leave that one with you. And Martin, can you get onto it right away. This could be pretty important.'

'I'm on it,' he said.

# Chapter 17

Sue arrived home at 8 pm. The temperature had plummeted again and a few snowflakes were floating lazily in the air. There was a blue Vauxhall Astra sitting at the end of the drive. Terry and Sarah! Sue groaned, she had completely forgotten that they were coming for dinner.

She parked the car and hurried into the house to the usual rapturous welcome from Oscar. 'Bill?' she shouted.

'In the lounge.'

The three of them were there, gathered around a blazing fire, glasses in hand. Sarah jumped up.

'Sue!' she exclaimed with pleasure. The two women hugged warmly, they had been inseparable since childhood and had even married on the same day. Bill looked round.

'Good heavens, what are you doing here at this time?'

'I do live here,' she told him.

'Really? I thought you just visited from time to time.'

Sue ignored the barbed comment and turned to Sarah. 'Sarah, I'm sorry I'm so late. I – er – couldn't get away before.'

'That's okay,' said Sarah.

Bill waved a bottle in the air. 'G and T?'

'I'd love one!' Sue said with feeling.

He poured her a large gin and tonic and added ice and lemon.

'Well, sleuth? How's it going?' asked Terry.

'Slowly,' she answered. 'We're gradually getting a few more pieces. But never mind that. Let's forget about work for tonight.'

Bill gave her an enigmatic look, then turned to Terry. 'Did I tell you I've a new rod?'

'No you didn't. Really? Well come on, let's see it.'

The two men exited, heading for the garage where Bill's fishing gear was stowed. Sarah looked shrewdly at Sue.

'Trouble?' she asked.

Sue gave a strained smile. 'Is it that obvious? Or has Bill been talking to you?'

'He didn't have to Sue - I've known you a long time. And Bill's greeting wasn't the warmest I've ever heard.'

Sue sipped her drink, feeling suddenly very tired and low. 'Things aren't good just now Sarah. I'm having to work some long and antisocial hours just now and Bill resents it. In fact he resents the whole job. He's all for me throwing it all in.'

'Seriously? He wants you to pack the job in completely?'

'Yes. Oh, I dare say he'd be happy if I could just get into a department that worked regular hours, but how can I do that? I need this experience Sarah. In any case, it isn't just this job, it's any job - any job that I wanted to make a career of anyway. He wants a family Sarah, and I'm not ready for that yet.'

They were interrupted by the return of the men. Terry was already wearing his outer coat. 'Sue, I'm sorry to drag Sarah away so soon, but we have to get going. Snow's falling fast and we need to get home.'

Sue muttered a curse under her breath. She needed to offload and it would have been good to talk things over with Sarah. She pulled back the curtains and peered out. It was indeed snowing heavily, not the big wet flakes that melted almost as they settled but the type of snow that was unlikely to thaw before morning. She accompanied her friend to the door. 'I've missed you Sarah.'

'Me too,' said Sarah. 'Listen Sue, ring me when you can – when you have time for a chat. And for God's sake Sue, don't let your marriage go.' She gave Sue a quick hug, then hurried to the waiting car.

Sue walked slowly back into the house. 'I suppose you've had dinner?'

'Of course. It wasn't much use waiting for you, was it?'

'Bill, I've said I'm sorry.'

'You could at least have rung,' he said.

'I would have done, but – well, I forgot. Bill, I really am sorry, I meant to be home earlier.'

Bill made a visible effort to contain his irritation. 'Bad day?'

'Not really. But it's a bit difficult with the murder being so close to home. Everyone knows that Pete Ashbourne's killer could be working right there in the station. It doesn't make for a good atmosphere.'

He poured another gin and tonic and handed it to her. 'From what little you've said, I thought it was pretty much a cut and dried case.'

'Yes, well, it did look like that at first, but it isn't turning out that way. Quite honestly Bill, I think they should have appointed someone from outside the force.'

'They more or less did,' he said. 'You don't know any of the people involved, you can be objective. Isn't that why they assigned you to the case?'

'Yes, but I'm still interviewing people I'll be working with in the future. I find it difficult to feel really detached, and I need to detach. I can't help feeling sorry for some of them. Especially people like Mandy.'

'Who's Mandy?'

Sue sighed, wishing she could discuss the whole case with Bill, knowing it wasn't possible. 'Mandy is a policewoman. Very young, very immature. She's already badly lacking in confidence and being involved in this is really going to knock her for six. I just hope it doesn't drive her out of the job.'

Bill picked up his glass. 'Well Sue, I don't even know Mandy. But looking at what the job's done to you I hope for her sake that it does drive her out of the job. Sue, have you any idea how much the job has changed you?'

'I was never as immature as Mandy.'

'Maybe not. But you used to be different, Sue. You were much gentler, a lot more sensitive, less independent.'

'Ah – now we're coming to the truth. That's what you want, is it? A gentle little woman who's totally dependent on her masterful husband?'

Bill slammed his glass down, the liquid splashing out onto the table. 'I didn't say that – you're twisting my words. I just want my wife back. I want the woman I married, the woman who wanted to spend time with me more than anything else. But now, the darn job's your whole life. Tonight is just typical. Your home life means so little to you that you forgot your best friend and her husband were visiting.'

'Sarah will understand. And I've said I'm sorry.'

'And that makes everything fine, I suppose? I'm scared of what's happening to us Sue. We're drifting apart on a fast current. Whatever you might think, I don't want a submissive little woman, but I do want a partner.' He paused. 'An equal partner.'

'No Bill – you don't. You want a dependent woman. That's what you said.'

'I said that's what you used to be.' He stood up. 'It's a waste of time talking to you nowadays. I'm off to bed. I'll sleep in the spare room so you needn't worry about disturbing me in the morning.'

# Chapter 18

Sue was operating on auto-pilot as she navigated her way along the treacherously icy roads on the following day. She had hardly slept all night, her mind churning non-stop as Bill's accusation played and replayed like a stuck record. Did Bill really want an equal partnership, or did he want her to take her place as a compliant, supporting wife? And what did she truly want?

She cast her mind back eight years, to their marriage day. There was no doubt she had been a different woman then. Not just younger; more naïve and more pliable. And yes, not so independent. But even then she had ambitions. She had only recently left university and was already exploring career options, including the one of joining the police service as a graduate entry, to fly through the ranks as quickly as possible.

They had talked about a family, but only in vague terms. That, she now realised, had been a major mistake. They had agreed not to try for a child immediately, but Bill had assumed that they would have children, and sooner rather than later. Sue, on the other hand, had never really wanted children. She had always jokingly said that she wasn't maternal; now she realised that it was no more than the truth. She had never been able to coo over babies.

As for leaving the job and sacrificing all her ambitions, that simply wasn't an option; there was no way she was prepared to do that. But for the first time, she had to face up to the fact that one day she might have to make a choice between her job and her marriage.

She was still dwelling on her marital problems as she parked the car in her designated space and made her way across the icy car park. She entered the reception area and headed up the stairs, then stopped short as she found her way unexpectedly blocked. Superintendent Horner had come up behind her and was holding his arm across the doorway to her office.

'Sue?'

She gave a start. 'Oh. Oh – sorry sir. I was miles away.'

'You certainly were, I said good morning twice and you walked past me as if I wasn't there.' He regarded her narrowly. 'You look fed up and tired out.'

She pulled herself together. 'No. No, I'm fine sir. Just thinking.'

'Not good thoughts by the look of you. Case going badly?'

'Oh no. There's a lot to do but I think things are going well enough.'

'There's something wrong though,' he persisted. 'Anything I can help with?'

She gave a smile. 'No sir, there isn't. I appreciate the offer, but there's nothing. Nothing to do with the case.'

He frowned, then nodded. 'Well, I won't pry into things that are none of my concern. But don't forget Sue, I'm here if you ever need to talk - whether it's work or personal.'

He gave her another appraising look then turned into the corridor and headed for the boardroom and the senior officers' briefing. Sue stood looking after him before turning back into her office. She didn't feel that she knew Michael Horner well enough to share her private problems with him, but she was nonetheless grateful for the offer. It was good to feel that support would be there if she needed it.

Martin was already in the office, talking to Chief Superintendent Wallace. She gave a surreptitious look at the office clock – five minutes to nine, so at least she wasn't late. As she greeted the chief superintendent she hurriedly searched her mind. Should she be expecting him?

His first words dispelled that concern. 'Good morning inspector – sorry to drop in on you without any warning but I thought I'd just catch up with how things are going. Of course I've had your updates but personal is always better. And yes please Martin – I'd love a coffee. Proper coffee, not that machine rubbish.'

Martin grinned. 'Rubbish is about right sir, I'll go and raid the canteen. Ma'am?'

'Yes please.'

Martin left the office and the chief superintendent sat in the chair opposite the desk. 'Right then Sue, before we talk about the investigation, how are things with you? How are you getting along with Sergeant Attwood?'

'Absolutely fine sir, no problems. He's a good DS – very sharp.'

'No problems accepting your authority?'

'Not now. We sorted that out on day one and I think we have a mutual respect for one another. I suspect he's a little more formal with me than he was with his usual DI, but that isn't a problem.'

'Good to hear. Now then, let's talk about the investigation. Put some meat on the bones of those updates.'

'Certainly sir. But before we do that I'd like to raise one concern. When you appointed me this looked like a very straightforward, cut and dried case. A good one for a newly appointed DI to cut her teeth on - you even said as much. Am I right?'

He chuckled. 'Very perceptive. Yes you are right, at least to a point.'

'But in fact it's turned out not to be so straightforward. Are you sure you still want me in charge of this investigation?'

He frowned. 'What makes you say that?'

She shrugged. 'Just the fact that it isn't so straightforward. Nichols is looking less and less likely as a suspect, which means that the murderer is most likely to be someone working at Fairfield Station. I just wondered if you wanted to appoint an outside investigator – someone from another force.'

'Do you want to come off the case?'

'No. I'd be very disappointed to leave the case, especially

now we've got this far and some of the strands are beginning to come together.'

'I'm pleased to hear that. I'm very happy to leave you on the case Sue. If I'd realised at the outset that the main suspects were going to be police officers then I would have asked for someone from another force to be brought in, but I don't really see that they would have any advantage over you. As I told you at the outset of this enquiry, your being new to the force was a big factor in appointing you as the investigating officer.' He paused. 'As far as I'm concerned you're doing a good job. And just for your information, your detective sergeant thinks so too.'

Sue raised her eyebrows, then smiled. 'I'm glad to hear that.'

'And you're sure you're happy to stay on the case?'

'Absolutely sure.'

Martin entered carrying a tray containing coffee and biscuits and the conversation turned to discussing the nuts and bolts of the investigation. Robbie Nichols had now been bailed to report back to the police station in two weeks time, but they were all agreed that as a suspect, he was looking more and more unlikely. At the moment no-one had given them any real grounds to suspect them of being involved in the crime, although both Sue and Martin agreed that there was a question mark over Jim Taylor and the black eye that he had allegedly received from Nichols. It would be interesting to see what Tony Woodford had to say about that.

# Chapter 19

They spoke to Tony Woodford the same afternoon when he dropped into headquarters on his way home from the early shift. Tony was 29 years old and just out of his probation, having joined the police service shortly before his 27th birthday. His demeanour was very different from Jim's. Where Jim had been cautious, occasionally bordering on hostility, Tony appeared relaxed, his manner pleasant and open.

The introductions over, she commenced the interview. 'Tony, obviously we're most concerned about your dealings with Pete Ashbourne – both on the day he died and before that. We need a complete picture. But first I'd like to go back to the afternoon of that day, when you arrested Robbie Nichols. I'd like you to talk us through that, from the time you arrived at Nichols' house.'

Tony looked slightly surprised. 'Well, of course, if you think it's relevant.'

'It might be,' said Sue.

'All right. Well, it was a blue-light job – the neighbours had reported hearing shouting from Nichols' house, followed by screaming. Jim was driving and he put his foot down because we've had dealings with Nichols before. He's a violent man with a lot of form. When we got there it was quiet in the street, but there were a few curtains twitching. We didn't hang about, we went straight in to Nichols' place.'

'Was the door open?'

'No, but it wasn't locked. We got into the hall and were greeted with a shout of 'fuck off!' from the kitchen, so we went straight in there. Nichols was standing with his back to the sink. His wife was on the floor, in the corner. She was conscious but there was a lot of blood.'

'Did Nichols still have his knife?'

'Yes, and pointed towards us. You could see the blood on it too. I got between him and his wife but kept my distance. Jim went straight to Mrs Nichols and checked her out. He got on the radio and told them to get the ambulance to us ASAP, then he looked after her. By this time the other panda crew had arrived, so we had back-up.'

'Did Nichols try to use the knife?'

'No. He's a very violent man but I think he realised that odds of four to one weren't good. He threw the knife onto the kitchen table. I told him I was arresting him for wounding and cautioned him. He just said that the stupid bitch had asked for it.' Tony shook his head. 'It isn't the first time he's attacked her, but it's the first time he's used his knife.'

'Did he put up any resistance?'

'Virtually none - just a token struggle. The other crew took over with Mrs Nichols and waited with her for the ambulance. I cuffed Nichols and Jim and I took him out to the panda and brought him in.'

Sue nodded. 'Just to clarify. Nichols put up no resistance at all? He didn't fight? He didn't strike you or Jim?'

'No. There was plenty of effing and blinding, but no violence.'

'All right. So what happened at the station?'

'Jim drove the panda into the cell yard. I took Nichols into the custody office while Jim checked the car over to make sure Nichols hadn't concealed anything. I was as sure as I could be that he hadn't, but we always check.'

'And the booking in? Purely routine?'

Tony frowned. 'Routine to a point, except for the fact that Pete Ashbourne hit Nichols. Twice in fact, although I only saw the first one.' He shrugged. 'I know it doesn't make any difference now – Sergeant Ashbourne is dead so it really isn't very relevant. All the same, I've reported it. I told him I was intending to, and I did.'

'What happened?' asked Martin.

'Sergeant Ashbourne told Nichols to take his woolly jumper off and Nichols gave him some lip, so the sergeant reached over and gave him a back-hander across the face. There was no need for it, Nichols was being mouthy, but that was all. Then he took Nichols down to the cells. I heard the sound of a thump and a yell from Nichols. When Sergeant Ashbourne came back he endorsed the custody record to the effect that Nichols had a black eye and a split lip, sustained on arrest. That wasn't true and I told him so. As I said ma'am, NIchols didn't put up any real struggle - not this time. I've already reported the incident and done a full statement.'

'Who did you report it to?'

'The super - Superintendent Horner. I had my annual appraisal that evening and I told him about it then. He was going to pass it on to complaints for a proper investigation.'

Sue nodded. 'What was Pete Ashbourne's reaction to your saying you'd report him?'

Tony gave a slight smile. 'If I remember correctly he called me a sanctimonious little nark. As I'm sure you already know, I really wasn't the sergeant's favourite officer.'

'Do you know why?'

'He likes men's men – hard drinking, hard swearing types. I don't drink very much and I don't swear. He used to try to get under my skin but I never gave him the satisfaction of a reaction. I think that rankled quite a lot.'

'Any other reason?'

Tony regarded her thoughtfully. He was slim and lightly built with light brown hair and quiet looking hazel eyes. He had regular features - one could even call him good-looking - but somehow unremarkable; the kind of man who wouldn't stand out in a crowd. Nonetheless there was something about him that was difficult to fathom. Sue generally prided herself on her ability to read people, to sense emotions, but Tony defeated her. She sensed that his apparently open manner masked a very private centre.

After a brief pause Tony shrugged. 'Well, I don't advertise it, but I think it's pretty widely known that I'm gay. So far as Sergeant Ashbourne was concerned that was the final nail in the coffin - he was homophobic, to put it mildly.'

'I see. And what did you think of Pete Ashbourne?'

Tony gave another slight smile. 'I thought of him as little as possible.'

'Did you dislike him?'

'Yes I did. I always tried to be polite and reasonable to him but he really went out of his way to make my life as difficult as possible, in every way he could.' He shrugged. 'It didn't bother me too much. He was only one man and everyone knew how he felt about me, so he couldn't really damage my career – only in irritating little ways, like making sure I didn't get the chance to see a case through when he was on duty. But I didn't like the man. That's not to say I'm glad he's dead, but – well, let's just say I'm not as sorry as I ought to be, seeing as I call myself a Christian.' He shrugged again. 'I'm only human.'

'Aren't we all,' said Sue dryly. 'Now, can you run through the rest of that day? When did you leave the custody office?'

'A bit after 5.30 pm. I went to the parade room and wrote out my statement of arrest. I dropped it back to Sergeant Ashbourne at six o'clock, then I went up to Superintendent Horner's office for my annual appraisal.' He paused. 'That took longer than usual because I also reported what had happened with Sergeant Ashbourne and Nichols - as I told you. The super asked me to do a full statement for the next morning and he'd get everything to complaints for investigation.'

'Was the super surprised?'

'You'll have to ask him that, but I think not really. Disappointed, but not surprised.'

'And how did he receive the complaint? Did he try to talk you out of it or anything like that?'

'No. He did point out that I might get a bit of stick from some of the lads though. Sergeant Ashbourne wasn't over popular but you know how strong police culture is - you don't shop your mates is the general rule.'

'And you were prepared to cope with the fallout?'

Tony shrugged again. 'No choice. Everybody knows I operate by the book, including Sergeant Ashbourne. Anyway I've coped with fallout before, being gay.'

'That's given you problems?'

'Of course it has - I expected it to. When I first came here I used to find graffiti sprayed inside my locker - words like fag, poofter, queer sprayed in bright yellow paint. It happened three or four times in my first month here, but now it just rears its head occasionally. But I thought it might start up again when they found out I'd shopped the sergeant.' He shrugged. 'Well, that's hardly relevant to Pete Ashbourne's murder.'

'The graffiti isn't irrelevant,' said Sue sharply. 'I mean, you're right it may be irrelevant to our murder investigation, but it needs looking into. Have you reported it?'

Tony shrugged. 'Yes, I've reported every case and there is a file on it - but so far there aren't any results. Short of catching him in the act - or her of course - there's not a lot anyone can do.'

Sue frowned. 'Well, so long as something's being done. To get back to the night of Sergeant Ashbourne's murder, what time did you leave the super?'

'About seven o'clock.'

'Did you go down to the custody office again?'

'No. There was no point, since I wasn't dealing with the case. I went straight home.'

'And the rest of the evening? What did you do?'

Tony smiled. 'Ah – an alibi! I got home around half seven and changed out of uniform. Then I went to my next door neighbour's house. It was his wife's birthday and they'd invited me round for a few drinks. Jill and Dennis, 35 Robertson Way.'

'How long were you there?'

'About two and a half hours. From eight o'clock until around half ten - maybe a little before that.'

Sue glanced at Martin, then looked back at Tony. 'Thank

you Tony, and thank you for being so open with us. I think that's all we need from you, for the moment.'

Tony nodded. 'I'm on long weekend from tomorrow so I won't be around the station. But I'm not going anywhere special. I'll be at home if you have any more questions.'

The office door closed behind him. Martin stood up and stretched. 'Well, that's interesting.'

'Which part?'

'Several parts. First of all, he seems to have a pretty good alibi. Tony lives a good twenty minute drive away so if that time of death is right, Tony Woodford has to be in the clear. Jim Taylor, however - - '

'No injury from Nichols.'

'No, and …'

They were interrupted by the shrilling of the telephone. Sue picked it up and hit the loudspeaker button. 'DI Bishop?'

'Inspector, this is Vinnie Richards from the control room at Fairfield. Martin Attwood was asking about some milk being taken down to the custody office on the night Pete Ashbourne was killed.'

'Yes,' said Sue. Opposite her, Martin sat forward, suddenly alert.

'I may be able to help.'

'Right,' said Sue. 'Could you pop over here?'

'I've just finished work so I can come now - just wanted to check you were there. With you in fifteen minutes.'

The phone went dead and Sue hung up. 'Who is he? she asked Martin. 'Is he a civvie?'

'No, he's a PC. Long serving man, almost done his thirty years.'

Twenty minutes later quick footsteps sounded in the corridor and a tall, middle-aged man appeared in the doorway. Sue stood up.

'Vinnie Richards? We haven't met. I'm Sue Bishop. Please take a seat.' Vinnie seated himself opposite her, next to Martin as Sue continued. 'You were saying you knew something about some milk possibly going down to the custody office on the night Pete Ashbourne died?'

'Yes. I was on 3 to 11 shift that day. Late in the shift Pete rang down to say he was out of milk and could we get some up to him.'

'Is that standard procedure?'

'Oh yes, when the canteen's shut. The custody office have their own fridge, but sometimes they run out and we let them have a drop of ours. It works the other way too. If there's no-one in the cells the custody sergeant might pop down to us and fetch it himself, but Pete said he had a prisoner in, so he couldn't leave the custody office.'

'So you sent the milk to him?'

'Yes. We had half a pint going spare, so we sent it down to him.'

'Did you take it down?'

'No. Jim Taylor happened to be in the kitchen making himself a brew, so I asked him to pop the milk down to Pete.'

'And he did?'

'Yes. Well, I assume so - he said he would.'

'And what time was that?'

'Five minutes to ten.'

Martin and Sue exchanged glances and Sue leaned forward. 'Can you be sure of the time?'

He smiled. 'I can be very sure. As Jim left the control room I was putting my coat on ready to go. I had an hour's time off that evening, so I'm afraid I was clock watching.'

'Which may be a very good thing in this case,' said Sue. 'Vinnie, can you do us a statement to that effect, including the time, and how you can be so sure of that time.'

Vinnie nodded and stood up. 'No problem. I'll do it right away if it's okay by you, I can squat in the admin office.'

Sue closed the door behind him and turned back to Martin. 'Well, well,' she said. 'It looks as if we need to have a few more words with Mr Taylor.'

# Chapter 20

Enquiries established that Jim Taylor was currently on half nights, starting work at 6 pm. Sue glanced at her watch.

'Only one o'clock - that gives me ample time to pop over to Fairfield and talk to the super.' She tapped the file in front of her. 'We've got his statement of course, but I just want to know if anyone can verify it.'

Martin laughed. 'Checking out the super?'

'Well, he was on duty that day. Says he left around half nine.' She shrugged herself into her coat. 'I'll meet you at Fairfield, quarter to six.'

Fifteen minutes later she was at Fairfield Station, knocking on the superintendent's door. As always he greeted her affably. 'Good to see you Sue, and looking a bit more cheerful.' He waved her to a chair. 'What can I do for you?'

'Well - actually sir, it's about your statement.'

'Statement?'

'On the date of Sergeant Ashbourne's death. I was wondering if anyone could verify the time you left the station? Sorry, but …'

He laughed. 'Ah - you want an alibi. You're quite right too, in a case like this, no one can be above suspicion. Well, I'm not sure whether anyone can verify when I left the station, but I think we can verify what time I got home.'

'I know you left the station around half nine sir, so what time would you be home?'

'Just before ten. It's usually a twenty minute run, but it was filthy weather that night so it took a bit longer.'

'And you say someone can verify that?'

'My gran. She's staying with me for a couple of weeks and

I talked to her when I got home that night. Of course close family can be a bit of an iffy alibi, but when you meet my gran I think you'll agree that telling a convincing lie of that sort would be beyond her.'

'Too honest?'

'Too vague. Oh, she still has all her marbles, but they're not rolling quite as smoothly as they used to. Understandably - she's in her late eighties.'

'She lives with you?'

He shook his head. 'Not all the time, no - she lives with my mother and father. But they're over in Florida visiting my brother and I'm looking after gran, just for a couple of weeks.' He glanced at his watch. 'Look Sue, why don't you come home with me now. I'll just introduce you to gran, then leave you to talk to her. I appreciate you have to check out all alibis and I'd really prefer you to someone like Martin. Martin's a first class interviewer but I wouldn't class him as being gentle with old ladies. I don't mean he's aggressive, but he could be a bit intimidating for poor old gran.'

The twenty minute car journey provided a good opportunity to get to know Horner a little better. He made no attempt to question her about the investigation itself, but Sue did confirm the fact that Pete Ashbourne had indeed been subjecting Mandy Cornwell to sexual abuse.

'It may well have affected her performance,' said Sue. 'I understand it's been going on for some time.'

Horner groaned. 'Why in the world didn't she say something before this?'

Sue shrugged. 'From what little she said to us, I'd say a mixture of reasons. It was her word against his, for one thing. And she was afraid some of her colleagues might think she was making a mountain out of a molehill, maybe even ostracise her for getting one of their mates into trouble. She so wanted to fit in - to be accepted as one of the lads, so to speak.'

'Ah yes,' said Horner. 'I can understand that - the need to be accepted. It's a strong culture in the police service.'

'And not always an easy one - for anyone, but maybe more so for people like Mandy.' She sighed. 'Sometimes I think there's a danger of sacrificing who you are to be one of the lads.'

The superintendent glanced sideways at her. 'Personal experience, by any chance?'

'I suppose it is. I remember a couple of years ago, when I'd just got my inspector's pips. I'd got just over five years service and I was feeling pretty young and inexperienced - which let's face it, I was. I had to do a presentation to a group of bobbies - old stagers, most of them. So I stood up there and tried to put on a tough façade - you know, a couple of risqué jokes; a few expletives. I suppose I thought it'd make them think of me as one of them.'

She paused. 'When I was going out to my car one of the bobbies I'd been talking to asked for a word. It so happened I knew Don pretty well - he'd been my tutor constable so I spent ten weeks with him after training school and I had a lot of respect for him. Anyway, he asked if he could speak frankly, then he said the person giving that presentation wasn't the Sue he'd known. He asked why I'd felt the need to make dirty jokes and swear like a sergeant major, because he knew I wasn't really like that.'

She paused. 'It rocked me, and it made me take a step back and take a good look at myself. I didn't have an easy answer for him, but thinking it through afterwards I knew exactly why I'd done it. I wanted to belong, to be regarded as one of the lads, able to fit in with all the banter and the rough and tumble. So I understand how Mandy feels. Don was right - it wasn't the real me. I wasn't being true to myself and when I thought about it I realised that.'

'Easier said than done, sometimes,' said Horner. 'And Sue, it isn't just women who find that difficult - it's hard for anyone who isn't naturally "one of the lads." Walking a lonely path is never easy, especially in a strong culture like this.'

'Of course,' said Sue. 'You're accelerated promotion too, aren't you sir?'

'I am indeed. And you of course are both a woman and special course, so you have two barriers to overcome.' He paused. 'For what it's worth, I think you're doing extremely well. As for becoming one of the lads - well, you may have to choose a different path in any case. You can't always be one of the lads if you want to really advance in the service.'

'Which I do,' said Sue. 'I'd certainly like to get to superintendent. Maybe it isn't realistic to expect much more.'

'One of the chief constable ranks you mean? I don't see why not.'

Sue shrugged. 'There aren't any women chief constables - or assistant chiefs, come to that.'

'Not yet, but give it time. Someone has to be first, Sue - and there's nothing wrong with being ambitious.'

Sue nodded. 'Well, I can only do my best. And you sir? Are you looking for ACPO rank?'

He nodded. 'Oh yes. I know there may be sacrifices along the way, but I'm determined to make ACPO rank before I'm forty - ACC at least, maybe even Chief Constable.' He smiled. 'After all, that's what accelerated promotion is for - to prepare selected officers for the highest ranks of the service. And that includes you and me Sue - both of us.'

They arrived at the superintendent's house and pulled onto the sweeping driveway. It was an impressive building, built in Tudor style, detached and standing in its own grounds; not massive, but nonetheless imposing. The grounds were extensive, overlooking the nearby golf course and sweeping down to a small river. Not bad for a man in his early thirties.

'What a lovely location,' she said.

Horner switched off the engine. 'Yes it is, and really handy for the golf course. I'm very lucky. Not entirely the fruits of my own efforts Sue, my paternal grandparents were fairly wealthy and I was lucky enough to inherit some of it. This way.'

The house was nicely decorated, with good quality modern furniture and plush carpets. It was very tidy - indeed immaculate - but Sue found it somehow impersonal. The mantelpiece was empty save for an ornate carriage clock and a photograph of a middle aged couple who Sue guessed were Horner's parents. The walls were magnolia emulsion, bare save for a large picture of galloping horses on the far wall. It was like a show house designed to be looked at rather than lived in, with nothing to hint at the personality of the occupier. Not what Sue would call a home.

Horner smiled, as if he read her thoughts. 'It's a bit spartan I'm afraid, probably needs the woman's touch. I don't go for much in the way of pictures and knick-knacks and I don't spend that much time here in any case.'

Horner led her into the lounge, where a tiny white haired old lady was seated in a chair, humming to herself as she crocheted what looked like a very intricate table cover.

'Hello gran,' said Horner cheerfully.' I've brought a lady home to say hello to you. Sue, this is my grandmother Mrs Atwell. Gran, this is Sue. She works with me.'

Mrs Atwell beamed and peered at Sue through blue eyes that appeared slightly cloudy with cataracts. 'Glad to meet you my dear, very glad to meet you.'

She peered up at Horner questioningly. He laughed.

'I'm sorry gran, Sue is a colleague – we just work together. She'd like to talk to you for a few minutes, about last Friday night. Absolutely nothing to worry about. You just chat with her about it while I make us all a nice cup of tea.'

He winked at Sue, then left the room, leaving her alone with gran. After a few pleasantries, Sue turned to the subject of the visit.

'Mrs Atwell, can you think back to Friday evening, just before the weekend. Your grandson tells me that's the day you arrived here.'

The old lady nodded. 'That's right. My daughter and son dropped me off here on their way to the airport. They're off to Florida for two weeks, to visit my other grandson. He lives there and they go every year about this time. I've been with them twice but I'm getting a bit old now to go traipsing half across the world, so now I stay with Michael while they're away.'

'And do you enjoy staying with Michael? It must be nice to spend a bit more time with him.'

The old lady sighed. 'Well, he's a good grandson and he does look after me very well, but it's a bit lonely when he's not here. He has to work so much you see.'

'Was – Michael – working last Friday? Can you remember?'

'Oh yes. He was here in the morning when Katie dropped me off, but then he went to work just after lunch. He didn't get home until after I'd gone to bed.'

'What time do you go to bed Mrs Atwell?'

'Well, usually around ten o'clock, but on Friday it was earlier. I was a bit tired I suppose, from the journey. Michael had said he'd probably be home around ten, but at nine o'clock I felt a bit drowsy, so I put myself to bed.'

'And can you remember Michael coming home? Did you hear him?'

'Oh yes. Something must have woken me up, I suppose it was him coming in. I called out, just to make sure it was him.' She smiled gently at Sue. 'I'm sure you understand dear, I'm used to living in my little granny flat in a semi-detached house, with neighbours all around. This house is very lonely and I get a bit nervous when I'm on my own. So I called out to make sure it was Michael. He called back "of course gran", then he came in to make sure I was all right.'

'And can you remember what time it was?'

'It was just before ten o'clock. I know it was because I asked him, then when he put on the light I could see it was. I've got a lovely big clock in my room, I can see the time even with my cataracts. So then Michael made me a lovely cup of cocoa, and I went back to sleep.'

Sue thanked the old lady and made small talk for a few minutes until Michael Horner returned, bearing a tray containing tea and cake. Mrs Atwell, she thought, was a delightful and guileless old lady whose world revolved around her children and grandchildren. She could see just what the superintendent meant about her being unable to maintain a careful lie such as the one that would be necessary to build up a false alibi. She had an engaging vagueness about her which Sue suspected was not entirely to do with age – the superintendent sometimes exuded the same air of abstraction. But more than that, she had an air of simplicity, of seeing the world in straightforward terms of good and bad, right and wrong, truth or untruth. Sue was as certain as she could be that the old lady had told her the truth - would indeed be incapable of lying with any degree of conviction.

Sue and the superintendent arrived back at Fairfield Station just before 3 pm, which gave her time to spend a couple of hours at home before returning to interview Jim Taylor again. Maybe she and Bill could have a serious talk about just where their relationship was going; at the moment it appeared to be going to the dogs and Sue was finding it difficult to think of a way in which they could rescue their marriage. But they were both supposed to be intelligent adults, for God's sake; surely there must be some way, some compromise they could make.

Terry's car was sitting on the driveway, to the side of the garage. Everything was quiet, not even a bark from Oscar. The front door of the house was locked. Sue peered through the window into the garage. No car. It looked as if Bill and Terry had gone out together, and taken Oscar along.

'Fishing!' muttered Sue in irritation. They must have gone fishing, and just when she unexpectedly had a few hours to spare. It was a beautiful winter's day, cold and frosty but with a clear blue sky. She really couldn't blame Bill for taking advantage of such lovely weather, he had no way of knowing that she would be home for the afternoon. That didn't stop her from feeling irritated at the waste of her time, there were plenty of things she could have been getting on with back at the station.

She washed up the crockery from lunch and loaded clothes into the washing machine. Then she made herself a snack, trying to relax and forget about work. As usual, she failed dismally. Shortly after five o'clock she scribbled a note to Bill, shrugged herself into her coat and headed back to Fairfield Station.

# Chapter 21

Martin had already spoken to the duty inspector at Fairfield Station and requested that Jim report to them after briefing. He arrived promptly at six o'clock, looking disgruntled.

'You asked to see me ma'am?'

Sue waved him to a chair. 'Just a few things we need to clarify, following on from our last interview.'

'I've already told you all I can.'

'I don't think so, PC Taylor.'

A flush spread up Jim's neck and he leaned towards her. 'Now just a minute, are you calling me a liar – ma'am?'

'I'm saying you haven't told us everything. PC Taylor, I suggest you calm down and think carefully about this. We are investigating a murder and any attempt to mislead us will inevitably lead to suspicion. I believe you have misled us – or tried to.'

'How?' muttered Jim.

'You told us you didn't see Pete Ashbourne at all on that day. We have information that contradicts that statement.'

'What information?'

'Milk!' put in Martin.

'Oh. Oh, yes, the milk. I'd forgotten about that. Yes, control room asked me to pop a pint of milk down to the custody office.'

'And did you?'

'Yes.'

'And you'd forgotten about it?'

'Yes. Well, it's hardly a major incident is it? Taking a bottle of milk down to the custody sergeant.'

Martin took over the conversation. 'Jim, if it was a normal run-of-the-mill day I'd agree with you. But it wasn't. We specifically asked you if you'd seen Pete Ashbourne that day and you categorically stated that you hadn't. Given what Mandy had told you earlier I find it difficult to believe you'd forget. Now, what time did you take the milk down?'

Jim shrugged, now looking distinctly uncomfortable. 'Ten o'clock, give or take a few minutes.'

'Which makes it highly likely that you were the last person to see Pete Ashbourne alive. And you must know that.'

'Apart from the murderer,' muttered Jim.

Sue and Martin remained silent, a silence that stretched until it felt uncomfortable. Eventually Jim resumed speaking.

'Yes, I do know that. And yes, I remember taking the milk down. But surely you can see why I didn't want to mention it? You know I've good reason to be angry with Pete. If you knew I'd been down there just before he was murdered - well, you were bound to be suspicious of me.'

Sue frowned. 'Not half as suspicious as we're likely to be now you've deliberately lied to us.' She held up her hand to forestall Jim's next comment. 'All right, listen carefully and please don't interrupt. You have just admitted seeing Pete Ashbourne just before he was murdered. You've also agreed that you had reason to be angry with him and you've admitted lying to us. This interview will now proceed under caution. You do not have to say anything unless you wish to do so, but what you say may be given in evidence.'

Jim blanched. 'You can't be serious. You're saying you think I murdered Pete Ashbourne?'

'No. I'm saying that we have sufficient grounds to suspect that possibility, hence the caution. Do you understand?'

'I suppose so.' Jim still looked stunned. Sue nodded to Martin, who continued.

'Jim, you told us you got that black eye when you arrested Nichols. Do you stand by that?'

Jim set his mouth and looked down at the floor, making no reply. Martin continued.

'Jim, you're really not helping yourself here. We happen to

know you didn't get that black eye from Robbie Nichols. Where did you get it?'

Jim shrugged. 'Don't know. We often get into scuffles in this job.'

'The forensic report shows that Pete Ashbourne had hair under his fingernails. Brown hair, Jim. The same colour as yours.'

'And lots of other people. Loads of people have brown hair.'

Sue cut in. 'PC Taylor, how much do you know about DNA?'

'Not a massive amount, it's a fairly new technique isn't it? I know they can match up skin samples, blood samples, stuff like that.'

'And hair samples.'

Jim blinked, but made no response.

'The hair samples from Pete are being analysed now. We're going to be asking you to provide us with a sample of your hair, for DNA comparison. Now then, bear in mind how it will look for you if there's a DNA match. Are you sure nothing happened between you and Pete Ashbourne?'

Jim groaned. 'Oh God, I'm just getting myself deeper and deeper in the shit.'

'Yes, you are.'

'Pete and I had a dust-up. A fight. Well, not a fight exactly - more of a scuffle really. I took the milk in to him and I didn't intend to say anything, I was determined to keep my temper. I'd promised Mandy I would – she was worried sick that I might have a go. But Pete asked me how my spaniel eyed little fiancée was getting on and I just lost it. I called him a pathetic little bastard and a dirty old man. Then the old red mist came down and I hauled off and hit him. He punched me back and then we were scrapping like a couple of little kids in the school playground. Bloody ridiculous when I look back on it. I suppose that's when he grabbed my hair – I don't remember that.'

'Anything else?'

'Not really. We both calmed down a bit. He said he'd report

me for hitting him and I told him that this time there would be an official complaint from Mandy because I'd bloody see to it that there was. Then I stalked out. And that's it. That really is it. As you say, I'm probably the last person to see him alive, apart from the murderer. I suppose it was stupid not to come clean before, but I was scared. Surely to God, you can see why.'

Sue drew a deep breath. 'PC Taylor, I'm not saying that you killed Pete, but I am saying that I'm not fully happy with your explanation. I am now arresting you on suspicion of Pete Ashbourne's murder. Before you respond, remember you are under caution.'

Jim shook his head but made no reply. His face was drained of colour, his expression one of profound disbelief.

It was approaching 10 pm. Jim Taylor had been taken down to Butt Lane Station and was now in custody. All his uniform had been seized, including shoes and boots; they would be examined for traces of blood. Sue and Martin were back at FHQ discussing the way forward. It was very quiet; most people at FHQ worked day shifts and Sue and Martin were the only people there, with the exception of security.

'Well?' asked Martin. 'What do you think?'

'About Jim Taylor? I think we have good grounds for arresting him, seizing his uniform, searching his place. But all the same I don't think we have a particularly strong case - not enough for a conviction anyway. It's pretty much circumstantial. Unless of course they find some of Pete's blood on his shoes or uniform.'

'The fight is good evidence.'

'It's evidence that Jim was angry enough to lose his rag. It's evidence that he initially lied to us. But it's not direct evidence of a murder. We still have the same problems, Martin. If Jim had committed that murder he would have been heavily blood-stained. But it doesn't appear that he was. He was seen around the station from ten o'clock until the end of his shift at eleven, but there's nothing to say he had visible blood-stains.'

'He could have got down to the locker room and done a quick change of shirt. Most of the lads keep a spare shirt in their locker and there weren't many people around at that time.'

'It's a possibility. But don't forget he'd already used his spare shirt. He was well blood-stained after Nichols' arrest, with Nichols' wife's blood. In fact, this fight could go against us. If there are traces of Pete Ashbourne's blood on his uniform, he can claim they came from this fight. And he could be right. If he carried out that murder there'd be a lot more than just traces.'

'He could have stuffed another blood-stained shirt in with the first.' suggested Martin.

Sue sighed. 'Yes he could, if he had two spare shirts at the nick. Trouble is he says he threw away the shirt with Nichols' blood on it because it was too badly stained. If there was a second shirt it would have gone the same way.'

'So we're buggered?'

Sue shrugged. 'We are so far as the shirt is concerned.'

'What about the hair?'

'Two things about the hair. First, it could only prove they had that fight – and we already know that. Second, it's unlikely the hair will prove anything anyway. We won't be sure until we get the forensic result, but they need the hair root for a matching analysis, and forensic didn't think they had that.'

Martin grinned. 'Well, well. So you were bluffing, were you?'

Sue shrugged. 'Not exactly. I told Martin we had hair samples. I told him DNA matches could be done from hair samples. I was hardly going to tell him that it was unlikely in this particular case.' She gave him a sideways glance. 'The rules of PACE don't say we have to be totally stupid and tell prisoners everything, Martin.'

The phone rang, startling them both. Martin pressed the intercom button.

'DS Attwood.'

'Martin, it's Paul. We're just heading for the Trumpeters. How're you fixed?'

Martin looked a query at Sue, who nodded.

'You might as well get a pint in while you can Martin, there's nothing more we can do here tonight. I'll just tidy up, then I'll be off home myself.'

'Heard that,' crackled Paul's voice. 'See you later.'

The phone went dead. Martin locked his briefcase into the cabinet and unhooked his heavy sheepskin from the coat rack.

'Goodnight Sue.'

'Goodnight.'

Martin's footsteps died away down the corridor. He was off to have a drink with the lads, as he did most nights. A warm, crowded pub, with laughter and camaraderie. Sue thought of her own home. It would be warm enough certainly; but no laughter, no camaraderie – unless you counted the dog.

The silence of the deserted building closed oppressively around her. She collected her coat and headed for the car.

# Chapter 22

Early the following morning Sue and Martin arrived at Fairfield Station to speak to PC Judith Saunders. In due course Sue intended to speak to all the women at the station, with a view to discovering whether any of them had experienced sexual abuse from Pete Ashbourne.

Judith Saunders was a tall, slim woman in her early forties, with severe, angular features. Her dark brown hair, liberally flecked with grey, was cut very short; her manner brisk and no-nonsense.

Martin opened the interview. 'Judith, as you know we're investigating the death of Pete Ashbourne. We've already spoken to everyone who was on duty the night he died; now we're starting to interview the rest of his colleagues. We need as full a picture as we can, of Pete Ashbourne, and his relationships with his colleagues.'

Judith nodded. 'Of course - I understand that. I doubt if I can tell you anything of value but I'll help in any way I can.'

'Thank you. To start with, how did you personally relate to Sergeant Ashbourne?'

'He wasn't my favourite person,' she responded bluntly. 'He used to throw his weight around too much for my taste, sometimes to the point of being a bully.'

'Did you have any problems with him, personally?'

'Personally? No.'

'Never?' Put in Sue. 'He never behaved in a - shall we say - improper way to you?'

'You mean did he try to touch me up or chat me up? No, he didn't. As you might have noticed I'm no spring chicken any more - I'm over forty and I've twenty years police service.

I'm really not - wasn't - Pete Ashbourne's type.' She paused. 'And even if I had been, I don't for a moment think he'd have tried anything on with me. He knew what kind of response he'd get.'

'Such as?'

'Such as a bloody strong verbal warning, or a swipe round the ear if he pushed his luck. Like I say, he wouldn't have tried it on in the first place. I'm not victim material ma'am.' She paused. 'To save you the trouble of tiptoeing around the subject, I'm well aware that he had been pestering young Mandy Cornwell.'

'Oh? Did she tell you?'

'No, but you know how fast the grapevine runs in the police service.' She paused. 'I'm afraid Mandy IS victim material.'

'Because she's young and attractive?'

'That's a factor of course, but probably not the main one. She's just the type of woman who has 'victim' stamped all over her, the sort bullies like Pete Ashbourne prey on. It's not just the sex thing with people like him, it's the dominance thing. And Mandy was just so easy to dominate.'

Her tone was dismissive and Sue raised her eyebrows. 'You don't sound too sympathetic.'

Judith frowned. 'I'm sympathetic to a point of course, but I admit I struggle a bit with people like that - women who turn themselves into victims because they let themselves be treated like doormats. And Mandy really should have been able to cope with it, whether she dealt with him herself or reported him.'

'Why?' Asked Sue quietly.

'She's a police officer for God's sake. She's supposed to be confident and decisive, or at least act that way.'

'I take it you haven't much time for Mandy,' said Sue dryly.

Judith shrugged. 'Not as a police officer, no. She's a nice person and she'd probably have been okay in the old-style peewee's department. But in the modern police service? No, I don't think she can hack it. Not yet, anyway; maybe when she's a bit more mature, but even then I doubt it.'

'I see. Just before you go, are you aware of any other women who Sergeant Ashbourne might have importuned? Police or civilian.'

Judith shook her head. 'None that I'm aware of.'

Sue nodded. 'Thank you for your time PC Saunders.'

'You're welcome ma'am.' Judith nodded to Martin and left the office.

'Well,' said Sue, 'I can understand why Mandy didn't confide in Miss Saunders.'

Martin grinned. 'Not very sympathetic is she? But I suppose the job can do that to you all too easily; she used to work in a department that dealt mainly with domestic abuse so she'll have seen all too many predators and victims.'

'I suppose so,' said Sue. She felt particularly sympathetic towards victims of domestic abuse, if Judith Saunders was the person supporting them.

Their arrival back at FHQ brought a new development. When Sue arrived at her office at eleven o'clock, DC Paul Redman was waiting for her. 'Morning ma'am,' he said. 'Thought you might be interested in this.'

'What is it?' She asked.

'It's the statement I took from Clive Stirling - you know, the woodentop who popped his head into the parade room the night Sergeant Ashbourne was killed.'

Sue drew a deep breath. 'DC Redman, do you really think it fosters good relations with the uniform branch to go around calling them woodentops? And why should they be woodentops just because they happen to wear a uniform? I suppose you skipped that stage of your career and joined CID direct from training school?'

Redman grinned, not looking in the least abashed. 'Sorry about that - just slipped out I'm afraid. It's what our old guvnor used to call the uniform branch.'

'Yes, well, I'm not your old guvnor and I'd be obliged if you packed it in. And it isn't funny,' she snapped at Martin, who had just walked in behind Redman and was grinning broadly. 'Now then, what about this statement?'

'He doesn't mention being at the nick that night. I didn't say anything about Jim seeing him there and I didn't ask him directly whether he was in the nick - I just asked him what he was doing at the time; told him we'd be talking to everybody in the nick sooner or later, which is true enough. Here, look for yourself.'

He handed the document to Sue and dropped into the chair opposite the desk. Sue read through the statement quickly. 'What's he say?' asked Martin.

'He says he left his house around seven o'clock to go to a meeting at his local church. He was at the meeting until just after ten, then went straight home. No mention of dropping in at the station - not a word.' She put the document down on the desk. 'Tell me about this man?'

Martin shrugged. 'Nothing special to tell. He's an old sweat, just a few months off his thirty years service. Had a minor heart attack last year, made a good recovery and didn't want to go on ill-health, so he's seeing his time out on light duties in the control room.' Martin paused, then continued. 'I'm not surprised to hear he was at a church meeting because he's very religious - like, I mean seriously religious. When I joined the job he was working in training and it was a standing joke that if you weren't interested in the lesson, you just had to mention something about religion to sidetrack him.'

'Religious in the same way as Tony Woodford?'

'More bigoted than Tony, I'd say. Maybe not exactly fanatical, but getting that way. I'm afraid the lads used to rib him a fair bit about it.'

'What was his reaction?'

Martin shrugged. 'No reaction really. If the ribbing was subtle he wouldn't even notice - he doesn't have much of a sense of humour, doesn't Clive. If the lads went a bit far he might give a bit of a tut or a haughty look, no more than that.'

Sue nodded thoughtfully. 'Thanks Martin, we'll be having a few words with Mr Stirling about this.'

# Chapter 23

Enquiries revealed that Clive Stirling was currently on rest days and was not due back at work for two more days; accordingly Sue decided that they would interview him at home. They arrived at his house early in the afternoon. He lived some ten miles from Fairfield Station but somewhat closer to FHQ. The property stood on the edge of a village - a small, detached cottage, surrounded by neatly trimmed Leylandi. The property was quite old but seemingly in good repair. A dark blue VW Golf stood in the driveway.

Stirling himself opened the door to Martin's knock. He looked to be around fifty, a little overweight but not fat. He had grey hair - thinning on the top but ruthlessly cropped - and a small, neat moustache. His eyes behind rimless glasses were lacking in colour, like dull ice. He looked surprised to see Sue and Martin standing on his doorstep.

'Martin. What brings you out here? Is something wrong?'

'Hopefully not,' said Martin, 'but we do need to talk to you. May we come in?'

'Yes - yes, of course.' He stood back to let them enter the house, then led the way to a small and very tidy lounge. A picture of Jesus on the cross was prominently displayed above the fireplace; a large crucifix was hanging on the opposite wall.

Martin introduced Sue, who went straight to the point. 'PC Stirling, I'm sorry to bother you on your day off, but we needed to speak to you and I didn't really want to wait two more days until you come back to work. It's about the statement you made to Paul Redman.'

He nodded, but made no reply. Sue continued. 'In your statement, you said you didn't go to Fairfield Station on the day

Sergeant Ashbourne was killed - not at any time.'

'Well yes, that's quite correct. I actually had the whole weekend off - Friday, Saturday and Sunday.'

'So I understand. But please think carefully - are you sure you didn't go into the station that day?'

'Of course I'm sure. Why would I travel all that way on my day off?'

'Only you can answer that,' said Sue. 'But our information is that you did in fact visit the station - quite late in the evening. One of your colleagues saw you there.'

Stirling blinked rapidly. 'Oh. Oh - yes - wait a minute. I'm so sorry - you're absolutely right. I had a church meeting that evening and the church is very close to Fairfield nick. So yes, I did just pop in on my way home. I'd forgotten all about that.'

'May I ask why you went into the station?'

'Oh, it was to - to pick up my torch, from my locker. I wanted to do some work on the car over the weekend and I didn't have another decent torch.'

'I see. And did you pick up the torch?'

'Yes, of course.'

Sue glanced at Martin, who took up the questioning. 'Clive, you're quite sure you collected the torch? From your locker in the parade room?'

'Yes, I'm sure I did.'

'Your colleague's account differs somewhat. He says you just put your head round the door, then left without going into the room.'

A flush had crept up Stirling's neck. The room wasn't particularly warm - was in fact on the chill side - but Sue could see sweat shining on the top of his balding head.

'Jim Taylor, wasn't it? Well, I'm afraid he must be mistaken. I mean, he had no reason to take any notice of me being there, had he? He was busy doing his paperwork, if I remember rightly.'

'He was,' agreed Sue. 'PC Stirling, under normal circumstances I could understand your overlooking a quick visit to the station on your way home, but these circumstances were hardly normal, were they? Given the fact that one of your colleagues was murdered that night, I'd have expected you to remember your visit.'

'Yes, well, I'm sorry but I didn't remember. In any case, I can't see that it matters. I appreciate you have to talk to everyone, but I certainly had no reason to kill Pete Ashbourne. I could never kill anyone. "Thou shalt not kill!"'

Sue looked at him closely, then nodded. 'Well, thank you for your time, PC Stirling. We'll leave you in peace now. Martin.'

She stood up. Martin looked at her with a slight frown, then he also stood and followed her from the room. He waited until they had reached their car before saying 'Sue, don't you think . . .'

'Not now!' She interrupted. 'Just pull away round the bend and stop - I want to see what he does. Of course I'm not happy with him - and neither are you.'

Martin did as she requested, driving the car out of sight of the cottage. They both left the vehicle and moved to where they could watch the property through the foliage of the tall hedge. After a few minutes the front door opened and Stirling went to the car in the driveway. He appeared to poke around in the boot for a few moments, then emerged carrying something in his hand.

'Come on!' said Sue. They hurried round the hedge and approached Stirling.

'Just a minute please,' said Sue. 'There are a couple more things we need to ask you.'

He spun round. His mouth dropped, then he put his right hand behind him. 'If you can just wait a moment . . .'

'What are you holding there?' Asked Martin.

Stirling backed away. 'It's nothing, really. Just a - a bit of paint, that's all.'

'May we see please?'

With obvious reluctance, Stirling brought his hand from behind his back. He was holding a can of bright yellow spray paint.

There was a moment of silence, then Sue nodded her head

towards the house. 'I think we should go back inside,' she said.

Stirling's face was ashen as he led the way back into the house and resumed their former seats. Martin was now in possession of the yellow spray can.

'PC Stirling,' said Sue. 'Why did you feel the need to go out to your car and remove this can?'

'Well - I - I suppose I just wanted to tidy the car boot up a bit. I remembered the paint . . .' His voice trailed off. Sue made no response, just sat and waited. Stirling moved restlessly on his seat; the sweat on his forehead was visible again. After a long pause, Sue nodded at Martin, who took up the interview.

'Clive, at this stage I'm going to caution you.' He gave the necessary caution, then continued. 'I believe I've seen paint this colour before - on the inside of a locker, at Fairfield Station.' Stirling looked down at the rug, but made no reply. 'Clive, you do realise we can get this checked out with forensics?'

Stirling's shoulders dropped; his whole body seemed to sag.

'I know that,' he said, so quietly they could hardly hear him. Then he looked up and his voice became firmer. 'It's just not right. As a God fearing man I can't condone it.'

'Condone what?' said Sue softly.

His mouth twisted. 'What Tony Woodford is. Homosexuality.'

'Being gay is not against the law,' said Sue. 'It hasn't been for some time.'

Stirling straightened his back. His colourless eyes took on a cold glitter. 'It's against God's law!'

Sue sighed. 'PC Stirling, do you admit spraying graffiti on Tony Woodford's locker?'

He nodded jerkily. 'I might as well admit it now, hadn't I? Now you've got the paint. Yes, I've sprayed the graffiti. I - well, I felt it was the only way I could register a protest about having a - a homosexual working at our station. And I hoped it might drive him away.'

'I see. And is that why you stopped off at the station that evening?'

'Yes. I - I hadn't done it for a while because I had to be

careful. If it kept happening on my shift someone would soon have rumbled me, wouldn't they? Then that evening we'd been reading the Bible at my church - Leviticus. "*If a man lies with a male as with a woman, both of them have committed an abomination; they shall surely be put to death; their blood is upon them.*" It reminded me how wrong it was, that I wasn't doing anything about what was happening at my own place of work. So I stopped off in the hope I might get the chance to proclaim again how sinful it was - but Jim was in the parade room so of course I couldn't do it.'

He paused. His voice remained quiet, but his tone was cold and his ice-chip eyes lacked all expression as he added 'I don't regret what I did, I was right to do it. What they do - what Tony Woodford and his ilk do - is wrong - evil. I don't care what our law books say; the Bible says that homosexuality is an abomination.'

Sue nodded and stood up. 'We'll continue this conversation at the station,' she said. 'PC Stirling, I'm arresting you on suspicion of causing criminal damage to police property.'

# Chapter 24

The next two weeks revealed few developments of any importance. Clive Stirling was formally charged with criminal damage regarding the graffiti, then bailed to appear at court. He was also suspended from duty and there was little doubt that once convicted he would be dismissed from the service. 'He was always a bit on the extreme side,' commented Martin to Sue. 'But there's no doubt he's got worse over the past few years. Fanatical.'

Sue nodded, remembering Stirling's implacability, his hard eyes and cold voice. 'I can just imagine him in the middle ages, putting the torch to the pyre when heretics were being burned.'

It was gratifying to be able to close the file on the damage to Tony Woodford's locker, but they seemed no further forward so far as Pete Ashbourne's death was concerned. There was nothing to connect Clive Stirling with that.

The DNA results on the hair under Pete Ashbourne's fingernails were, as expected, disappointing. None of the hairs appeared to include the root. Notwithstanding these results, samples of hair had been taken from Jim Taylor, but more as a matter of routine than with any real expectation of a result. Jim Taylor was by no means in the clear, to the best of their knowledge he was the last person to see Pete Ashbourne alive and he had admitted violence between them. Still, the evidence remained circumstantial. Enough to suspect, but unlikely to be enough to convict. He was currently on bail, but under suspension. They were still awaiting the results of tests on his boots and uniform.

Sue was no longer spending every available hour at FHQ; pending further developments, she was working a basic day shift on most days. This gave her more time at home, which she had hoped would help her and Bill to pick up the pieces of their marriage. But the main bones of contention remained. Bill wanted children, sooner rather than later, and had conceived an active dislike of Sue's job. They were now in a state of guarded truce. The outright rows had ceased, but the volcano was still bubbling beneath the surface.

It erupted one day in mid-February. Bill had an interview that day, for a job in their nearest town. He was well qualified for it and had driven off that morning in a confident mood. Sue was keeping her fingers crossed for his success; she was convinced that a lot of his problems stemmed from his unemployment, worsened by the fact that Sue was not only employed, but highly successful in her job and probably destined to go far.

Winter had returned with a vengeance, heavy snow driven by gales to form deep drifts. She had navigated her way home through minor roads made treacherous by snow and ice. There were no tyre tracks in the drive, so she assumed Bill hadn't returned. She was surprised to see lights blazing out from the lounge and kitchen.

She opened the front door, which was unlocked. Oscar greeted her with his usual boundless delight, tearing up and down the hall with one of Bill's shoes. At least he no longer chewed them.

'Bill?'

'Kitchen.'

He sounded irritable. Sue pushed open the door. He was sitting at the kitchen table, sipping tea and looking moody.

'How'd it go?' she asked.

He shrugged. 'Not well. They didn't tell me straight away, but I could tell they weren't too impressed. Being late didn't help.'

'Late? You left here in loads of time.'

'Pranged the bloody car!' he muttered.

'Oh no! Bill, are you okay? You're not hurt?'

'No. I was a bit shaken up though. Lost it in Common

Lane, just short of the main road junction. Bloody great sheet of ice. There was nothing I could do, the whole car skidded – all four wheels. Couldn't brake, couldn't accelerate, couldn't steer. Horrible feeling. I knew I was headed for the ditch, but I could do sod all about it.'

'Much damage?'

'Enough. The front nearside ended up against a tree and took a good hammering. Otherwise it's just scratches.'

Sue put her hand on his arm. 'Bill, I'm so sorry, but look on the bright side. At least you're okay. Cars can be replaced.'

He shrugged her off irritably. 'Yeah, I know, but it had to be today. I got to the main road and managed to pick up a bus, so I wasn't very late. But the fact remains, I wasn't on time. And it had rattled me. It's the worse interview I've ever had.'

'Did you tell them what had happened?'

'Of course I did, so they knew why I was late. But it wasn't only that - I just fluffed the interview.'

'Have they recovered your car?'

'Yes, I arranged that as soon as I'd had the interview. But it's going to be at least a week before they can do it. They're darn busy at the moment, you can imagine.' He scowled at her. 'So now we're down to one car and we both know who's going to have that.'

'Bill, that's not fair. I've got to have the car, to get to work.'

'Whereas I haven't. I'm just the unemployed house husband.'

'Well, that's hardly my fault is it? Look Bill, I'm sorry you smashed up the car and I'm sorry the interview didn't go well. But there's nothing I can do about it.'

Bill threw the newspaper onto the table. 'Well, maybe it wouldn't have happened if I'd had my own car.'

'What do you mean?'

'What I say. You've been using my car, while I made do with yours. But mine's better on the ice than yours is. You know that.'

'But Bill, that's why I've been using your car. I've been driving to and from work on snowy roads, every day.'

'So you agree with me. If I'd been in my own car I probably

wouldn't have had that accident.' He picked up the newspaper again and disappeared behind its pages.

Suddenly Sue had had enough. She grabbed the paper from him and screwed it up before throwing it onto the floor.

'You could have had the bloody car if you'd asked for it,' she shouted. You could have kept it here all the time if that's what you wanted. Maybe then I'd have been the one to pile up against a tree. Maybe I wouldn't have been lucky enough to walk away from it. Maybe I'd have been injured. Then I'd have been off work and you'd have been happy. Bill, I've had it with you, up to here! You should be bloody glad one of us has a job, we'd be well buggered without my wage and you know it. But you mope and moan around the house all the time. You hardly lift a finger to help with the house work, even though I'm working full time. I suppose you think that's just women's work – too good for you. I'm surprised you summon up the energy to feed the bloody dog. Well, I've had enough!'

She stormed out, slamming the kitchen door behind her with all her force.

# Chapter 25

The following morning dawned dark and murky. The snow was beginning to thaw, leaving the roads treacherous with slippery slush. The wind had risen and the air was filled with driving sleet. The weather suited Sue's mood. Nothing seemed to be going right; in the absence of further evidence the murder investigation was almost at a stand-still, and her marriage was well and truly on the rocks. She and Bill hadn't spoken since she had slammed her way out of the kitchen. He had - yet again - spent the night in the spare room.

Sue left home a little after 8 am. The drive to work would normally take thirty minutes at the outside, but given the weather conditions it could well be double that time. The sleet poured down the windscreen, with the wipers working overtime as she drove cautiously down the drive and along the narrow rutted track at the end of it. At least Bill wouldn't miss not having a car today, only a madman would go out in this lot if he didn't have to.

She was about two miles from home when the engine spluttered, caught, spluttered again, then failed. She brought the vehicle to a cautious halt and turned the key. Nothing. The engine was dead as the proverbial Dodo.

Sue swore softly to herself. The wipers had stopped and the sleet was now pouring down the windscreen and hammering on the roof. She had, it seemed, two choices. She could walk on a further mile to the main road and try to get a lift to the station, or she could return home and ring in. Staying where she was really wasn't an option, not many people would be using this lane in weather like this.

She thought it over. Even if she walked the mile to the main road, that didn't mean she would be able to pick up a lift easily. No, she would have to return to the house and ring the station. If there had been any significant developments they could send a car for her. Otherwise she would have to spend the day at home and hope that the car could be fixed quickly. Or she would have to hire one. It really was sod's law, this car breaking down just when the second car was out of commission.

The decision made, she buttoned her coat, collected her briefcase, got out of the car and turned for home. She was soaked through in seconds – her shower proof mac was adequate against light rain, but useless in this driving sleet. The only mitigating factor was the fact that the wind was blowing towards home, meaning that she had her back to the sleet. Even so, walking was far from easy. The minor road was bad, but when she turned into the rutted farm track that led to their house it became a lethal quagmire of thick slush, with patches of ice in the shady parts where the thaw was only just beginning to take effect. At least, she thought, she wasn't wearing high heels, but her shoes were still not suitable for the conditions underfoot. She slipped and slithered her way along the road, making slow progress. By the time she reached the house she was soaked to the skin, frozen and completely exhausted. It was already almost ten o'clock, they would have expected her at work an hour ago.

A blue Peugeot was parked in front of the garage - Terry and Sarah's car. She gave a tired smile of relief. With a bit of luck she wouldn't have to miss work after all, hopefully Terry would give her a lift in.

She opened the door to the kitchen and went into the welcome warmth and the usual enthusiastic welcome from Oscar. She threw off her soaked coat and grabbed the nearest towel to get the worst of the water off her face and hair, then headed for the lounge. There was no-one there. Sue gave a groan. Surely to God they hadn't gone out fishing in this weather – no-one in their right mind would do that. Well, she would worry about that later. She was still wet through and frozen; her first priority was to shower and change, then she would telephone the station.

She climbed slowly up the stairs, too stiff and cold to move swiftly. She opened the door to the bedroom she shared with Bill, then stopped in disbelief. There was movement in the room – in the bed. Black hair and blond intermingled, bodies closely entwined. Bill - and Sarah.

For an endless moment Sue just stood there, body and mind numb. Her husband, and her best friend. Her best friend, for God's sake – her best friend! Then she slammed the bedroom door behind her. The two people in the bed jumped convulsively and rolled apart.

'Sue!' exclaimed Bill. 'Oh my God, what . . .'

Sarah was already scrambling around for something to put on, as if covering herself up would somehow make a difference. Bill climbed out of bed and began pulling on his trousers. Sue hadn't said a word. She was beginning to shake as reality hit her and shock started to set in. A little voice at the back of her mind was talking to her as she came out of her cataleptic state . *Be strong Sue, be dignified.*

'WHAT THE FUCK IS GOING ON?' she screamed.

Sarah was sitting on the bed now, wrapping Sue's dressing gown around her with shaking fingers. 'Sue – oh my God. Sue, I never meant to . . .' her voice also tailed off.

Sue took a deep breath, trying desperately for calm.

'Get out of here!' she said.

Bill was pulling on his shirt. 'Sue, please listen. We have to talk about this.'

'There's nothing to talk about. Just get out. Both of you – get out!'

'Sue, please …'

'GET OUT!' she yelled.

Sarah was shaking almost as much as Sue. She grabbed Bill's arm. 'Please Bill, let's go. Please. We can't talk about anything now. Let's just go. Please Bill – I have to get out of here.'

She started towards the door, then stopped, eyeing Sue in

trepidation. Suddenly Sue's temper snapped completely.

'YOU FUCKING TWO FACED BITCH!' she yelled. She flung herself at Sarah, hitting out wildly - a punch, not an open handed slap. She caught Sarah on the left side of her jaw and Sarah collapsed onto the floor as Bill grabbed Sue, pulling her back and throwing her across the bed.

'Sue, for God's sake calm down.'

Sue scrambled off the far side of the bed, fighting for self control. Far back in her mind, a voice was telling her that she must calm down; that this kind of behaviour was self destructive; that it wouldn't help. She was trembling badly now as she fought for rationality and self control. Bill was kneeling next to Sarah, who was holding her jaw and looking dazed. Still watching Sue warily, he helped Sarah up and led her from the room.

# Chapter 26

Sue was brought back to reality by the strident ringing of the telephone. She was sitting on the floor of the bedroom with her head buried in Oscar's fur, still wet through and shaking with cold and reaction. She reached up and grabbed the receiver.

'Sue Bishop.'

'Sue, it's Martin. Sue – are you there?'

'Yes. Yes Martin, I'm here.'

'Is there something wrong? I thought we were meeting up at nine o'clock this morning for a confab. Or have I got it wrong?'

Sue glanced at the bedside clock, which showed 10.30 am. With an effort, she steadied her voice and tried to control her shaking. 'No Martin, you haven't got it wrong. I'm sorry, I was about to ring in. The car broke down partway to work and I had to walk back home. I – er – haven't been in long.' She glanced down at the carpet, soggy with water all around the area in which she was sitting. 'In fact, I'm still freezing cold and soaking wet,' she added truthfully.

'Can you borrow your husband's car?'

'No, he pranged it yesterday. Actually Martin, it might be better if we postpone the confab, given the circumstances. I'll arrange to get the car sorted and come in tomorrow. '

'I think you need to get in here today Sue.'

Her attention sharpened. 'Why?'

'Because there may be a development. When I got in this morning there was a message waiting for us – from Tony Woodford. He says he needs to talk to us and that it's important. He's on late shift today but he's coming in here first, at one o'clock.'

'When did he ring?'

'Yesterday evening, at 9 pm. He left the message with control room and they sent it up here. That's all there is – I've no idea what it's all about. But the message does say it could be important.'

Sue pulled herself together. 'Right. Give me time to have a shower and change into some dry clothes. I'll try to get a taxi down.'

'No need for that, I'll pick you up. If I leave now I'll be there by the time you're ready.'

'Right,' said Sue. 'See you later.' She hung up the phone and looked down at Oscar, who gazed back at her with his melting spaniel eyes full of sympathy. Sue sighed as she fondled the dog's fur, he was going to be another complication. Her mum and dad would certainly be prepared to help out in the short term, but after that ... She pulled herself up short. After that was too far to look at the moment, it was enough to cope with the present. She picked up the phone and dialled her parents' number.

By the time Martin's car pulled up outside Sue was showered, changed and outwardly calm. She had arranged for her father to pick up Oscar on his way home from work. Her mother had of course guessed that there was something amiss, but Sue had parried her questions for the time being.

She opened the door and gestured Martin inside. 'I'll just pick up my coat, then I'm ready.'

'What's wrong?' he said.

'What do you mean?'

'What I say. You're as white a sheet and you've an expression like a rabbit caught in headlights.'

She shook her head. 'It's nothing Martin. Just personal problems. nothing you can help with.'

'Whatever it is Sue, it isn't nothing. Obviously you haven't looked in the mirror.' He took her arm and led her back into the house. 'All right, you don't have to tell me anything – it's probably none of my business. But at least you can sit down and have a cup of tea before we go. No, you just stay there, I can manage to find tea and milk.'

Leaving Sue sitting on the sofa, he disappeared into the kitchen. Sue leaned back and tried to relax. Things were beginning to come back into focus now, but her thoughts were still chaotic.

Martin returned with the tea and put the cup into her hand. Here, you need this. You look like a volcano that's about to erupt.'

Sue gave a shaky laugh. 'Actually Martin, I'm a volcano that has just erupted - but I could very well blow again.' She looked at him squarely. 'My husband has just walked out on me.'

'Oh God,' said Martin softly.

Sue nodded. 'Well, really he didn't walk out. I told him to get out. Him and his – his . . .' she took a deep breath. 'I told you the car broke down this morning?'

Martin nodded.

'Well, I'd driven about two miles, so I had to walk back here. The weather was filthy and so was the track, by the time I got here I was soaked through, frozen and pretty much worn out. Bill didn't seem to be at home and I wondered about that, but to be honest I was more concerned with getting out of my wet clothes and getting warmed up. I went straight up to the bedroom.' She paused. Why on earth was she blurting out her personal affairs like this, to someone who was no more than a colleague? Well, shock often led to strange behaviour and whatever the reason she felt a compelling need to offload.

'Bill was at home all right,' she continued. 'He was in bed – with my best friend, Sarah.' She laughed expressionlessly. 'That should now read "my former best friend Sarah."'

Martin made no response, just waited for her to continue. Despite her distress, she subconsciously noted the technique. Good use of silence – he always used that well in interviews.

'I just lost it - totally lost it. I screamed at them to get out, both of them. I think Bill tried to calm me down, but I was beyond that.' She looked down at her left hand, thinking back over the short but distressing scene. 'In fact I hit her. I've only just remembered that.'

'Hard, I should imagine,' said Martin dryly.

Sue laughed shakily. 'It certainly wasn't a ladylike slap. I punched her on the jaw, as hard as I could.' She paused, thinking of the possible consequences of that blow. 'It really was a punch Martin, I knocked her down. She's going to have one hell of a bruise. God, that would be a bit of a turn-up wouldn't it? The local detective inspector charged with ABH.'

'Is she likely to complain? I shouldn't imagine she'd want that little scenario aired in public.'

Sue shook her head. 'Probably not. But it's frightening, that I just lost the plot like that. I've always had a temper, but never physical. I've never hauled off and punched someone like that before. I think – well, I was already tired and cold and feeling pretty low emotionally. And she was supposed to be my best friend. That made it worse.'

'Of course,' said Martin. 'It's bloody betrayal, from both your husband and your friend.'

They sat in silence whilst they finished their tea. Then Sue looked up.

'Martin, I don't know why I've offloaded on you like this - it really isn't your problem. Let's just forget about it.'

'Forget it?' he queried softly.

'Well, not forget it exactly, but move on. I still have a job to do – we still have a job to do.'

'Are you sure? I can cover for you if you want to take a day or two off.'

'No. I want to get back to work, God knows that's all that's left now.' She put down her cup and stood up decisively. Let's go!'

By the time they reached the station Sue was feeling a little better, at least she had stopped shaking and her mind had begun to focus again. Her marriage, she thought, had effectively been over even before she had discovered her husband in bed with her friend. Maybe a clean break like this would be better, once she recovered from the shock. She would just have to take things one day at a time and concentrate on her job - the job that had cost her marriage. No, that wasn't fair, she had always had choices and she had made those choices. She had chosen to move half-way across the country, dragging a reluctant Bill with her. She had chosen to reject the idea of having a baby, knowing Bill desperately wanted a family. But why? Was that just to get Sue into her "rightful place" as a wife and mother? She groaned to herself. This was doing her no good, her mind was just going round in circles.

She and Martin lunched in the canteen at FHQ, then returned to the office to wait for the arrival of Tony Woodford. One o'clock came, then one thirty, but no Tony. At two o'clock Martin turned to Sue.

'What do you think? Changed his mind?'

'He may be stuck in traffic or something. Or yes, he may have changed his mind. But whether he has or not, we're going to want to talk to him now. He must know that. We'd better contact Fairfield and see whether he's turned up for work.'

Martin nodded. 'And if he …'

He was interrupted by the telephone. Sue pressed the loudspeaker button.

'DI Bishop.'

'Chief Superintendent Wallace. Inspector, I'd like to see you and DS Attwood. In my office. Right away please.'

'Right sir. We're on our way.'

She hung up. 'Well, well,' said Martin. 'He sounded a bit brusque. I wonder what that's about.'

Sue groaned. 'Maybe Sarah has complained about that punch.'

Martin frowned. 'In which case he would hardly include me.'

'True enough. Come on Martin, let's find out what's up.'

Chief Superintendent Wallace was waiting for them in his office, and he wasn't alone. With him was Superintendent Horner.

Both men looked worried. No, more than worried - distressed.

'Come in!' said Wallace tersely. 'Shut the door and sit down.'

Sue and Martin complied, looking enquiringly at the chief superintendent.

'We've just had some disturbing news,' he said. 'Some bloody awful news. PC Tony Woodford has just been found – dead!'

There was a stunned silence, broken by Sue. 'Where? How?'

'In his car, in Repton Woods. It's too soon to draw any conclusions, but there seems to be a strong possibility of suicide.' There was a long pause whilst Sue and Martin absorbed the shocking news of Tony's death. Sue eventually found her voice. 'Why?' she said. 'Why do you think it might be suicide?'

'He appears to have been killed by exhaust fumes – a pipe from the exhaust and through a small gap in the front window of the car. He was found about an hour ago, by a passing motorist. Control sent a car to investigate. The officer they sent was Mandy Cornwell – of course she recognised Tony straight away. There's a forensic team on the way to the scene now.' He stood up. 'Come on, let's get over there. Michael?'

Superintendent Horner was sitting in the far corner of the room, looking white and shaken. He spoke for the first time.

'No. I'm not going to be involved in the investigation and the less people tramping around the scene the better. I'll go over to Fairfield and see if there's anything I can do there.' He shook his head. 'Poor young Mandy's going to be in a bit of a state, what with her fiancé being arrested and now finding one of her shift dead.' He turned to Sue and Martin. 'I'd be grateful if you could keep me informed as much as possible. I know it's not my enquiry, but . . .'

He nodded to them, then walked out without finishing the sentence. Wallace took his coat down from the hook. 'Come on – let's go.'

## Chapter 27

Repton Wood was on the outskirts of the town, a twenty minute drive from FHQ. The sleet had stopped, but it remained dismal and overcast. By the time they arrived at the scene it was just after three o'clock and dusk was already falling, but the forensic team already had floodlighting installed while they searched the scene.

The entrance to the wood was cordoned off, as was the entire car park. Most of the activity was centred around a red Corsa hatchback, parked adjacent to the entrance to the woodland path. Martin parked by the side of the road and they approached the cordon. The only entrance was controlled by a uniformed officer with a clipboard. He recognised them immediately.

'Can we go through?' asked Sue.

He nodded. 'Yes ma'am, but please would you keep to the designated route forensics have marked out .'

The doctor was already in attendance, the same man who had attended Pete Ashbourne's murder. He walked across to them, accompanied by a severe looking middle aged man with a thin face and greying hair. Sue recognised Patrick Ferguson, the head of the force's forensics department.

'What can you tell us?' asked Sue.

'I can certainly confirm the man is dead and that's about it up to now,' said the doctor. 'There's a pipe running from the exhaust into the car, but there's no way I can say for certain whether that caused his death – not at this stage. There are some strong indications of course, but we'll have to wait for the post-mortem to be sure. But this is interesting - take a look at this.' He led Sue to the driver's side of the car, where Tony's body was slumped in the seat. He lifted the head and gently pulled up one of the eyelids of the corpse. 'See that red mottling in the eye? That's petechiae. Could just be caused by the carbon monoxide but some drugs do that. Can't rule anything out at this stage.'

'Any idea how long he's been dead?'

He shook his head. 'It's really difficult to be accurate on that one. He's still in complete rigor mortis, which would normally indicate he's been here at least twelve hours - maybe considerably longer in these cold conditions. So we're probably talking about any time between yesterday evening and the early hours of this morning.'

'He was on duty until ten o'clock last night,' said Martin softly. 'So it couldn't have been before that.' He nodded towards the body. 'And he's still wearing his uniform under that coat.'

'That's helpful' said Ferguson. 'It ties the time down to quite a narrow margin because what we can say with a fair degree of certainty is that the car has been here all night. It was sleeting heavily from midnight onwards and it only let up about an hour ago.' He pointed to the car, standing a few yards away in the glare of the floodlights. 'But underneath the car is relatively dry - relative to the rest of the ground around here, that is.'

'So he left work at ten o'clock,' said Sue. 'Then he had to drive here, and you say the car's been here since before midnight. Realistically we're looking at a window of less than two hours.'

Ferguson nodded. 'Looks that way.' He paused. 'There's also a note.'

'Note? You mean suicide note?'

Ferguson shrugged. 'Could be. It's just one word - "sorry."'

'Typed or hand written?'

'Hand written, but with only five letters - well four really - the chances of proving a hand-writing match are pretty unlikely.'

'Okay,' said Sue. 'Who else knows about the note?'

'The young policewoman who called us out knows there's a note, but not the contents. It was folded and she had the sense not to touch it.'

'Good, let's keep it that way. Keep the contents just between us. Now then, how long before we can have a good look round?' She paused. 'Obviously I'm not suggesting you'll miss anything, but I just like to get a good feel for the scene.'

'Quite frankly inspector, I'd prefer you to wait until tomorrow before you start tramping around. We'll do what we can under floodlights but I also want to examine the scene in daylight.' He paused. 'The surrounding woodland too, as far as we can.'

'Fair enough,' said Wallace. 'We'll leave you to it and come back here in the morning. You'll still be here?'

The forensic officer gave a humourless smile. 'Not personally perhaps, but the team will be here for the whole of tomorrow. At least that.'

'Was the engine running?' asked Sue. 'When he was found I mean.'

'Apparently not, but the ignition key was still turned. The car is right out of petrol – as you might expect if the engine's been running all night.'

'Wouldn't that have helped to keep the corpse warmer? I mean, that might have affected rigor mortis.'

The doctor shrugged. 'Maybe. We have no way of knowing how long the engine's been dead.' He looked at his watch. 'If it's all the same to you, I'm off home, I've done all I can here and it's too cold to stand around when it isn't necessary. We'll get the PM done first thing in the morning and be in touch.' He looked at Sue. 'I take it one of you will go with the corpse and attend the PM?'

Sue gave an inward groan; she hated post-mortems - especially the inevitable smell. 'I'll do that,' she said, trying to sound unconcerned. The doctor nodded goodbye and headed towards his car, parked at the entrance to the little car park. Martin eased Sue out of earshot of Ferguson and Wallace, speaking quietly. 'Look Sue, I know you're perfectly capable of going to a post mortem, but under the circumstances don't you think I should do it?'

'What circumstances?'

'What happened this morning. You may not realise it, but you're still in shock and you're probably functioning on pure adrenalin.' He paused. 'This is nothing to do with your being female, I'd say the same thing to a male colleague. You can do without any unnecessary trauma. Let me do the PM bit.'

Sue paused, then nodded. 'All right. And thank you Martin. To be honest, post-mortems aren't high amongst my favourite things.' She shivered as Wallace came over to them. 'He's not wrong about that cold.'

Wallace nodded. 'Come on inspector, we might as well go too. There's nothing we can do here – we'll just be in the way. Oh – and we need to keep a couple of plain-clothes people here, day and night I'm afraid, but they can sit in a nice warm car. There are bound to be regular users of these woods – dog walkers, lovers and the like. We need to find out if anyone was here yesterday evening, and whether they can remember seeing this car – or any other car. Given the filthy weather it's a long shot.'

'It wasn't quite so bad last night,' Martin pointed out. 'As Mr Ferguson said, the wind and sleet didn't really kick in until around midnight.'

'That's true, so we may have a small chance of a witness coming forward. Let's keep our fingers crossed. Come on, let's get back to HQ and see if we can make any sense out of any of this.'

'There's just one thing I'd like to do first,' said Sue. 'Given what happened just a couple of weeks ago, I'd like to drop in on Clive Stirling. Preferably before he gets the chance to hear about this on the grapevine.'

Wallace frowned. 'Good idea.' He called across to the white haired scenes of crime supervisor, huddled in his scarf and overcoat as he directed his team. 'Mr Ferguson, any idea how long it'll be before you can move the body?'

'Couple of hours yet, at least,' responded Ferguson briefly.

'Thank you. Sue, that gives you ample time to talk to Stirling and get back here in good time to go with the body, to the morgue.'

'Martin's doing that,' said Sue. 'He volunteered.' Wallace raised his eyebrows but made no further comment.

Martin and Sue went back to their car and Martin drove off towards Stirling's house. 'Is there any way he can legitimately know about Tony's death yet? Asked Sue. 'Given it was only discovered this afternoon.'

'It's already been put out on local radio,' said Martin. 'It was on the four o'clock headlines - I heard it while you were talking to the boss.'

'How much info did they give?'

'Body found in car at Repton Woods. Identity not yet released but believed to be that of a serving police officer.'

Sue groaned. 'Bummer! Who the devil authorised that?'

Martin shrugged. 'Don't know, but it's done now. There's still no reason why he should know it's Tony.'

Ten minutes later they pulled up outside Stirling's house. Lights showed behind the closed curtains of the lounge. 'Looks like he's home anyway,' said Martin, as they approached the house and rang the bell.

Stirling's mouth thinned when he answered the door and saw them standing on the doorstep. 'Thought you might turn up,' he grunted. 'You'd better come in.'

They followed him into the lounge, where he waved them towards the sofa. 'Why did you think we might turn up?' asked Sue.

Stirling shrugged. 'Isn't it obvious? When I heard about Woodford I knew you were bound to come here.'

'What have you heard about Tony Woodford?'

'That he's been found dead in Repton Wood.'

'I see,' said Sue. 'Might I ask how you obtained the information?'

'On the local news. They showed the woods, and the forensic team still working on the car.'

'And they mentioned Tony Woodford's name?'

'No, they didn't, but I wanted to know who it was, so I rang Fairfield Control.'

'Why were you so anxious to know who it was?' asked Sue.

'Why? Isn't it obvious why? I wanted to know because I've worked at that station for the last six years. Thanks to you I know I'll never work there again, but of course I wanted to know who it was.'

'And they told you it was Tony?' Stirling nodded. 'Who did you speak to?'

'Geoff Robertson. I told him I'd heard about a police officer being found and asked who it was, and he said it was Woodford. He said it might have been suicide but that wasn't official yet.'

'And so,' said Sue, 'you expected us to come and talk to you.'

'I knew you would. You know how I felt about Woodford so you're going to regard me as prime suspect. If it isn't suicide.'

Sue leaned forward. 'Mr Stirling, we don't necessarily regard you as prime suspect; it's much too early in the enquiry for that. But surely you must understand why we need to talk to you. After all, you are a police officer.'

'Was. We both know the result of the disciplinary hearing is a foregone conclusion.'

'Be that as it may,' said Sue, 'you are still, at this moment, a police officer. You've been one for many years. So again I say, you must understand why we need to talk to you.'

'Just because I've no love for the likes of Woodford?'

'It's a little more than that, isn't it?' Put in Martin. 'You actually committed a criminal offence against said Tony Woodford - on more than one occasion.'

'I sprayed graffiti on his locker. That's hardly an indication of wanting him dead.'

'And Leviticus?' Said Sue. 'I seem to remember you quoting Leviticus at us, last time we were here. Something about men who lay with men being put to death, wasn't it?'

Stirling paled, but made no reply.

'Didn't you say you regarded that as God's law? asked Sue softly.

'I do, but in the name of God, that doesn't mean I wanted Woodford dead. I'd never go that far, of course I wouldn't.'

'PC Stirling, could you tell us your whereabouts from ten o'clock yesterday evening, until two o'clock this afternoon?'

'I was here. I was here all evening and all night, and all day today. I don't go out much now, with the neighbours all knowing what's happened. You know it was all in the papers, don't you? The whole court case? The local media made a big thing of it.'

'Were you here alone?'

'Yes I was, I've lived alone since my wife died. I don't have an alibi, if that's what you're driving at. But that's hardly evidence, is it?'

'That alone doesn't indicate much,' agreed Sue.

Stirling leant back and folded his arms. 'Then there really isn't anything else I can tell you.'

Sue nodded and stood up. 'Please understand PC Stirling, that we may need to come back and talk to you again. In the meantime, could we please have a look at your car?'

'My car? Why?'

'May we look?'

He shrugged. 'You can search it if you want to - you'll find nothing incriminating this time because I've done nothing.'

He led the way to the garage, where his blue VW gleamed under the fluorescent lights. Sue and Martin walked round, examining the paintwork carefully. Martin got down onto the floor and peered underneath. The car was immaculate - it could have had pride of place in any showroom.

'You keep your car very clean,' commented Sue. 'When did you last wash it?'

'This morning. I wash it most days, especially in the winter.

This morning I polished it as well - it gives me something to do.'

Sue thanked him and left the garage. As they walked back towards their car they saw that a couple were just getting out of their car on the next driveway. Sue and Martin walked across to the couple, introduced themselves and established that the couple lived at the property.

'Do you know Mr Stirling next door very well?' Asked Sue.

The neighbour shook his head. 'I know him of course, but I'd never say well. He's always kept himself to himself. We knew Clara better - that was his wife - but she died three years back.' He hesitated. 'Clara was quite friendly, but Clive - well, he's never been very sociable. We just pass the time of day and that's about all.'

'Did you by any chance notice whether he went out at all, yesterday evening or today?'

The couple looked at each other and both shook their heads. 'Sorry,' said the man, but we both work during the day and we were both out yesterday evening, until nearly midnight.'

'Thank you,' said Sue. 'This might seem like a strange question, but have you ever noticed how often Mr Stirling cleans his car?'

The neighbour glanced at his wife; both of them laughed. 'Clean it?' said the woman. 'He cleans it so often, it's a wonder he hasn't worn the paint off it. He's always been like that with his cars, never a speck of mud to be seen.'

Sue nodded. 'Thank you - you've been very helpful.' The couple looked at her curiously, but made no comment as Sue and Martin headed back to their own car.

'No mud!' said Martin, as he slid behind the wheel. 'And the floor of the garage was as clean as the parquet floor in the chief's office.'

'No mud,' agreed Sue. 'No way to say whether there ever was and no evidence to suggest he's washed the car to get rid of it. Ah well, there's nothing else we can do here for the present. If it turns out not to be suicide he's got to be up there on the suspect's list, but there's nothing to hold him on at the moment.'

Martin put the car into gear and they headed back towards the crime scene.

# Chapter 28

The preliminary report on the post-mortem was inconclusive. It revealed that carbon monoxide inhalation was indeed the most probable cause of death, but that there were also alcohol and drugs in the system. Analysis of these would take somewhat longer. The analysis of the one word 'suicide note' was, as predicted, disappointing. The handwriting was certainly similar to that of Tony Woodford, but with so few letters to go on the match was far from certain. As evidence in court, the note would be virtually useless.

With little to do but wait, Sue and Martin sifted endlessly through every statement and report, searching for any tiny clue they might have over-looked. It was tedious work, but even so Sue spent as much time as possible at the office. Being at home was no longer a pleasant experience for her. Every time she entered the bedroom she had shared with Bill, the whole scenario would replay in her mind - Bill and Sarah in the bed, blond and dark hair intertwined on the pillow. She had taken to sleeping in the spare room now.

The house felt empty and the quiet she had once loved pressed down on her. It didn't help that it was still deep winter, with spring seeming a world away. Sue had never before lived alone, before her marriage she had lived at home with her parents, then in halls of residence with her peers. Even the dog was gone, living at her parents' house. Of course Sue could also have moved in with her parents – they would have been delighted to have her – but that would have meant a round trip of over fifty miles to work. And somehow it would have felt like defeat.

Martin broached the subject one day, remarking on the

amount of time she was spending at the office. 'Don't worry,' she told him. 'I'm not booking overtime.'

'I didn't mean that.'

'Sorry Martin,' she muttered. 'I know you didn't. But I can't explain it to you. You wouldn't understand.'

'Oh I think I might, only too well. It happened to me too, a couple of years ago. Exactly the same thing.'

'Oh, Martin, I'm sorry; but not really exactly the same thing. You mean you found your wife in bed with another man?'

He shook his head. 'No Sue. I said exactly the same thing and that's what I meant. I found my wife in bed with another woman.'

Sue looked up, startled. 'With another ... oh, well.... I'm sorry Martin...'

Her voice trailed off. For a moment they gazed at each other, then suddenly, at the same time, they started to laugh. Once started, Sue just kept on laughing. There was, she recognised, something hysterical about the laughter, but she couldn't stop. At last she managed to calm herself down and slumped back into her chair, trying to get her breath back.

'Martin, I'm so sorry. That was unforgivable of me.'

'Was it? I was laughing too.'

'But it isn't funny. It really isn't funny.'

'Not to most people, but we're coppers. We laugh at things like that because we have to – because we need to. It helps us cope.'

'I suppose so.' She paused. 'I don't know whether that's better or worse. The other woman, I mean.'

Martin shrugged. 'I'm not sure either, but at least I can tell myself she didn't prefer another man over me - that's got to be better for my ego.' He paused, then continued. 'In the end we parted fairly amicably; there were no children, thank goodness.'

He turned away, picked up a file and began to read it, signalling the conversation was at an end. Sue surreptitiously wiped the last of the tears from her eyes, still stunned by her highly inappropriate outburst of laughter. But she felt much better, as if the uncontrollable laughter had released a spring that had been holding her emotions down tight. She knew that real tears were not far away, but the grief would be cathartic. There was a long road ahead, but at least she now felt ready to get her feet on that road.

The following day provided a potential break-through in the case of Tony Woodford's death. When Sue entered the office a little before 9 am Martin greeted her by waving a piece of paper at her.

'What's that?' she asked.

'It's a message from control'

She sighed. 'I can see it's a message. What's special about it? Someone wants to confess to both murders?'

He laughed. 'Nothing so dramatic I'm afraid, but still very interesting. On the evening before Tony was found, a local bloke pulled into the woodland car park to take a leak. He says there were two cars on the car park, one of which was parked at the entrance to the woodland track, right where Tony's car was found.'

Sue's interest quickened. 'What time?'

'Just before eleven o'clock.'

'Have they sent anyone to see the witness?'

'No. They thought we might like to look after this one ourselves.'

'Good idea,' agreed Sue. It might turn out to be nothing of value, but on the other hand it just could provide the breakthrough they needed to get things moving.

They arranged to visit the witness in the early evening, after he had finished work. He was a middle-aged man with an easy and pleasant manner, who nevertheless struck Sue as a shrewd individual He would probably be a good witness if it ever came to that; calm and reliable, not easily ruffled

He had, he said, pulled into the woodland car park to 'take

a leak' on his way home.

'What time was this?' asked Sue.

'Around eleven o'clock in the evening, maybe a few minutes before. I was on my way home when I suddenly needed to take a leak and I still had a few miles to go before I reached home. So I stopped in the Repton Wood car park.'

'And you say there were other cars there?'

He nodded. 'There were two. One of them was parked near the entrance to the woodland track. The other one was tucked away in the far corner, under the trees.'

'Anything else about the cars?'

'I can't tell you much about the one under the trees because I didn't get a good look at it - it was quite big and dark coloured and that's about all I can say. But the one at the entrance to the woods was definitely red.'

Sue's heart quickened. A red car! That fitted in with the possibility that it was indeed Tony's car. The position was right too.

'How can you be sure it was red?' she asked. 'It must have been pretty dark.'

'Black as pitch, but my headlights lit it up. The road around there is unlit so I had the lights on high and they swept across that car as I drove in. I can't tell you the model, but it was a hatchback and it was definitely red. A darkish red.'

'Could you see if there was anyone in it?'

He nodded. 'I think two people. I can't be one hundred per cent certain on that, but I'm pretty sure the lights registered two silhouettes, in the front seats.'

'And the other car? The one under the trees? You're sure you can't remember anything more about it?'

He shook his head. 'Nothing. I'm sorry, but it was tucked away in the far corner. I registered it was there, but nothing else about it. As you say, it was pretty dark, and you have to realise, I had no reason to notice those cars. They meant nothing to me at the time.'

'You didn't get a closer look at the red car?'

'No. If people are parked up in that car park at that time of night, at this time of year, they're usually only there for one thing. It was a bit dark and dismal to be having a picnic in there, or to be walking the dog.'

Sue questioned him at some depth, but there was nothing he could add, so Martin recorded a detailed statement.

'Just one more thing,' said Sue. 'This all happened a couple of weeks ago and it's been pretty prominent in the press. May I ask why you didn't come forward before?'

'Didn't know about it,' he said. 'I keep a café down on the coast and this time of year is about the only time we can shut up shop and take our holidays without losing business. We took off for the Canaries the day after I saw those cars. We only came home yesterday.'

'I see. Well, thank you for coming forward now. This could prove to be very useful to us.'

They took their leave and returned to their car for the journey back to the station. 'Well, well,' said Martin, 'if that's right about the other person in the car, it'll drive a coach and horses through the suicide theory. Pity we've nothing on the second car - we could have a good witness at the very least.'

Sue nodded. It was a shame they didn't have some kind of description for the second car, but all the same it was an interesting development. The second car might or might not have anything to do with the death, but the fact that there had been two people in Tony's car was very, very interesting. The great problem, of course, would be finding out the identity of that second person.

# Chapter 29

The full post-mortem report arrived some weeks after Tony's death. It confirmed that the actual cause of death was carbon monoxide poisoning. It also confirmed the fact that there was alcohol in the system, though not to excess. The drug also present was now identified as Gamma Hydroxy Butyrate or Gamma Hydroxybutyric Acid, generally shortened to GHB. A brief description of the effects of the drug was included -

*Low doses of GHB induce a state of euphoria, intoxication and increased social abilities. At higher doses, however, it can cause nausea, seizures, convulsions, vomiting, dizziness, depressed breathing, unconsciousness, amnesia, visual disturbances. Possible coma and death. The effects generally last between one and two hours and are dose dependent. In liquid form the actual concentration of GHB is usually unknown, which makes accurate dosing difficult.*

*Deaths fron GHB alone are rare, but severe effects may result if it is mixed with another depressant, such as barbiturates or alcohol.*

Sue looked across at Martin. 'Know anything about this drug?'

He shook his head. 'Drugs aren't really my thing. Hang on, I'll get Paul up here - he's ex drug squad.'

'Good idea – and while you're about it, get hold of Doctor Clarke. He can put some flesh on the bones of this report for us.'

Paul joined them shortly afterwards. 'What can I do for you?'

Sue handed him the part of the report describing the drug. 'Have you come across this drug in your line of work?'

He scanned the report quickly, then nodded. 'Oh yeah,

this is quite widely used in the club scene because of the high it gives. Widely used on the gay scene too.' He paused. 'It's also a date rape drug because it doesn't take long for the victim to become disorientated - unconscious if the dose is strong enough. Amnesia too, so the victim is generally pretty useless as a witness.'

'How's it sold?'

'Generally in liquid form, dissolved in water. Doesn't take much.'

'So it would be pretty easy to lace a drink with it - say whisky, for example?'

Paul nodded. 'Or any other drink, just so long as it's strong-tasting enough to kill the taste. If you just knock back the straight dose in water it would taste slightly salty, but no more. In alcohol, you wouldn't notice it - especially if you'd already had a few. That's why it's so handy as a date rape drug. But if it is mixed with alcohol, it's dangerous. We've had a couple of fatalities.'

Sue leaned forward. 'Paul, you mentioned that the drug is widely used on the gay scene. I think it's widely known - or at least suspected - that Tony Woodford was gay. Are you able to give us any info on that?'

He shook his head. 'Only negative info. We keep tabs on the gay scene, just as we do on the club scene or any other scene where recreational drugs are used. Tony Woodford wasn't on the gay scene - not at all. There are a couple of coppers that are - no names no packdrill - but Tony wasn't one of them.'

'Are either of those coppers from Fairfield Station?'

Paul shook his head. 'No, they're both off the Eastern Division. So far as I know neither of them has ever had any contact with Tony Woodford.'

'Did Tony have a partner?' Sue included both men in her question. Paul shrugged. Martin shook his head.

'I don't know. Tony was a very private individual and he kept his personal life well and truly to himself. He lived alone.

As you know, we've left no stone unturned over the past few weeks and we've turned up nothing and no-one. If he did have a partner he was very discreet about it.'

'I see. Well, thanks Paul, that's very helpful. Now, I'd like you to do something else for us. I want you to go through this entire file with a toothcomb. Re-read every statement - twice if possible - and take your time. You've been less involved than Martin and me; a fresh pair of eyes just might turn up something we've missed.' She paused. 'I've cleared it with Mr Wallace - he's happy for you to drop everything else for a couple of days.'

'Sure, no problem,' agreed Paul.' He turned to Martin, 'see you in the pub later?'

'Should be there, so long as nothing comes up here.'

Paul left and Sue turned to Martin. 'Anything from Doctor Clarke?'

'He's happy to see us but he's a bit tied up with his surgery. Suggested we might take a drive over there, then he can see us during his lunch break.'

'Good idea,' approved Sue. 'It'll be good to get out of here for a couple of hours - especially today when the sun's shining for once.'

The drive to the doctor's surgery took around twenty minutes. The weather was indeed bright sunshine, although still cold. It was early March and at last there were unmistakable signs of spring, with bright crocuses and even a few early narcissus braving the end of winter. Doctor Clarke greeted them cheerfully and led them up to the surgery's rest room area on the first floor.

'Now then,' he said affably, 'what can I do for you?'

Sue handed over the report. 'I was wondering if you could answer a few questions on this report. Specifically, the use of this GHB drug.'

'I'll help if I can. What would you like to know?'

Sue quickly recapped what Paul had told her about the use

of the drug. The doctor nodded. 'That all sounds fair enough. It is one of the easiest drugs to take and the hardest to detect. As your man says, it would be very simple to slip some into an alcoholic drink - or any other drink.'

'But it would be dangerous in alcohol?'

'Highly so.' He tapped the report. 'This gives the cause of Tony Woodford's death as carbon monoxide. But if he hadn't breathed in carbon monoxide he could very well still have died - from the effects of the drug/alcohol cocktail. Of course we can't be sure, but it's a possibility.'

'And how long would it take before the drug took effect.'

'Variable depending on the dose. Generally ten minutes up to an hour, but the alcohol would tend to speed up that time.'

'Is there any way of knowing how long it had been in Woodford's system, before death?'

The doctor shook his head. 'Can't be too accurate on that one I'm afraid. But it had been absorbed, so probably not too recent.'

'What's the likelihood of a man being able to drive a car safely, after taking the drug?'

'In this case, with alcohol? Once he started to feel the effects he wouldn't be able to drive safely at all. He'd be a menace - the equivalent of a badly drunk driver.'

Martin and Sue were silent on their way back to FHQ, both pre-occupied with their thoughts following the doctor's revelations. Back in their office, they poured themselves the inevitable coffees and sat down to dissect the information they had.

Unfortunately much of it was still largely speculation. From what the doctor had said, it appeared increasingly unlikely that Tony had driven himself to the wood after taking the drug/alcohol cocktail, but no trace of any container had been found in the vehicle, not even the tiniest bottle.

'Which means,' said Martin 'that either someone else

drove Tony to the scene in Tony's car, or they met there and the other person provided the drug and alcohol.'

'The second car?'

Martin nodded. 'Possibly, but with absolutely no description we've as much chance of finding it as a virgin in a whorehouse.' He swigged some coffee, peering gloomily into the polystyrene cup. 'You happy it definitely wasn't suicide?'

'What do you think?'

'I think it's bloody doubtful, given what we've got with the drug, and the possible second person in the car.'

'I agree,' said Sue. 'The note is meaningless, since it can't even be positively identified as being Tony's writing. The fact he was apparently so far gone on the drug is another indicator. How likely is it he could have rigged that pipe up, in that state? And another thing, there were no prints on that pipe - absolutely nothing. It had been wiped clean. Why on earth would he bother to do that?'

Martin nodded. 'So we're left with another murder.'

'As the most likely option? I think so. I think either that second person drove Tony there in Tony's car and managed to get Tony into the driving seat, or the second person was in the other car and they rendezvoused there by arrangement. Either way, Tony knew the man. Always assuming it was a man.'

'It could have been a lover's tiff or something like that,' suggested Martin doubtfully.

'It could. He could also have been killed by the same person who killed Pete Ashbourne.'

'And that's where your money is?'

Sue nodded gloomily. 'I'm trying to keep an open mind and I'm open to any other suggestions. But yes Martin - that's what I think.'

'Yeah, me too,' he agreed. 'It's just too much of a coincidence, two murders in such a small and - shall we say - unlikely little community. Especially when you add that Tony had asked to see us about something that might have been relevant to Pete's death. I strongly suspect that Mr Woodford was killed to keep him silent, about something.'

'Most likely. The million dollar question, Martin, is what.'

Once again, they ran through the list of people who were on duty that night and who might have killed Pete Ashbourne - and now Tony Woodford. Martin himself had an alibi for Pete's murder, as did the superintendent. Mandy Cornwell was a theoretical but highly unlikely candidate for Pete Ashbourne's murder, but an even more unlikely one for Woodford, given the state that finding the body had reduced her to. Martin ran his hand through his curly hair, as he often did when distracted or worried.

'That still leaves Stirling and Jim Taylor as the only really viable suspects, and Jim only because of his possible connection with Pete's murder. He did have both motive and opportunity with Pete, and if Tony did know something - but Jim has an alibi for that evening. He and Mandy both say they were together at Mandy's house, from when she got home just after 6 pm, to her going to work at ten o'clock the following morning.' He shook his head. 'Of course it isn't the most reliable alibi in the world, given that they're engaged, but we've no evidence to suggest it isn't true.'

Sue nodded. 'And so far as Pete Ashbourne is concerned, we can't rule out the chance of someone not on duty using their pass key to come in that back door and getting out the same way. That back door isn't even on the surveillance camera.'

Martin grunted. 'Possible, but not very likely.'

'Possible is all the defence would need,' Sue pointed out. 'We have the beginnings of a case against Jim Taylor, but it's not enough. If we only had to prove balance of probabilities we might - MIGHT - get it home; but we certainly couldn't prove it beyond all reasonable doubt because clearly there is a doubt. Even you and I aren't sure.'

Martin groaned. 'Oh for the days of good old verballing - an admission would simplify things so much.'

'Martin! You're not seriously suggesting . . .'

He shook his head quickly. 'Just a joke Sue. No, of course I'm not suggesting we try to verbal Jim. That's unthinkable. But I must admit there have been times in the past when I have been sure about someone's guilt - really sure. As in they've admitted it openly but the admission can't be given in evidence - that kind of thing. That's when verballing could be very useful. It's just so frustrating. Oh, in this case I agree with you. I wouldn't be overly surprised if Jim had killed Pete, but I'm not sure. And Tony - well, he's another kettle of fish altogether.'

Sue sighed. 'Martin, you're a good detective, but you've got to kick some of your ideas. Do you realise they're introducing tape recorded interviews here at the beginning of next year?'

'So soon?'

'Yes. Training starts in the summer and the whole force will be up and running by January. The days of verballing are well and truly over.'

Martin sighed and nodded.

## Chapter 30

The next lead - if it could be called a lead - came just two days later. Sue had just returned from the weekly CID briefing when Martin walked into the office, closely followed by Paul. Sue looked up.

'You look very purposeful?'

'Not half. You're going to be very interested in this one.' He glanced at Paul, who nodded.

'I've got to say, I'm bloody uncomfortable about this,' he said slowly. 'It feels like I'm shopping a mate and coppers don't do that. But then what the hell? Tony and Pete were mates too - at any rate they were coppers and if it comes to helping find their killers I'm up for it.' He paused, shifting his weight from foot to foot, then continued. 'Anyway, I've been going through the statements like you told me to and I've just been reading Jim Taylor's statement. The one where he claims to have been with Mandy Cornwell on the evening of Tony's death.'

He paused again. Sue stared at him intently. 'And?'

'And that isn't true.' He pulled out a chair and sat down. 'That evening I was in the Red Lion on the High Street with Colin McArthur from drug squad. I remember it well because we were on a job, on the QT. Just after eight o'clock Mandy Cornwell came in. She was with a load of mates - about half a dozen I'd say, all women.'

'Just women? Jim wasn't with her?'

'Just women. Looked like a hen night or something like that.'

'Did she see you?'

'No. Like I said we were on a job, the last thing I needed

was for a bloody woodentop - sorry ma'am, a uniformed officer - to recognise me and let the cat out of the bag. We nipped into the other bar and kept out of her way - or at least I kept out of her way. We were there for about an hour, till nine-ish. Then we left.'

'And Mandy and co were still there?'

'Very much so, you couldn't have missed them unless you'd been bloody deaf - a couple of them were getting very noisily drunk. I don't think she was, but she was still with them, for sure.'

'Shit,' muttered Sue, sotto voce. She wasn't sure whether to be glad or sorry, this could put Jim Taylor in the frame or it could just muddy the waters even more. 'Okay Paul, well spotted and thanks for coming forward with this - I do appreciate it's not been easy. We'll need a statement from you - soon as you can.'

'Right away boss.' Paul left the office and Martin let out a whistle. 'This could rather set the cat among the pigeons.'

'You can say that again,' agreed Sue. She looked closely at Martin. 'Something else bothering you?'

He shrugged. 'Just something Paul said. It's a real bugger, having to investigate my own mates like this. It's the first time I've ever felt sorry for the rubber-heel squad, investigating their own all the time.'

'Rubber-heel squad? Oh - complaints of course.'

'The atmosphere at Fairfield is dreadful now,' continued Martin. 'Oh, not aimed at me in particular, but people are different with me, sort of a bit cautious and careful what they say. With two coppers dead - one certainly murdered and the other maybe - well, you can imagine what it's like. It's worse because everyone knows the murderer could be the bloke they're out on the panda with.' He looked at Sue with a hint of resentment.' It's not so bad for you - you don't know these people, I've worked with some of them for years.'

'I appreciate that,' responded Sue. 'But let's not forget I may well have to work with them for years, after this is all over. And Martin, we're talking about murder, not nicking the tea fund money or giving a prisoner a black eye.'

'I know, I know!' He sighed and stood up. 'Well, here we go again. Let's go and arrest ourselves a copper.'

'And interview another one,' said Sue dryly. 'I've every sympathy with young Mandy and I can understand why she felt the need to cover for her fiancé, but even so it's not behaviour we can condone in a police officer. Just a small matter of perverting the course of justice.' She picked up her briefcase and followed Martin from the office.

Sue decided to interview Mandy first in order to establish just how long Jim had spent with her on that fateful evening. 'And then,' she said, 'we move straight on to Mr Taylor, before they can get their heads together. Let's find when young Mandy's next on and pull her straight in for interview, then we'll get Taylor picked up and brought in while we're talking to her.' She paused. 'Paul and Dave can do that.'

'Under arrest?'

'I'd rather not. Lying about whether he was alone or not that evening isn't really enough evidence for strong suspicion - not on its own. But if he won't come in of his own accord I'm prepared to take the chance and arrest him.'

Enquiries established that Mandy started duty at 2 pm. Sue and Martin cleared her release from her beat for the necessary time with her sergeant and awaited her arrival in the interview room. Shortly after two o'clock there was a tentative knock on the door.

'Come in' called Sue.

The door opened to admit a nervous looking Mandy. 'You asked to see me, ma'am?'

Sue nodded but didn't offer the reassurance of a smile. 'Yes we did - sit down Mandy.' She nodded to Martin, who closed the door and pressed the engaged button.

'Right Mandy, we need to talk to you about Jim Taylor.'

'Yes Ma'am.'

Sue tapped the statement on her desk. 'We have here a statement from you referring to the evening before you found Tony Woodford's body. In this statement you say you were with Jim Taylor all that evening and through the night.'

Mandy looked wary. 'Yes ma'am, he stayed at my house that evening - and all night.' She reddened. 'We are engaged ma'am.'

'I'm not concerned about the moral issue,' said Sue crisply. 'This is 1987 not 1887 and your private life is your own business. But I have to ask you whether you now wish to amend your previous statement.'

'I'm sorry - I don't understand.'

'I think you do. You know the law Mandy, in fact I understand you're very gifted in that department and know the law very well. You appreciate it's a serious matter if you deliberately lie on a written statement.'

'It's not perjury', muttered Mandy

'No it isn't. But it's still a criminal offence. A serious criminal offence - even more so for you. Mandy, I don't think you appreciate the trouble you're getting yourself into. This is a murder enquiry; you're supposed to be a police officer. Aside from the false statement - and we know it's false - there's also the question of attempting to pervert the course of justice.'

Mandy looked obstinately down at the desk and made no reply. Sue sighed and continued. 'I'm sorry Mandy, but because we're talking about criminal offences here, we're going to have to proceed under caution.' She rattled off the official caution, then resumed. 'Now then Mandy, do you wish to stand by your original statement?'

Mandy now looked terrified, freckles standing out on a face that was suddenly pasty white. 'Yes - no - oh God, I don't know.'

She burst into noisy tears. Martin and Sue exchanged covert glances and waited. After a while Mandy stopped crying and blew her nose. 'Sorry,' she mumbled.

The silence held. After a few seconds Mandy pulled

herself together and continued.

'I'm sorry. But - but I love Jim. He's my fiancé, the man I'm going to marry. And he'd never have killed Tony - not in a million years. He liked Tony.'

'Would you say they were friends?'

'Yes. Well, not close friends I suppose, but colleagues who got on well anyway.'

'So did you see Jim at all that evening? The whole truth please Mandy.'

She took a deep breath.' Most of it is true - I swear it is. He did come round just after six, just as I said. And he stayed all evening - all night. It's just . . .'

She trailed off, then continued.

'It's just that I wasn't there with him all evening. I'd already arranged to meet some friends from my old job. They were having a bit of a hen night, one of them was getting married. I'd promised to go and Jim said I should.'

'How long were you out?'

'I left about half past seven, got back a bit after ten o'clock. I didn't stay till the end because I wanted to get back to Jim.'

'Where did you go?'

'To the pub. Well, to a couple of pubs. We started off in the Trumpeters and then to the Red Lion for a pub meal. After the meal I went home and the rest went on to a night club.'

There was silence save for the scratch of Martin's pen, then Sue spoke again.

'Mandy, I need you to keep telling me the truth. I'm really trying to keep you out of hot water on this one, but you have to be truthful now. Any more prevaricating and I'm afraid we'll be throwing the book at you. Now then, did Jim put you up to this?'

'What?'

'Don't play games,' said Sue.

'We talked about it,' muttered Mandy, 'but it wasn't really

his idea, I offered to do it.' She looked up, no longer sobbing but with tears still streaming. 'Can't you see what it's like for him? He hasn't done anything - I know he hasn't. He told me about the - the scuffle he had with Sergeant Ashbourne but that's all it was. He didn't kill him - I just know he didn't. But he's scared - he's so scared! He knows he's under suspicion for Sergeant Ashbourne's murder and then when poor Tony was found dead . . . he said if it wasn't suicide you were sure to suspect him and he didn't have an alibi. I said I'd give him one. I offered. He didn't ask me.'

Sue nodded. 'Anything else? Please think hard Mandy - we need the whole truth. No omissions please.'

'I'm sure ma'am. That's all there is, I swear to God it is.'

'Thank you. Now, I need a full statement from you, right now, before you leave the station. You'll stay here with us until PC Taylor arrives in a few minutes, then you'll find yourself a little niche and get that statement done. Before you do anything else. Clear?'

'Yes ma'am' mumbled Mandy. 'Am I - in a lot of trouble?'

Sue sighed. 'I'll keep you out of it as much as I can but you appreciate these are serious offences. I'll have to talk to Mr Wallace about it.'

'And Jim? I've got him into trouble haven't I?'

Martin and Sue exchanged glances. Sue nodded slightly and Martin leaned forward. 'No Mandy. We knew you'd given him a false alibi - we had hard evidence - that's why we asked to talk to you. All you've done today is to dig yourself a little way out of the mess you've got yourself into.'

'And Jim?'

Martin shrugged. 'You know we can't discuss that with you.'

A knock on the door announced the arrival of Paul. 'PC Taylor's here,' he said. 'He's waiting in the inspector's office.' He paused. 'Dave's with him.'

'Thanks Paul. Mandy, go with Paul and find somewhere

to write your statement. Paul, give us just five minutes, then ask Dave to bring Taylor here.'

Paul left with a tearful Mandy. Sue shook her head sadly. 'That wasn't pleasant,' she said. 'I have to say I really feel for that girl - she's had a hard time of it what with Pete's assault, Jim's suspension, finding Tony's body. And now this.'

'Will you be able to keep her out of it or will she be charged?'

Sue shrugged. 'I'm not sure. I'll do my best but it's really up to the boss. I've got a feeling all this will end up being too much for her in any case. I'll be surprised if she stays in the job.'

Martin nodded. 'Might be best if she goes. Best for her. Now then, do we interview Jim under caution, or not?'

Sue frowned. 'Tricky one. Do we actually have grounds to suspect him of Tony's murder - real evidence? No, we don't. Obviously I'm not happy with him lying about an alibi, but that alone is hardly evidence of murder.' She paused. 'On the other hand, we do have some pretty strong circumstantial evidence so far as Pete Ashbourne is concerned. Let's play safe.'

'So we caution?'

'Yes. He isn't likely to clam up on us, is he?'

Martin shrugged. 'Shouldn't think so.'

There was a firm knock on the door. Sue stood up and stretched. 'Ah well, here we go again. You front this one Martin, before you get writer's cramp.'

Jim Taylor came in and took the proffered seat, looking wary. Martin opened the questioning.

'Jim, we need to talk to you again about your alibi for Tony's murder.'

Jim frowned but made no reply. Martin continued.

'In your earlier statement you said you and Mandy were together for the entire evening before Tony was found dead - and the whole night. We now have reason to believe that isn't true. Before you answer, I must tell you that we're doing this interview under caution.' He gave the official caution.

Jim shook his head. 'Shit! I should have known it was a crap idea.'

'What was a crap idea?'

'Lying - about Mandy being there all the time. It was . . .' he stopped. Martin waited, then prompted him.

'It was what? Jim, whose idea was it? To lie about an alibi?'

Jim shrugged. 'Doesn't really matter, does it? It was a crap idea.' He paused, then continued. 'I'm already under suspicion of Pete Ashbourne's murder, for God's sake. I know I didn't kill Pete but I also know you've got bloody good grounds for suspecting me. I was there just before he was killed, we had a fight. Dear God, do you think I don't know how bloody serious this looks for me? I had the means, the opportunity and the motive and the only person who knows for sure I didn't kill Pete is me.'

'And Tony? Why did you feel the need for an alibi for Tony?'

Jim shrugged. 'I don't know. What possible reason could I have to kill Tony? I liked Tony - he was a mate. Well, a colleague, but we got on okay and worked well together.' He stopped, looking down at his hands and absently turning his engagement ring around his finger. 'But the alibi - I was shit scared when I heard about Tony being dead. Mand said it looked like a suicide but even so it scared me. I knew I didn't have an alibi for that evening and I suppose - well, I suppose I just wanted to put myself out of the frame - in the clear.'

'Instead of which you've put a suspicion in our minds that probably wouldn't have been there,' said Martin. 'Jim, did you know Tony had asked to speak to us?'

Jim frowned. 'What do you mean? Talk to you when? What about?'

'The "when" would have been the day he was found

dead. The "what about" - well, I was hoping you could tell us.'

'I haven't a bloody clue, why should I have? Don't forget I'm on suspension from work. I haven't even spoken to Tony for a couple of weeks. At least that.'

Martin leaned forward. 'Jim, I want you to think really hard about this. So far you've taken refuge in denials and false alibis and none of it has done your case any good at all. Are you quite certain you don't know what Tony wanted to talk to us about?'

'I'm completely certain. I swear to you, I haven't a clue. Why would I have?'

'Not even a guess?'

Jim shook his head. 'Any guesses I made you could make yourself. Maybe he wanted to talk about Pete's murder, maybe he knew something, maybe he wanted to confess to it.' He shrugged. 'How the bloody hell should I know? Given the stupid lies I've told you I don't expect you to believe me, but this time it's the truth.'

Martin nodded. 'So what did you do that evening?'

'I stayed at Mandy's. That was true - it's just that she wasn't actually there all evening. She left - oh, a bit after seven I guess. She got home around half ten.'

'And you were in the house, all the time?'

'Yes - I just had a couple of beers out the fridge and watched TV.'

'All right,' said Martin. 'Are you now prepared to make a further statement, retracting that false alibi?'

Jim nodded. 'Yes. But I don't want Mandy mixed up in it.'

'Jim, she's already mixed up in it. She gave you a false alibi.'

'Keep her out of it,' muttered Jim. 'Please. God knows, she's been through enough.'

Martin looked at Sue. She shook her head slightly. 'PC Taylor, we can't promise to keep Mandy out of it, given the circumstances. I can only say that we'll do our best for her.

We're not unsympathetic, believe me - but that's the best we can do.'

Jim nodded, looking defeated. 'Well, thanks for that anyway. All right - give me the forms and I'll get a new statement written.' He paused. 'You want it under caution?'

'I'm afraid so,' said Sue.

# Chapter 31

The week following their interview with Jim was uneventful, save for an unexpected encounter with Bill. It was Friday lunchtime, a hint of spring was in the air. Having trawled through the evidence one more endless time, Sue and Martin agreed to give themselves a break and have their first full weekend off for weeks.

Sue pulled into her driveway just after 2 pm, to find Bill's car there. Her heart jumped, then began to race. She hadn't seen or spoken to Bill since catching him in bed with her best friend. She had consulted a solicitor who had advised changing the locks on the house, but given it was rented accommodation - and a short term rent at that - she hadn't done so. Now, seeing Bill's car, she wasn't sure how she was going to react. If he had Sarah with him . . .

She got out of her car and approached the front door, but it opened before she got there to reveal Bill standing in the doorway. He looked as stunned as she felt.

'Sue! I thought I heard your car. What the devil are you doing here at this time?'

'I think that should be my question,' she said icily. 'Is the bitch with you?'

'Sue, I haven't come to row with you. I only came to pick up a few clothes - nothing more.' He paused. 'The solicitor said I should do everything through him but that seemed silly. I deliberately picked a time when I was sure you'd be at work.'

'Bad guess. Is Sarah with you?'

'No. I had more bloody sense than to bring her, after what you did last time.'

Sue's quick temper boiled. 'What the hell did you expect

me to do? Hold the door open and usher you politely from the room. Carrying your underpants and trousers?'

Bill flushed and held up a hand. 'Sue, I'm so sorry for what happened and so is Sarah. Truly we are. It wasn't planned. It just sort of - happened.'

Sue took a deep breath, fighting for control. 'Bill, I'm not ready to hear about it. Have you got what you came for?'

He nodded. 'Pretty much, it's all in the car. I've only taken my own clothes Sue, nothing more.' He paused. 'Sue, can't we sit down and talk things through, like adults?'

Sue shook her head. Suddenly tears were not far away and she was determined he wouldn't see her cry. 'No Bill. Not yet anyway, it's too close. Maybe one day, but not yet.' She looked at him, still fighting back the tears. 'And whatever we have to say Bill, our marriage is over. You must know that.'

He nodded. 'I know, but I'd still like to talk things over - maybe get rid of some of the bitterness.' He began to say something else, then seemed to change his mind. 'Where's Oscar?'

'At my parents' house and he's bloody staying there until I can have him back. He's fine there - better than here really - mum's home all day with him.'

He nodded awkwardly, then walked to his car. She watched him reverse, swing around the tarmac circle and head down the driveway as he had so many times before; then she turned and went towards the front door of the empty house. The tears she had successfully suppressed in front of Bill were now streaming down her face.

## Chapter 32

It was late afternoon on the following Friday. Sue and Martin were in Chief Superintendent Wallace's office, discussing the progress - or rather lack of progress - of the two murder enquiries. Things seemed to have reached a stalemate. No one left uninterviewed, no stone left unturned. All statements, interview notes and forensic results had been read through, again and again. All alibis had been checked and re-checked.

Wallace threw down the file he was reading and sighed heavily. 'Sue, I don't see where else we can go with this. We're certain Pete Ashbourne was murdered, but we're still no closer to identifying a *bona fide* suspect, so far as I can see. I think Robbie Nichols is definitely out of it now, which leaves Jim Taylor. We've got evidence against him, certainly, but not enough to charge him - any half decent barrister would have him walking down the road in no time. But we can't just leave things in limbo much longer.'

Sue nodded glumly. 'I appreciate that sir. And if we haven't enough evidence to charge PC Taylor, we're going to have to lift his suspension. We can't leave him dangling indefinitely.'

'Quite. Which means he'll have to be allowed to return to work. With the suspicion of murder still hanging over him and everyone knowing it. It's a bloody mess!' He sighed. 'And as for Tony Woodford, that's even worse in a way.'

'No suspects,' agreed Sue.

'No suspects and not even a definite murder, though most things point that way.' He sighed heavily. 'All right, let's just suppose for a moment that it wasn't murder - that it was a suicide. Let's run through it again - what's the evidence against that?'

'The drugs and alcohol in his system. And the fact we found no evidence of drugs or alcohol at the scene. No containers - nothing.'

'All right. So Tony drives himself to the woods. He sets up the tube from the exhaust but doesn't start the engine, not yet. He takes his drug, then goes into the woods before it takes effect and disposes of the container.' He paused. 'Let's face it, if he took a small container or whatever into those woods and buried it or something, we'd have no chance of finding it. Then he goes back to the car and when he feels the drug taking effect, he starts the engine. Comments?'

'Why?' said Sue. 'I mean, why would he bother with the drug? He would only need the exhaust pipe. And why would he take the drug then hide the container? It makes no sense.'

Wallace shook his head. 'No it doesn't.'

'And there's the witness sir - the witness who saw the other man in Tony's car. And the other car.'

'There's the witness,' agreed Wallace. 'A good witness. A witness honest enough to admit he only caught a glimpse of the two profiles, not enough to be one hundred per cent certain.'

'I know,' agreed Sue. 'But sir, I still think there's enough evidence to keep this going as a murder enquiry.'

Wallace sighed and nodded. 'So do I Sue, I'm sorry to say. Suicide would have been a bloody sight easier - especially if he'd left a longer note coughing to killing Pete Ashbourne. Ah well, things aren't often so nicely cut and dried as that, are they?' He looked at his watch, pushed the file away and stood up. 'Half past five - time to call it a day I think. We'll reconvene on Monday with the whole team and see where else we can take this. Are you off home too?'

'Soon,' said Sue. 'I just want to sit down quietly and read through some of the stuff on Tony's case, then I'll be off. Martin, what about you?'

He glanced at his watch. 'I'll hang on for an hour or so and give you a hand. Tell you what, I'll pop down to the canteen and pick up some decent coffee.'

He left the room. Sue said goodnight to Mr Wallace, gathered up the files and returned to her own office. A few minutes later she was deep into the statement of the witness who had seen the two profiles in Tony's car when there was a gentle tap on the door. Superintendent Horner strolled into the room. 'Working late, Sue?'

She shook her head. 'Not really sir - I'll call it a day soon. But what brings you to headquarters so late on a Friday evening?'

He laughed and dropped into a chair. 'Just making arrangements for my move.'

'Move? to where?'

'To here - to headquarters. I'm being promoted to chief super in charge of admin. It's a bit earlier than I'd expected, but I'm certainly not moaning on that account.'

'Good career move?'

He nodded. 'Oh yes, and a necessary one. Twelve or eighteen months in an HQ admin role and I'll be looking for an ACC appointment in another force somewhere.' He sighed. 'I have to say, I won't be sorry when that time comes. I've enjoyed my time here, but the last couple of months have been hell. Especially at Fairfield - I'm sure you can imagine the state of morale there.' He paused, then continued. 'I don't suppose you've had any breakthroughs with the enquiries?'

Sue smiled wryly. 'I only wish we had - a breakthrough is what we desperately need. In either case, because I think a breakthrough in one would lead to a breakthrough in the other.'

'You definitely think the cases are linked then?'

'Yes, I do - though I can't prove it.'

'And Tony's case was definitely murder? There was talk of it being a suicide.'

'Yes there was, but I don't think so.' She shook her

head. 'Difficult to prove, either way.'

Horner nodded, looking sympathetic. 'I can see that, especially with just a one-word note to try to match up.' He stood up as Martin came back into the office. 'Well Sue, I'd best be off. I want to get back to Fairfield by six to wish Mandy Cornwell all the best - today's her last day.'

'Today? I thought she was leaving at the end of the month.'

'So she is, but by the time you've taken into account rest days and annual leave today is her last day of actual working.'

Sue nodded. 'Well, please wish her well from me, sir. She's had a pretty rough time of it.'

'I will,' he promised. 'Goodnight Sue - Martin.'

He strolled out of the office and Sue returned to her file. But she found herself struggling to concentrate. Something was coming between her and the words on the page - something the superintendent had said. Suddenly she had it. She threw the file down onto the desk.

'The note! How did he know about the note?'

Martin looked up from the file he was reading. 'What note?'

'Tony's note - the so-called suicide note. Superintendent Horner was talking about the case just before you came back in. He said something like "especially with just a one-word note to match up." Think about it Martin.'

'Think about it? Well - ah, I see where you're going. The instructions about the content of that note were bloody specific . . .'

'Yes they were. Not to go beyond the immediate murder team, if I remember correctly. So Martin, how did he know about that being a one word note?' She shook her head, feeling confused as to where her thoughts were taking her.

'He shouldn't have known,' said Martin positively. 'But I suppose it's possible . . .'

He was interrupted by the strident ring of the telephone. 'Damn!' said Sue explosively. 'She pressed the intercom button. 'DI Bishop.'

Mandy Cornwell's soft voice came over the loudspeaker. 'Oh ma'am, thank goodness you're still there. Ma'am, I need to talk to you. Urgently - it's really important.'

'Well, of course,' said Sue. 'Can you give me some idea what it's about, Mandy?'

'Yes. It's about Sergeant Ashbourne's . . .'

The line went silent and Sue frowned. 'Mandy? Mandy, are you still there?'

'Yes ma'am.' Mandy's voice sounded hesitant now.

'So what's it all about Mandy? Pete Ashbourne?'

'Yes ma'am.' Mandy stopped speaking again. Sue and Martin exchanged puzzled glances. 'Mandy,' said Sue, 'is it difficult for you to speak right now?'

'Yes ma'am.' Mandy sounded relieved.

'I see. Where are you speaking from?'

'The parade room ma'am, at Fairfield.'

'Right. Stay where you are Mandy, and we'll come to you.' She glanced at her watch - just before six o'clock. 'I just need to make a quick phone call and we'll be on our way. Should be with you somewhere around half six, maybe a few minutes after.'

'I'll be here,' Mandy promised. The line went dead as she hung up.

Sue raised her brows at Martin. 'Interesting,' she said, 'we'd best get over there - just as soon as I've made this call. I just hope he's still here, given it's Friday.' She was already punching numbers on the telephone handset. After a moment the ringing stopped and a male voice announced 'Ferguson.'

Sue drew a breath of relief. 'Mr Ferguson, I'm glad I've caught you. DI Bishop here.'

'Oh - evening ma'am. You've only just caught me - I was about to go home.'

'I won't keep you long,' Sue promised. 'It's really just a quick question, about the Tony Woodford case. You remember the note he left - the possible suicide note?'

'Of course.'

'To your knowledge, was the content of that note discussed outside the immediate investigating team?'

'To my knowledge, certainly not.' The voice sounded irritable now.

'I'm not trying to say that it was,' Sue assured him, 'and I have a good reason for asking.' She paused. 'How many of your team knew about the contents? The fact that there was just the one word?'

'Me,' said Ferguson. 'Kathy, who I can certainly vouch for. And of course the handwriting expert.'

'Mr Ferguson, did anyone ask you any questions about that note? Any police officer?'

'No-one asked me anything, but of course I can't answer for Kathy.'

'Is she there?'

'Sorry, afraid not. It is Friday evening inspector - I'm the only one still here, and I'm hoping to be away as soon as I can.' He paused. 'If you need to speak to Kathy I'm afraid it'll have to wait until Monday now, she's in London for the weekend. But I've worked with Kathy for a long time and I can assure you, she understands the meaning of discretion. If the chief constable asked her about that note she wouldn't tell him anything.'

'I'm not thinking about anyone quite so exalted,' said Sue. 'Thanks very much Mr Ferguson - enjoy your weekend.'

'You too,' he grunted.

Sue hung up the phone and turned to Martin, who looked as confused as Sue felt. 'The superintendent? You seriously think . . .?'

'Don't know,'. said Sue. 'There may very well be a perfectly simple explanation, but it's certainly something we need to ask him about next time we see him.' She glanced at her watch. 'Come on Martin, let's get over to Fairfield and see what young Mandy has to tell us.'

# Chapter 33

Sue and Martin pulled into the car park at Fairfield Station just after 6.30 pm. Martin nodded towards the main car park. 'There's Mandy's car, so she's still here.'

They hurried through the front office, nodded to the constable on duty behind the desk, and entered the parade room. It was empty save for Judith Saunders, who was busily scribbling away at the far end. She looked round at their entry.

'Oh, hello ma'am - sarge.'

'Evening Judith. Is Mandy about?'

'Well, she was here earlier on.' She looked round the room and pointed towards a holdall standing on the floor, overflowing with odds and ends. 'She's not far away, that's her bag. Lucky you caught her ma'am - today's her last day at work.'

'Yes, I know, but she won't have gone without talking to us. She's expecting us.'

'Is she? Oh - was it you she rang? About half an hour ago?'

'It was. Were you here?'

'Yes.' She tapped the statement on the desk in front of her. 'I've been here all afternoon trying to get this paperwork finished for the weekend.'

'Did Mandy seem agitated to you?'

'Yes she did. She came rushing in here looking like a flustered rabbit and asked me for the internal phone book - I guess to look up your number.'

'Did she say anything to you?'

'Not exactly to me, she was more talking to herself - well,

thinking aloud anyway. She was muttering something about a coat.'

'A coat?' Sue's mind snapped to attention. 'What did she say? Please try to remember - it could be very important.'

'As far as I remember, she said something like "the coat - he was wearing the coat! I have to ring …" she found the number and started talking to you. You know the rest.'

Sue took a deep breath. 'Judith, Mandy started to tell us something then suddenly stopped short and started speaking in monosyllables - as if she suddenly had to be careful what she was saying. Did something interrupt her? Can you remember?'

'Well, not exactly. Someone came into the parade room - maybe she didn't want him to hear. Though I can't think why if she wasn't bothered about me hearing her.'

'Who came in?'

'The super. Superintendent Horner.'

Sue and Martin exchanged startled glances. 'Judith,' said Sue. 'It's essential we know what he heard. Can you remember what Mandy was saying?'

Judith frowned. 'Not really - I wasn't paying that much attention. He came in, then Mandy put the phone down and left the parade room.'

'Did she mention the coat? In his hearing?'

'Don't think so.' She paused. 'The super asked me about it though.'

'The coat? He asked about the coat?'

'Not exactly, no - he asked me if something had upset Mandy. As I said, she seemed like a flustered rabbit when she came in. When she went out she looked more like a terrified rabbit. Anyway, I told the super what I've just told you - that Mandy came in here looking agitated and said something about a coat and someone wearing it. It didn't make any sense to me.'

Sue's brain was spinning. The superintendent! Surely he wasn't - -

'Judith, what was his reaction to that?'

'Well, nothing spectacular. He looked a bit - kind of stunned. Then he stood there for a couple of seconds as if he was in his own little world. You know he does that, ma'am. Then he went out the door.' She paused, then continued. 'Is there a problem here? Shouldn't I have told him? I couldn't see any reason not to …'

Sue interrupted her. 'You had no reason not to answer him and you've certainly done nothing wrong. But yes, there could be a very serious problem. I need to know whether Mandy is still in the station and I need to talk to her. I'd like you to go and check the ladies cloakroom, then check the entire first floor. Martin, check the rest of the building, including the super's office. Use the cleaner's keys if you have to. I'm going to talk to control.'

A few words with the control room sergeant soon established that none of them knew Mandy's whereabouts. Her car was indeed still on the car park. 'What about the super's car?' asked Sue. 'Superintendent Horner.'

The sergeant operated the video camera giving on to the car park. 'Not there ma'am - his space is empty.' He paused. 'Can't have been gone long though, he popped in here just after six, checking messages.'

Martin entered the room, closely followed by Judith Saunders. Judith looked a little confused, but Martin looked worried.

'No sign of her ma'am, and we've checked the entire building. No sign of the super either.'

'Did you check his office?'

'Of course. Didn't need the cleaners' keys - it was still unlocked.' He paused. 'There were two cups of coffee on the table - well, cups with coffee dregs in them. And the coffee machine was still pretty warm.'

Sue pulled Martin into the tiny kitchen adjoining the control room, out of earshot of the curious watchers. 'I don't like the feel of this Martin. If Mandy knows something about that coat - that's been the missing piece all along. And if the super is involved…'

'Dear God, what possible motive could he have?'

'I don't know. If we knew that he'd have been in the frame before this…' She broke off. 'Martin, this may be career suicide but I don't see I have any choice.'

She led the way back into the control room. 'Sergeant, I want an all stations out on Superintendent Horner's car. Sightings to me. I also need to know if he has a passenger. Do you have the number?'

The sergeant chuckled. Of course ma'am, everybody knows the super's car - he likes to swan around in it, surprising the troops. But what's going on? You just want sightings? Why…'

Sue took a deep breath and made her decision. 'I want this out force wide, not just on this sub-division. If possible he's to be stopped and detained. Arrested on suspicion of the murder of Pete Ashbourne.'

'You have to be joking!'

'Is it likely I'd be joking?'

'Well, no. But…'

'Do it now,' said Sue. 'On my authority. I'll take full responsibility and any future flack will be mine. The buck stops here.'

'Right ma'am.' Sue heard the beginnings of the all stations and turned to find Martin over at the racks where the radios were kept. He was already fitting batteries into two of the handsets. 'Good man,' said Sue. 'Let's go!'

They hurried down the stairs together and across the darkening car park. It was just approaching sunset, but cloud cover was heavy, with an intermittent drizzle. Martin slipped into the driving seat of the CID car and fired the engine.

'You've really stuck your neck out on this one!' he commented.

'I know. But what else can I do? If I'm wrong the shit's going to hit the fan in a big way; but if I'm right - - - If I'm right, Mandy Cornwell could be in a lot of danger, right now!

I can't take the chance of not getting him picked up.'

Martin shrugged. 'For what it's worth I agree with you. But I have to admit this is one time I'm glad you're the boss.'

'Wouldn't you have done the same thing?'

'I'm not sure, but I think I would. I hope I would. Career versus someone's life.' Sue groaned inwardly, Martin's comment was probably only too true.

'Where are we going?' asked Martin.

'I wish I knew. Head away from town.'

As they swung out onto the main road the radio burst into life with their call sign. Sue acknowledged.

'We have a sighting of Superintendent Horner's car, one of the traffic lads saw it heading up the A149 towards the coast. Just passed through Bilston. About ten minutes ago.'

'No chance to detain?'

'No ma'am, the sighting was before the all stations. He just remembers seeing the car. Sorry ma'am, but he can't give any certain information as to whether there were passengers. He thinks the super was alone, but he can't be certain.'

Sue acknowledged as Martin accelerated towards the A149. 'What's up there?' she asked him. 'Is there anywhere he might try to do away with someone, or dump a body?'

'It's a pretty quiet road,' said Martin. 'Couple of lay-bys, small villages. Then there's the golf course, not far past Bilston.' He looked sideways at Sue. 'Now wouldn't that be a sod, if he was heading for a round of golf.'

'In this muck, and this light?'

Martin chuckled. 'Maybe not, but he could be heading for a function or something. He does play there ... oh bugger!' He suddenly banged on the brakes. The car went into a four wheel skid before he regained control. Sue swore under her breath as the seatbelt cut painfully into her.

'Martin, what the devil...'

'Sorry! I've just remembered something.' He manoeuvred the car into a narrow lane, really little more than a cart track. 'There's a lake at the side of the golf course - first a bit of woodland, then a lake in the middle. Just a small lake - not many people know about it but it's popular with some of the local birdwatchers. You can bet the super knows it.'

The car bumped and skidded down the track, sometimes grounding on the high grassy centre. Half a mile or so along the track swung left and entered woodland. The sun had set now and it was dark under the trees and bushes that closed around them. Soaking leaves and branches slapped at the windscreen as the car slid and bounced down the uneven and muddy track. Martin groaned. 'Our wheelbase is too low, we need a four by four.'

'Tough!' said Sue. 'Isn't there another way down?'

'Yes - a better track, more like a minor road. But it's the other side of the golf course and it'd put another three or four miles on the clock.' He shrugged. 'You take the rap for arresting the local super - I'll take the rap for wrecking the car.'

It was growing lighter ahead, where the trees stopped at the edge of the lake. It was indeed a small lake, probably no more than sixty to seventy feet across, but Sue paid no attention to that. In the deepening twilight they could just make out a car standing on the far side of the lake, with a figure clambering up the bank towards it. It was too dark to recognise the person but Sue knew who it had to be.

The track ended at the edge of the lake where the land dropped away into a three foot high bank. The last part of the track was a sea of mud and the car went into an uncontrollable four wheel skid, tearing into the foliage surrounding the lake and almost carrying on into the water. As the car finally came to a halt Sue found herself staring at a thick tree trunk, just six inches from her door.

Martin leapt out of the car, tearing off his overcoat and throwing it down onto the bank. Finding it impossible to get her door open, Sue clambered across the gear stick and exited by the driver's door. Martin had already dropped down the bank and was wading across the water towards the far side, flailing around and searching as he went. Sue slid inelegantly down the bank after him, to find herself above her ankles in viscous red mud. Martin, chest high in the water, had passed the centre of the lake when he stopped and let out a shout. Next moment his head and shoulders disappeared under the water.

Sue plunged into the lake, shuddering as the extremely cold water penetrated her clothes. She made her way towards Martin, half wading and half swimming. Chest deep for Martin meant neck deep for her and it was hard going. Weeds wrapped themselves around her arms and shoulders. The bottom was muddy and also full of weed and at the back of her mind she was afraid of getting stuck - maybe even drowning because she wasn't a particularly strong swimmer at the best of times. But she kept going.

Martin had surfaced again, holding an inert form in his arms and lifting it above the surface with apparent difficulty. 'Coat!' he gasped. 'Get her coat open - there's something in there.' Sue tore at the buttons of what had once been a stylish rain coat but was now a mud-covered, weed draped mess. She managed to tear the coat open and a large, heavy boulder fell out, splashing into the water and narrowly missing her foot as it settled to the bottom.

Still chest deep in the water, Martin was already performing mouth-to-mouth on Mandy. After a few breaths they struggled with her to the far bank, which fortunately was less steep. As they dragged her up Sue subconsciously registered the roar of a car engine - undoubtedly the superintendent making his getaway. But he wasn't their first priority - Mandy was. As Martin hauled her onto the comparatively level ground, Sue was already pulling out her personal radio, praying it would still work after the soaking it had just received.

'DI Bishop to control' she gasped. 'Urgent message.'

'Go ahead.' The voice from control was calm, unhurried.

'Ambulance,' gasped Sue. 'Side of the lake alongside Bilston golf course . . .'

'Access from Briar Road end,' prompted Martin. Sue

passed on the information.

'Will do. Can you give us an idea of the problem?'

'Possible drowning,' said Sue breathlessly, still recovering from the effort of rescuing Mandy. 'We've just pulled Mandy Cornwell out of the water. Not conscious.'

'Stand by.' The control operator was no longer so calm and laconic. There was a pause. 'Ambulance en route. Can you give any more information?'

'Put out another all stations for Superintendent Horner's car, just left lake side and headed up the track towards Briar Road. To be stopped and arrested on suspicion of attempted murder of Mandy Cornwell.'

'Received and understood.' This time Sue could hear the shock in the voice. The all stations began to come over the air as she dropped to her knees alongside Martin. He had stopped mouth to mouth resuscitation and was trying to check Mandy's pulse.

'How is she?' asked Sue.

'Don't know. She's certainly breathing, but I can't tell about the pulse - my bloody hands are too cold.'

Sue realised that not only her hands but her whole body was shaking uncontrollably with cold. Her feet were completely numb and she was literally soaked through to the skin, with slimy weed coating her hair and clothes. Martin was in the same state and as for Mandy . . . half-drowned as she was, being as cold and wet as this was going to do her no good at all. Sue slid down the shallow bank and squelched her way round the side of the lake to where Martin had dropped his coat. It was muddy and the side where it had lain on the ground was wet, but the other side was relatively dry. Sue slipped and slithered back to Martin and they pulled Mandy onto the coat and laid her in the recovery position. It was virtually dark now, but in the trees above them they could glimpse the lights of the superintendent's car, making its way up the zigzagging track towards the road. Then another light became visible. A flashing blue light, coming down the track.

'Ambulance.' said Sue unnecessarily.

'And the super hasn't made the road yet. Two vehicles can't pass on that track - he'll block the ambulance.'

'And it'll block him,' said Sue. But Martin had already stood up and was groping his way towards the track. The lights were stationary now. There was the sound of a horn, then doors slamming and some shouting. Martin called up the track. 'Ambulance! Ambulance men. Get down here with a stretcher - we're right at the side of the lake. Possible drowning.'

A pause, then a shout of 'on our way.' There was the flash of a powerful torch, then two ambulance men materialised out of the darkness, one of them carrying a stretcher, the other a miscellany of kit. Sue stood and moved back out of the way as they both bent over Mandy. One of them spoke over his shoulder to Martin. 'Who was the lunatic in that car? Instead of trying to back up he just jammed his anchors on and left the bloody car blocking the track.'

'Where did he go?' asked Martin.

'No idea. He just got out of the car and dashed away through the trees.'

Sue tried to raise control again but this time there was no response. She looked at the radio despondently. 'I think this time it's packed up for good - the water will have had time to soak right into the works.'

'Mine's in the car,' said Martin. 'I'll call in and update them. We'll get a cordon thrown round and see if we can get the dog down here.' He dropped down the bank and made his way cautiously through the mud. Sue turned back to the ambulance men. They had an oxygen mask fitted and were strapping Mandy to the stretcher. 'How is she?' asked Sue.

'Pulse is a bit slow, but not too bad. Breathing quite well. I don't think she's suffering from the effects of drowning, but she doesn't seem to be coming round.'

Sue thought about that, and about how the superintendent had got Mandy to go with him. 'She could well be drugged,' she said. 'Possibly GHB.'

He nodded. 'Right, we'll make a note of that. Ready Phil? Okay, up we go.' He looked at Sue. 'It'd help if you could light us up.'

Sue took the heavy torch from him and followed them up the track, shining the light ahead of them. Martin caught up with them as they reached the ambulance.

'Everyone's scrambled and Brad's on his way, with Caesar - should be here within ten or fifteen minutes.'

'Brad and Caesar?'

'Dog handler and dog. Sue, I know one of us needs to go with Mandy, but the other should stay here and wait for the dog.'

Sue paused, longing to be in at the kill; but much as she hated to admit it, Martin did have certain advantages over her when it came down to tearing through woodland without even the benefit of a machete. 'It makes more sense if I go with Mandy,' she said. 'You wait here for the dog - and keep me posted.'

She scrambled up into the ambulance and settled down opposite Mandy as the ambulance reversed slowly back up the woodland track.

# Chapter 34

Two hours later, Sue was sitting in the deserted dayroom at the Queen Elizabeth hospital. She had been able to shower at the hospital and was now clean and dry, but incongruously dressed in the only things the hospital had available - hospital gown and dressing gown. Her own soaked and filthy clothes were tied up in a plastic bag. Shortly after 9 pm a man popped his head round the door, then came into the room. He was middle-aged, small and chubby and looked as tired as Sue felt.

'Inspector Bishop? I'm Doctor Lenton.' He shook hands then sat down next to her. 'Sorry you've had to wait so long, but obviously Miss Cornwell was our first priority.'

'How is she?' asked Sue.

'Hopefully she'll be all right. All her vital signs are good now - strong pulse, breathing steadily. She's still unconscious - almost certainly from the drug - but she's not down as deep as she was. She should be back with us soon.'

'Thank goodness for that. Can I talk to her when she comes round?'

Doctor Lenton frowned. 'It all depends on how she is - you're welcome to wait if you want to, but I'm not guaranteeing you can see her. If I do let you speak to her it won't be for long and you certainly won't be interviewing her. Her full recovery is what matters to us - I'm sure you understand.'

'Thank you - I'll wait.'

'I'll get someone to bring you a cup of coffee,' he said. He stood up to leave, then turned back. 'By the way, a Sergeant Attwood rang a few minutes ago and left a message for you. He said to tell you they've arrested their man and he'll be in contact with you as soon as he can.'

'He's coming here?'

Doctor Lenton shook his head. 'Sorry, but I don't know any more. The message came up from reception, just as I've told you.'

'Thank you,' said Sue. When he had gone she sank back into her chair, suddenly more tired than ever as she relaxed for the first time in hours. She could hardly believe that the hunt for Pete Ashbourne's killer was almost certainly over. At the back of her mind was a tiny regret that she had after all not been involved in the final stages, but that was an unimportant and totally selfish issue. And of course the final stages were still to come, with the interview and almost certainly charges. There were still a lot of questions to be answered - they now had the 'who' but not yet the 'why.' What could be Horner's motives for killing Pete Ashbourne, and in all probability Tony Woodford as well?

One of the nurses brought her a strong coffee and some chocolate biscuits, which she devoured gratefully. Shortly before ten o'clock Doctor Lenton returned.

'Miss Cornwell is conscious now,' he said. 'She's reasonably alert and you can speak to her, but only for a few minutes.' He paused. 'She's still very tired and normally I'd be reluctant to let her see anyone, but she's been asking for you and I think she'll rest better when she's spoken to you. By the way, she can't remember anything about why she's here - she certainly can't remember being pulled out of the lake, half drowned. Please don't try to question her about that, at this stage.'

'Is she likely to remember, later on?'

He shrugged. 'Depends when and how quickly the drug took effect. If she was unconscious when she was taken down to the lake, she'll never remember. Come this way please.'

Mandy was in a small private room, propped up on several pillows and looking tired and washed out. Her pupils, Sue noted, were still abnormally dilated. Sue took a seat by the bed.

'Mandy, glad to see you awake again.'

'Yes ma'am, but I don't really know what I'm doing here. I asked the doctor and he just said not to worry about it for the moment.'

'That sounds like good advice.'

'Yes. He wanted me to go back to sleep again, but he mentioned you were here so I asked if I could see you first.' She paused. 'I wanted to tell you - about the coat, Sergeant Ashbourne's black coat.'

'Is that what you were trying to tell me on the telephone?'

'Yes - but I had to stop because Superintendent Horner came in.' She paused, seeming to find concentration difficult. 'Take your time,' urged Sue.

'Yes - sorry, I'm still a bit woolly. Well, you know today was my last day at work and I was just clearing the last few bits and pieces from my locker.' She paused. 'Memory's such a funny thing. The rain was hammering on the windows, just the way it was the day Sergeant Ashbourne died, and I - well, I suppose I was feeling pretty emotional, the way I was that day. You know - in one way glad to be leaving and in another way sorry. Anyway, I pulled my black uniform mac out from the back of the locker and suddenly this image kind of flashed into my mind and I remembered it all.'

She paused. Sue waited patiently, then Mandy continued.

'On the night Sergeant Ashbourne died I was on office duty - you probably remember that. I finished at ten o'clock and just after ten I went down to the parade room where Jim was doing some paperwork. On the way I passed the side corridor - the one that leads to the back door, into the yard. I saw someone at the end of the corridor, just opening the door. They were wearing a long black trench coat and for a moment I thought it must be Sergeant Ashbourne because he's the only one who's got a coat like that. Then the person turned side-on as he opened the door and I realised it was the superintendent.'

'Superintendent Horner?'

'Yes. And he was wearing Sergeant Ashbourne's black coat - or else one exactly like it.'

'Mandy, have you ever seen the superintendent in a similar coat? Or any black coat?'

'Only uniform. He never seems to wear dark colours out of uniform and his overcoat is a kind of light fawn colour.' She paused. 'I've never seen anyone else at the station in a coat like Sergeant Ashbourne's.'

Sue breathed out and closed her eyes for a moment. At last, the main key to the puzzle. 'Thank you Mandy. Now then, I'm going to need a really full statement from you, but obviously not tonight.' She smiled. 'Doctor Lenton would probably throw me out on my ear if I even thought about it. But I should be grateful if you could do it for me tomorrow - or as soon as you feel up to it.'

'Yes ma'am. Ma'am, before you go, what am I doing here? I can't remember anything after being at Fairfield.'

Sue paused, mindful of the doctor's demand not to question Mandy. She had to proceed carefully here.

'Mandy,' she said. 'What happened after you put the phone down in the parade room? After you had spoken to me?'

Mandy frowned. 'Well, as I said I had to stop talking when the superintendent came in. It panicked me a bit - well, quite a lot really. I was pretty flustered. When I got off the phone I went straight out and went down to the ladies loo. When I came back out the super was walking up the corridor. He stopped and started to chat. He was - oh, perfectly normal - just talking about it being my last day at work and how pleased he was to have caught me before I went. Then I thought, well, why shouldn't he be normal? He didn't know anything about the coat because I hadn't said anything he could overhear, I was just being twitchy because of what I knew.'

She paused, thinking back. 'I don't see how he could have known anything. Anyway he suggested we just pop up to his office for a farewell chat. I didn't want to go, but then I told myself I was being silly and it would look funny if I refused to go. So I went with him and he gave me a cup of coffee. We chatted for a while, and then - then I started to feel really peculiar. Kind of drifting, not unpleasant really, but strange. I remember him saying he'd get me home and I think I remember him helping me down the stairs. And that's it. I can't remember anything else until I woke up here.' She paused and looked at Sue. 'Did he drug me?'

Sue nodded. 'He did, but nothing dangerous Mandy. It's GHB - sometimes known as the date rape drug. I'm sure he had no designs of that kind,' she added hastily. 'He just wanted you out of it for a while.' She had no intention of telling Mandy about her narrow escape at the lake. It was inevitable that she would find out about it sooner or later, but she certainly shouldn't have to cope with it just yet.

Mandy was looking confused. 'I don't really understand this ma'am - he couldn't have known anything, could he?'

'I'm afraid he did know Mandy, or at least he knew you wanted to speak to me about a coat. When you left the parade room he asked Judith Saunders if you were all right because you seemed distracted. Judith told him it was something about seeing someone wearing a coat.'

'Oh my God! But - I hadn't said anything to Judith.'

'Not directly, but apparently you were mumbling to yourself when you were looking for my telephone number. Just under your breath, kind of thinking aloud I suppose. Loud enough for Judith to hear anyway.'

There was a gentle tap on the door and Doctor Lenton entered, accompanied by a nurse. He looked sharply at Sue. 'Inspector, I did ask you not to question Miss Cornwell.'

'She isn't,' said Mandy. 'Really doctor, I just wanted to know what had happened - why I was here.'

'All right,' he said. 'But I think that's enough now. We'd like to get you settled down for the night.'

He looked at Sue again and she took her cue, standing up to leave. Mandy called her back. 'Ma'am, could you tell Jim I'm here? I know he can't see me tonight, but - well, I'd be really glad for him to know where I am.'

'Of course,' promised Sue. 'Goodnight Mandy.' She nodded to the doctor. 'Goodnight Doctor Lenton, and thank you.'

He nodded, still looking irritated. 'Oh, by the way inspector, there's someone waiting for you in the dayroom.'

Sue hurried back to the dayroom to find Martin seated there, sipping a cup of coffee. He stood up at her entry.

'Sue, good to see you. I like the outfit - are you being kept in?'

'Very funny! The little hospital shop was closed and this was all they could provide.'

He handed her a battered carrier bag. 'Try these.' She looked inside to see her own jeans, T-shirt, woolly jumper. 'I raided your locker on the way here,' he explained.

Sue smiled. 'Martin, thank you - I take back anything bad I've ever said about you. Well, most of it anyway.' She looked around the room, spotted the inevitable hospital screen and moved behind it. 'Right, while I'm changing, get me up to date.'

'How's Mandy?' he asked.

'She'll be fine - they're just settling her for the night.'

'She's conscious?'

'Conscious and coherent. I'll tell you about it in a minute, but come on - you first. I gather Superintendent Horner's been arrested?'

'He has indeed. He led us quite a chase across the golf course, but he really didn't have much of a chance, once the dog arrived. The rain had stopped and there was a beautifully undisturbed, fresh track for Caesar to follow. Added to that, Brad had a powerful torch and Horner had nothing - it was as black as pitch out there and he couldn't have had much idea as to where he was going.' He paused. 'We finally caught up with him right near the middle of the course.'

'Did you get to make the arrest?'

'No, Brad did that. I kept up as long as I could but by

God, these handlers are bloody fit. Once I fell behind I lost the benefit of the torch, so that slowed me up even more. By the time I caught up with them it was all over and the cuffs were on.' He paused. 'Oh - and Caesar had a taste of prime rump steak.'

'Prime rump - Martin, he didn't?'

Martin laughed. 'He did - took a good bite out of our former super's backside. Actually it's not too bad because he had a couple of good layers of clothing, but it still broke the skin. We took the super to Bilston station because it was the nearest one and called the police surgeon out. He stuck a couple of stitches in and gave a tetanus jab and we bedded Mr Horner down for the night.'

'Does Mr Wallace know?'

'Got control to call him out while we were waiting for the dog. He was at Bilston by the time we arrived with Horner. He got things moving right away - got a team searching the car and a team turning over the house. We seized all Horner's clothes too - he needed to change in any case because he was as wet as I was. We've wrapped him in brown paper until we can get hold of some of his other clothes from his house.' He stood up as Sue emerged, still pulling her jumper over her head. 'Ready? We're to go straight to Bilston to talk to Mr Wallace.'

'Ready,' she said. 'Let's get going - I'll fill you in with Mandy's side of the story on the way.'

It was shortly after 11 pm when they arrived at Bilston station, to find Mr Wallace waiting for them in the CID office. 'Inspector Bishop,' he greeted her. 'Before I say anything else, very well done this evening.'

'Sir?'

'I understand you stuck your neck right out and made some pretty risky decisions. I also know that had you not taken the risk, we'd probably have lost another officer tonight.' He paused. 'I contacted the hospital earlier on - I gather Mandy

Cornwell will be all right?'

Sue nodded. 'They're keeping her overnight but that's just a precaution; they seem happy enough with her condition. She doesn't actually remember much about what happened this evening - just being in Horner's office, then feeling woolly.'

'Nothing about the lake?'

'Not a thing. She was apparently unconscious by then. It's likely she may never remember - which may be a good thing for her.'

He rubbed his chin. 'Mmm, I can see that, but of course she's going to have to know all about it, given he'll certainly be charged with her attempted murder. I'm guessing she has some crucial information, for Horner to take such a long shot on silencing her?'

'Very crucial,' agreed Sue. She explained to Wallace all that Mandy had told her about the coat. 'Though I'm afraid the actual coat is long gone,' she concluded.

'Almost certainly' Wallace agreed. 'It may turn out to be a good thing for us that Horner panicked tonight - we might still have struggled to prove the case against him. But now - I have a feeling he's not going to give us a lot of trouble any more. Though of course we can't be sure of that.'

'Has he spoken to a solicitor?'

'Very briefly. The solicitor is coming back at nine o'clock in the morning to interview his client fully. We'll conduct our interview straight after that.'

'Inspector Bishop and me?' asked Martin.

Wallace thought for a moment. 'Yes, I think so. I did consider taking over and doing the interview with Inspector Bishop, but you two have proved yourselves a good team and you certainly know the ins and outs of the case completely. Better than I do, though I've got a good overview.' He glanced at his watch. 'In view of which, you two need to be on the ball tomorrow; it's getting on for midnight and you both look pretty well bushed. I suggest you get yourselves home, get what sleep you can. I'll see you back here at nine o'clock and we can plan our way forward while Horner talks to his brief.'

# Chapter 35

Sue arrived at Bilston shortly before nine o'clock the following morning, to find that Horner was already in consultation with his solicitor. They still didn't have Mandy's written statement but Sue had made detailed notes, especially with regard to her sighting of the superintendent in Pete Ashbourne's coat. Wallace sighed as he laid the notes on the desk.

'It's a real tragedy she didn't remember this sooner, there's a good chance Tony Woodford would still be alive. Always assuming that Horner killed him too.'

Sue nodded but said nothing. There was nothing to say. The truth of Wallace's comment was indisputable, but it was too late for 'what ifs' and regrets. Her thoughts were confused. On the one hand she was relieved - immeasurably relieved - that one murder was now almost certainly solved, probably both murders. At least, it was solved to the point of having discovered the person responsible; they still had no idea as to the motive for either killing. Then there was Horner himself. He had been so supportive to her and she had begun to think of him as a friend, someone she could trust and confide in. Well, so much for that.

There was a tap on the door and the PC assisting in the custody office poked his head round the door. 'Sergeant Morris asked me to tell you sir; the solicitor has finished talking to Mr Horner. He'd like a word with you before the interview.' He paused, 'that's the solicitor sir - not Mr Horner.'

Wallace nodded. 'Bring him down here, will you.'

The solicitor was Mr Seymour, one of the leading partners in a local firm. Not surprisingly he already knew Mr Wallace and Martin and Wallace quickly introduced Sue. They shook hands, then the solicitor dropped into a nearby chair.

'Well,' he said. 'I've spent over thirty years in this job and I have to admit this one's set me right back on my heels. Never expected anything like this.'

'Neither did we,' said Wallace quietly.

'I should imagine not. Now then, who's going to be conducting the interview?'

'I am,' said Sue. 'With Sergeant Attwood.'

'Right. Well, I've obviously discussed the case in some detail with my client and I have to say he is inclined to - shall we say - put his hands up to all that's happened.'

'By which you mean a full admission?'

'Yes. After what happened last night he feels there's no point in denials any more.'

'Is that your advice?' asked Wallace.

Seymour shrugged. 'I think it's the best course of action, yes. I might have preferred him to give me a little more time, the chance to see just what evidence you have against him; but quite frankly I think he's had enough. He wants to finish it.'

'Has he given any indication as to why?' asked Sue. 'I mean, what his motives were?'

'He has, but that's not for me to say, inspector. However, I think you'll find he's prepared to answer all your questions. So, if you can spare me twenty minutes for a quick cup of coffee, I'll be ready when you are.'

Wallace nodded and stood up. 'In that case I'll leave it to you two - please make sure you keep me updated. In the meantime I'd better get over to headquarters and drop the bombshell on the Chief's toes. And stand by to fend off the press.'

Half an hour later Sue and Martin were in the interview room, with Horner and his solicitor. Horner was now dressed in his own jeans and open necked shirt. He was unshaven and looked as if he had slept very little. He also had what Sue thought of as a shell-shocked look - a look that suggested he still couldn't quite believe what had happened. The preliminaries were over and the interview proper was under way. Horner shifted uncomfortably in his chair.

'I'm not quite sure where to start,' he said.

'Why not just start at the beginning?' suggested Sue.

Horner shrugged. 'The beginning? I'm not quite sure where the beginning really is.'

'Then take us through the events on the day of Pete Ashbourne's death. The relevant events.'

He nodded. 'You might remember from my statement that I had an appraisal interview with Tony Woodford on that day, at 6 pm? I was also scheduled for an appraisal interview with Pete Ashbourne, at 7 pm?'

'I remember that.'

'Okay.' He looked at the floor, seeming reluctant to carry on. After a short silence he continued.

'You know, of course, that Tony Woodford was gay?'

'We do, he told us so himself.'

'Yes' he mumbled. 'Well, as it happens, so am I.' He looked up again. 'I didn't broadcast the fact - in fact I took pains to hide it. I'm sure you understand why.'

'Not really, no,' said Sue. 'Being gay is perfectly acceptable nowadays.'

Horner sat up straight and a flush spread over his face. Suddenly he became animated - more animated than she had ever seen him. 'Sue - inspector - I'm sorry to say that you're talking nonsense. It isn't acceptable - it still isn't. Oh, things are better, but there's still a long way to go. Remember the graffiti on Tony's locker, and the damage to his car? And it was a lot worse when I joined back in the mid 70's. That was before the Sex Discrimination Act or any legislation like that. If they'd known I was gay I'd never have got into the job. And as it was I had to hide the fact. Have you any idea what that's like? I know you face a degree of discrimination as a woman, but it's not the same thing. I'd go back to the training centre after the weekend and everyone would be chatting about their weekend - what they'd done, who they'd been with. But I could never do that - I had to lie. Have you any idea what that does to you, having to live a lie, constantly? And having to sit through the lessons on sexual offences and laugh at all the jokes about poofters and the queers' charter, as they called the '67 Act.' He sat back, still flustered. 'Yes, things are improving, but it still takes a lot of courage for a man to be openly gay in the police service. And I don't think it would be good for his career, even now.'

There was a silence as he regained his composure, then Sue prompted. 'Can you please tell us where this fits in to what happened that day?'

'Yes - I'm sorry - but it has everything to do with what happened. I suppose in a way that is the beginning - my being gay, and afraid to say so. Tony realised and we had a few heart to heart chats. I - well - we were attracted to one another, you see. We - we had what you might call a fling, but then Tony called it off. He said it could never lead to anything, what with the rank difference and working at the same station, and having to hide it from everyone. I accepted that - reluctantly.'

He took a deep breath, now appearing back in command of himself. 'Well, Tony came up at six o'clock and we conducted his appraisal. It actually took around half an hour, then we got to discussing other things. Tony told me about his encounter with Pete Ashbourne - about Pete hitting his prisoner - and a few other things. We were both upset that we couldn't safely have a - a more permanent relationship and Tony was upset about the whole thing with Pete Ashbourne. Tony didn't show his feelings easily, but believe me he was upset that day.' He paused. 'Well, one thing led to another. I started to console Tony and before I knew it we were embracing - kissing. That's all it was - we weren't naked over the table or anything like that. In fact Tony was just beginning to break off when suddenly a voice said something like 'well, well - how interesting.' We broke apart and there was Pete Ashbourne standing in the doorway'

'You left the door open?'

'Of course not, but it wasn't locked. I asked him why he didn't knock and he said he had knocked, but we must have been too busy to hear him. He said something to the effect that he was so sorry to disturb us. He'd just popped in to see if I could fit in his appraisal a little earlier but he could see it was a bad time. Then he closed the door and left. But his expression, especially when he looked at Tony - he looked as if Christmas had come early for him.

'We were both devastated of course - Tony said there wasn't a cat in hells chance that Pete would keep that little snippet to himself, especially since Tony was involved. It would be all over the station the next day and all over the force the day after that. Tony was typically philosophical though. He didn't see what we could do about it, he said we'd just have to ride out the storm.'

'And you? What did you think?'

Horner shrugged. 'At first I thought the same as Tony, that there was nothing to be done. Then I thought it was at least worth a try, to talk to Pete. After all, there was nothing to lose now. If being gay wasn't going to be good for my career, this was going to be a damned sight worse - being caught in a passionate embrace with another man, a subordinate, in my own office. So I went down to the cell block to see Pete.'

'What time was this?'

'Just after ten o'clock.'

Sue nodded. 'Please carry on.'

Horner shook his head. A look of confusion had come over his face.

'Looking back on it I still can't quite believe what happened. I just went down there to talk to him, to try to make him see reason and persuade him not to ruin two careers. That was the only thing in my mind, I swear it was.' He sighed. 'It was a bloody stupid idea on my part. As you might guess, Pete was totally unsympathetic. He was - sarcastically polite with his "sirs" and he made it very clear that he felt it his duty to report the whole matter to the divisional commander, and he intended to do so first thing in the morning. He gloated over it, especially over the fact he could now bring down Tony. He'd always hated Tony.

'By this time I'd realised it was hopeless. There was no way I could persuade him to keep quiet - my career would be finished. Pete had gone over to the sink and started to wash up the plates and mugs, he was just ignoring me. I turned to leave - and then I saw the knife.'

'Please can you clarify that for me?'

He shrugged. 'Isn't it obvious?'

'Yes it is. But for the record?'

'Oh yes of course - for the record. The stiletto that Nichols had used to stab his wife earlier was still sitting on the back shelf, all bagged up and ready to go in the safe until the following day. I was thinking that even if Pete had agreed to keep quiet he would still have a sword hanging over our heads. And then - it was as if I was someone else, watching this - this stranger that was me. I pulled off the seal and took out the knife. I held it down at my side, out of sight, and I walked over to Pete. He was still washing up and he had his back to me. He must have sensed I was there but he ignored me, so far as he was concerned the discussion was over. So I was able to get right up close to him and….and I stuck the stiletto into his back, right around where the heart would be.'

Horner took a deep breath, his face was grey and he had broken into a cold sweat. 'It went in to the hilt. Pete didn't even cry out, just a kind of gasp, then he dropped. There was a lot of blood - well, you know that. My hands were well covered and there was a lot on my shirt too - I was still in shirt-sleeves.

'I started to shake then. It was as if - as if I'd been away from my own body and now I was back again and just realising what I'd done. I was terrified, but I was also desperate. I rinsed my hands in the sink then I wiped off the hilt of the knife with the tea towel. It was ten past ten by then and I had to think about getting out of there. I fetched Pete's coat from behind the counter and put it on, I knew I needed to get away from the station without being seen, but if my luck was out and I was spotted - well, better not to be visibly covered in blood. I realised I'd left prints so I took off my shoes and washed them thoroughly - I tried to avoid the blood after that. Then when I was putting on the coat I noticed the keys to the cell block.

'That gave me an idea. I picked up the keys and quietly unlocked the entrance to the cell block, then I went down to Nichols' cell. He was lying on the bed facing away from the door and he looked to be asleep. I unlocked his door too, then I wiped down the keys and put them back on the hook.'

'Putting Nichols squarely in the frame,' said Martin quietly. Horner nodded.

'That was the idea. At best - at very best for me - he'd be convicted of the murder. I certainly hoped he'd be charged even if the evidence was a bit too circumstantial for a conviction. And if Nichols had come out of his cell earlier than he did he'd have been securely in the frame, because it's odds on he'd have at least tried to make a run for it.' He sighed again. 'As it is, the time of death was just wrong.'

'Anything more to add?' asked Sue. 'Relating to Pete Ashbourne I mean.'

'No, that's it really, for Pete. I left via the back door and made it to my car without being seen. Well, at the time I thought I'd made it. I didn't see Mandy Cornwell and I certainly didn't know she'd seen me.' He paused. 'Why did she leave it so long? To tell you?'

Sue ignored the question. 'So then you drove home, still wearing Pete's coat?'

'Yes. Needless to say I got rid of the coat. I burnt it up the same night and slung the ashes into the rubbish bin. I'd have buried them but the ground was too hard.'

'And your alibi? How did you fix your alibi with your gran? Did she lie for you?'

Horner gave a slight, sad smile. 'No. No, I don't think gran would know how to lie. But gran was asleep and she's also quite deaf, so she didn't hear me go into the house.'

'What time was that? When you got home?'

'A bit after half ten. As I expected and hoped, gran was fast asleep in bed. I crept into her bedroom and turned the clock back, then I went back out again and made lots of noise coming home. As far as gran was concerned it was just coming up to ten o'clock. It was easy enough to creep back in later and put it back to the proper time.' He leaned back in his chair, a drawn, defeated look on his face. 'And that's it. That's really all I can tell you - about Pete at any rate.'

'Right,' said Sue. She glanced at the clock on the wall. 'It's just past twelve o'clock, so we'll take a break now. We'll resume at two o'clock this afternoon. Before we break, just one final question to put things beyond doubt. You fully and freely admit that you killed Pete Ashbourne?'

Horner nodded wearily. 'Yes. Yes - this time you really do have an open and shut case.'

# Chapter 36

The afternoon found them once again in the interview room. This time the interview concerned the death of Tony Woodford. Horner looked dreadful, tired and drawn. He looked like a man haunted by a recurring nightmare - which, thought Sue, he probably was. The killing of Pete Ashbourne had been almost a crime of passion - the killing of Tony Woodford was likely to be something else again. And Tony had been more than a friend. Martin was leading the interview.

'Did you discuss Pete's death with Tony Woodford?'

'Of course I did, how could I not? We talked about it at some length, naturally.'

'And what was Tony's reaction?'

Horner shrugged. 'Mixed I suppose. There's no doubt that relief was in there. It was a load off his mind - off both our minds. But Tony is - was - strongly Christian. In action, not just words. You could see he was trying not to be pleased about Pete's death.'

'Did he have any suspicions?'

'About me? Certainly not then he didn't. At that stage everyone simply assumed Nichols was guilty - after all, word quickly got round that Sergeant Hawkins had found him standing above the body, holding the knife. Don't forget Hawkins hit the alarm button - half a dozen other people also saw the same thing.'

'And when it became clear that Nichols wasn't the sole suspect?'

Horner shrugged. 'That didn't become clear that quickly - you did a good job of clamping down on leaks from the investigation. But then when Jim came into the frame - well,

Tony was surprised, same as we all were. But I think even then his money was firmly on Nichols. He wasn't surprised that Jim had taken a swing at Pete, but he didn't think it likely Jim had committed the murder.'

'At what stage did Tony realise Jim had taken a swing at Pete? In your opinion of course?'

'Once you arrested Jim it became common knowledge. Jim talked to Mandy about it just before his arrest. Mandy told Tony first, then after Jim's arrest she made no secret of it.'

'So when did Tony become suspicious?'

Horner shrugged. 'Do you know, when I think back on it I'm not sure he ever did. Not really suspicious. He came up to see me after Jim had been bailed and suspended. He said the enquiry obviously wasn't as straight forward as it had seemed, and we shouldn't be with-holding evidence that might prove important. As far as he was concerned we both had first class alibis, but he still felt we should open up and tell you about us. About me and him having a - an embrace and about Pete walking in on us.'

'And how did you feel about that?'

'Well, you can just imagine how I felt. I was running scared, to say the least. Tony was giving both of us a clear motive and that would make you focus in much harder on us. Tony would still have been in the clear, but me - I didn't know how strongly my alibi would have held up. I could picture gran under cross-examination in the courtroom, the barrister tying her in knots about the time I came home. She was sure in her own mind - she wasn't lying for me - but she wouldn't have been a good witness.' He spread his hands, palms upwards. 'I don't think you'd have had enough to get a murder conviction - not without that damned coat - but my career would have been done for. I just couldn't let that happen.'

He paused, staring down at his hands. The silence held, becoming uncomfortable and still no-one spoke. Eventually Horner continued.

'I told Tony I'd do as he asked and I suggested we meet

up that evening to discuss the best way to approach things. He was working until ten so we agreed to meet after that - he wasn't really keen about meeting in the woodland clearing, but I talked him round. We'd - we'd met there before a few times, back in the summer and autumn. Anyway I decided then I couldn't afford to let him tell anyone about us - about me. It was easy enough to get hold of the drug from a friend - for obvious reasons I'm not on the drug scene, but I have contacts who are.

'I sorted out the length of hose and put it in my car. An hour before Tony was due to arrive I drove my car to the woodland car park and left it there, back in the corner away from the entrance and the headlights.

When Tony arrived it wasn't difficult to persuade him to have a swig from my hip-flask - he's not a big drinker but he was almost as stressed as I was. He wouldn't have any more because he was driving, but it was enough, laced with GHB. Pretty soon he was virtually out of it. I fetched the pipe from my own car and trailed it from the exhaust in through the front window. Then I switched to engine on and left him. I drove back home in my own car.'

'And the note?' asked Martin.

Throughout his narrative, Horner had remained staring at the floor; he seemed to be talking to himself rather than responding to their questions. He jumped at Martin's question, staring at them as though he had forgotten they were even there.

'The note? Oh, yes. That was just an attempt to muddy the waters a little, to add a bit of credibility to the question of suicide.'

'You copied Tony's writing?'

'I did my best. I kept it short in the hope it would stand scrutiny, but it was always a long shot.'

Martin raised his eyebrows to Sue, who nodded. 'All right,' said Martin. "Do you want to break for today, or can we look at what happened with Mandy.'

Horner shrugged. 'Let's get it over with now.' There was a pause, then he continued. 'I think - no, I know I just went into a flat panic over Mandy. Before that I really thought I was home and dry - with Pete and Tony I mean.' He nodded towards Sue. 'I knew you weren't happy about it being a suicide because you hadn't tried to close the case, but I was pretty sure you couldn't connect anything with me. But with Pete Ashbourne - my one big fear was that coat. If anyone saw me leaving the station that night I was going to be snookered.

'After all this time I thought I'd got away with it though. Then that evening . . . I just popped into the parade room to have a word with Mandy - you know, to wish her well. I didn't even hear what she was saying on the phone - it was her attitude. When she saw me come in she just stopped talking and went bright red, then pale. She looked terrified for a moment, then she started talking again, but in monosyllables. It was absolutely obvious she didn't want to say anything while I was there.

'When she put the phone down she gave me a quick glance, then bolted from the room. I went across to the phone and the internal directory was still open at the headquarters section - your section. I felt a bit uneasy at that but I thought I was probably putting two and two together and making five. So I went across to Judith Saunders and casually asked her about the call.' He shook his head again. 'The moment she mentioned the word "coat" I knew the game was up and that she must have seen me. But I don't understand that - if she saw me, why would she wait so long? Do you know?'

'Can we continue with your account for the time being?' said Sue.

Horner shrugged. 'Well, you're never going to tell me that in any case, are you?' He ran a hand through his hair, looking distracted. 'Where was I? Oh yes. Well, the moment Judith said 'coat' I started to panic. I guessed from the end of Mandy's phone conversation that you'd be coming over and my first thought was to get out - fast! I'd had arrangements in place for a quick getaway, ever since the Pete Ashbourne - since I killed Pete Ashbourne.

'I went back into the corridor intending to grab a couple of things from my office and get going. Then I walked right into Mandy just coming out of the ladies' loo. I just began to improvise then. I started to talk to her, being as pleasant and normal as I could, then suggested she pop up to my office for a quick chat and a coffee.' He gave a strange smile, with no real mirth in it. 'It's always been very easy to read Mandy's reactions - she wears her heart on her sleeve. She looked worried, then you could almost hear her thinking "well, he doesn't know I know anything." So she came up to the office with me.'

'What were your intentions then?' asked Martin.

'I'm not really sure. I was kind of making it up as I went along. I think at that stage I just intended drugging her and locking her into my office, to gain time. But then I started to think - what if I could actually get rid of her? Completely. I decided to try it. When she was well gone but still just conscious I helped her down the stairs to my car. If I'd been seen then, I'd have said she'd been taken ill and just left her with whoever was there. Then I'd have made a bolt for it. But I got her to the car safely without being seen.'

He paused again, looking at Sue and Martin. 'You think I'm mad, don't you?'

'I think you were being - optimistic - to think you could get away with snatching Mandy,' commented Sue.

Horner shrugged. 'I know it - I wasn't thinking straight. I thought if I did get rid of her it would buy me a bit more time. Of course you'd have been suspicious - very suspicious - but I wasn't planning to hang around while you added up the evidence. I put Mandy on the back seat of the car then drove down to the lake below the golf course. Then I pulled her out of the car, put a big boulder under her coat and buttoned the coat over it to hold it there. She was completely out by then. I was just dragging her into the water when I heard a car - then

I looked up and saw the lights across the lake.' He shook his head in remembered disbelief. 'I knew right away it had to be you - though how the hell you got onto it so fast I don't know. Anyway, I dropped Mandy and scrambled back up to my car.'

'Didn't it cross your mind to pull Mandy out of the water first?' asked Martin. 'Surely at that stage you must have realised you couldn't possibly get away with killing Mandy?'

Horner shrugged. 'No, it didn't cross my mind. The only thing I could think about was to get away. But then my bloody car had got itself bogged down in the mud and by the time I got it moving the ambulance had blocked the track out of the woods. And you know the rest. I just ran for it and blundered about in the dark until the damned dog took a chunk out of me.'

He slumped back in his chair, looking drawn and exhausted. There was a silence, then the solicitor spoke. 'Inspector, I think it's time for a break.'

Sue glanced at her watch, then nodded. 'I agree. In any case, I think we have all we need now. Thank you Mr Horner - if you'd just go with DS Attwood we'll return you to your cell and get you a meal.'

Horner nodded and stood to precede Martin out of the room. At the door he turned and looked back at Sue.

'Tony,' he said, his voice close to breaking. 'Why did I have to kill Tony? I didn't care so much about Pete or Mandy, but Tony - Tony was special. If only Mandy Cornwell had remembered sooner about the coat. I'd have been no worse off and Tony would have still been alive.'

Sue made no reply and Martin led Horner from the room.

# Chapter 37

Sue stood by the window gazing out across the extensive grounds of FHQ; beautiful grounds, with sweeping lawns and flower beds bright with golden daffodils. The lawns ended in a narrow belt of woodland, trees verdant with the clean green of new leaves.

It was a lovely and peaceful scene; she only wished she could feel as much peace within herself. The investigation was now well and truly over; yesterday Horner had been charged with the murders of both Pete Ashbourne and Tony Woodford and the attempted murder of Mandy Cornwell. He was now kept in custody pending a remand appearance at court. Everything had gone very smoothly, with full written admissions to both murders.

Martin came in, shrugging himself into his coat. 'Right then, I'm off to the pub. See you tomorrow.' He looked at her more closely. 'Why so melancholy? It's all over bar the shouting. Case solved - both cases - fantastic result.'

Sue turned back into the room. 'I know, and I'm relieved. But I can't help thinking of the waste.'

'Of two lives?'

'Of two lives, and how many careers? Mandy's - and Jim's.'

'Jim has resigned?'

Sue nodded. 'Mandy came up to see me. Apparently he just doesn't feel he can be a copper any more, after all that's happened.' She sighed. 'Horner too - his career is certainly over. You know Martin, I really liked Horner.'

'Most people did.'

'Yes I know. But - well, he was particularly supportive to

me, when I really needed it. I thought we were on the way to becoming real friends. Oh, I don't mean in a romantic sense, just good friends who could confide in each other, support each other. And in the end…'

'In the end?' prompted Martin.

She shook her head. 'I can't help remembering one thing in particular Horner said. He said that before Mandy remembered the coat he was pretty sure we wouldn't have had a case against him. Not a case we could win.'

'I remember that. What of it?'

'Martin, he was pretty sure he wouldn't be going to prison, that he would never actually be convicted of Pete's murder. But he still killed Tony. Don't you see? He didn't kill Tony to avoid a murder rap, he killed him to avoid damage to his career. He sacrificed Tony for his own ambition - nothing else. Pete too. Pete more so, because Horner would hardly have lost his job, even if his relationship with Tony had come out. Of course it wouldn't have done him any good in the short term, but it would probably have been a nine day wonder - all forgotten when the next scandal reared its ugly head.'

'What are you leading up to Sue?'

'I suppose I've just been thinking about ambition. How it can get hold of you - what it can do.'

He frowned. 'Are you by any chance thinking about yourself?'

'I suppose I am. Oh, I'm not putting myself in Horner's league - I'm not that obsessed with success. But there's no doubt my ambition was the biggest factor in my marriage breaking up.'

'More so than finding your husband in bed with another woman?' said Martin dryly. Sue gave a shaky laugh.

'I suppose not - but then, would he have gone with Sarah if our marriage hadn't been on the rocks? I don't think so.'

'You mean you should have thrown the job in because Bill wanted you to?'

She shook her head. 'Not really. I don't think I could have

done that - quit the job, I mean; it's got too tight a hold on me. But I don't think it would have come to that if I'd just agreed to put things on hold while we had a family. We could have compromised. I could have gone back to the job after my maternity leave. Of course I probably wouldn't have gone up the ranks - or not so quickly anyway.'

'And just supposing you'd have chosen to give up the job or put your career on hold. How would you have felt about that?'

Sue gave a hollow laugh. 'Resentful, of course. It was a no-win situation really, whatever I did.' She squared her shoulders. 'It's just reaction I guess, the anti-climax now the investigation is over. I don't really regret my decision - it's just - well - food for thought I suppose.'

There was a tap on the door and Paul stood in the doorway. 'Off to the pub Martin - you coming?'

Martin nodded. 'Yep - coming now.' He walked out of the door and Sue turned back to putting the final touches to the case files.

'Sue?'

Martin was back. 'Why don't you come along?' he said.

'To the pub?'

'Sure. It'll do you good.

Sue looked at the case files spread out in front of her.

'They'll keep until tomorrow,' said Martin. 'Come on guvnor - you've earned a break.'

Sue hesitated, then pushed the files into the drawer and turned the key. She took her coat from the rack and followed Martin from the room.

**Also by C. A. Shilton**

**Barricades - the Journey of Javert**

In 18$^{th}$ Century France a storm is brewing. A boy finds the strength to turn his destiny around – but at a price.

The son of a convict and a gypsy, Javert is born in prison. His harsh upbringing and the horrors of the French Revolution turn the vulnerable boy into an implacable adult, unyielding in his beliefs and ashamed of his gypsy heritage.

When forced to question those beliefs and confront the truth about his background, Javert faces the greatest challenge of his life.


**About the Author**

Born in the Midlands of England, C. A. Shilton spent 22 years as a police officer, providing an ideal background and ample material for the writing of crime novels. She served in both operational and specialist capacities and in 1987 - when this novel is set - she was working as an operational police sergeant.

She now lives on the North Norfolk coast. Hobbies include travel, walking, theatre, sketching, 'wining and dining' and swimming.